Unbury the Dead

by

Laurel Hanlon

Unbury the Dead

Cover Art by *Teddi Black*

The Wild Rose Press, Inc.
PO Box 708
Adams Basin, NY 14410-0708
Visit us at www.thewildrosepress.com

Publishing History
First Edition, 2025
Trade Paperback ISBN 978-1-5092-6310-3
Digital ISBN 978-1-5092-6311-0

Published in the United States of America

Dedication

For all my family and friends that made this dream a
reality.

Chapter 1

I was so close to freedom.

The concrete under my hand built up into a silky pile; a harsh contrast to the unforgiving prison that hardened and encased my entire body. When I wasn't scraping away at the sandpaper-like walls of my impossible predicament with my fingers, the rest of my body rotated through different muscle groups, grinding away at the material one section at a time.

Initially, only my jaw could move. The grit of the walls reminded me of my predicament with every twitch of muscle. Teeth ground back and forth until the motion created enough space to move my lips and let the saliva moisten the stubborn rocks. Bit by bit created a crevice. This repetitive motion threatened to drive me to madness however and required me to shift focus to another part of my body. In the beginning, my feet were snug in leather oxfords, but to my elation, time caused the material to fail and toenails scraped directly against the concrete.

Bless my nails. With their strength, I finally started to make significant progress. The fine grains of the gray rock pooled under my freed hand and feet with every retraction. It grew a bit more with every movement. Scrape. Scrape. Scrape.

It happened so fast. One moment, the deep rays of the morning sun were pushing me back into the shadows, and the next, the heavy mixture heated up as it started its chemical reaction against my skin. It oozed around every orifice and suffocated any wiggle room I would have otherwise had, leaving no room to open my eyelids, flare my nostrils, or shift away from the pocket watch that pressed into my buttocks this entire time.

For so long, the little machine announced the passing of time. Each click of the second hand reassured me the world moved into the future. It kept me company for what could only be surmised to be about a year before it too succumbed to the madness. Since then, it had been very quiet.

Even if I could pry my eyes open, I'd only see absolute darkness pressing down on me from the suffocatingly low ceiling of my figurative coffin. This place kept me prisoner for God knows how long. Time did not exist here. There was no sun, no moon, no stars to gaze upon. Only my memories reminded me of what they looked like. Even so, they started to leave me too. Images of my past blurred and combined like cream in tea. As hard as I tried to hold on, they were slipping away. The reality of my current situation was my constant companion and the only thing that reminded me of a different future rasped through the coffin like nails on a chalkboard. The rhythmic motion of rubbing my finger up and down, up and down, up and down brought me no pleasure, but it kept me going.

And revenge. It would take an utter fool to betray me like this. Only a coward would ambush a man at his weakest. They must know that this prison could not hold me forever and my vengeance, spurred by their heartlessness, encouraged every sweep of my finger.

****

A person in my predicament had to keep focused and set goals, make the task easier. Milestones that would hopefully give me the strength to crack open my own personal hell. First, get my hand free enough that it could rotate at my wrist. Then, work my way up the arm. Once my shoulder could move, there would be enough momentum to shatter the rest of my cage. Alas, I had a long way to go.

So, to keep myself from completely going off the deep end, I hummed. A particular favorite of mine translated easily from its origin as a lively ensemble piece that highlighted the string section with hints of brass and an enthusiastic harpist. Perhaps the memory of it brought me the most comfort. A wave of warmth, like the sun's rays, circulated through me at my fondness for the evening. A Czech composer visited London for just one performance, inviting an oversaturated attendance, but our connections granted us entry. Most people would have considered it a rather late appointment, but the candles flickering around the stage only added to the atmosphere. The piano melody floated easily from one act to another, touching emotions from excitement to sorrow with just a series of notes. Then again, it could have been my company.

The last note of the symphony died in the back of my throat briefly before moving onto the sea shanties overheard from the ships roped in the harbor. Seamen often used the tunes to get through their work as joyfully as they could before the sun dipped below the horizon. Watching them from the shadows of a nearby attic made me an expert to their habits, which brought me comfort. Their movement came through the wavy glass, disjointed and unfocused, providing an excellent vantage point to watch them from sunrise to sunset.

Naturally, spending so much time conducting business from such close vicinity, their songs resonated my thoughts long after their day concluded. The charm of bellowing out such tunes would have been preferable, but humming it instead would have to do. At the end of their day, they would put down their tools and meander deeper into the town in search of food and drink. It never took long for one of them to wander off alone and into a particularly secluded alleyway. They had no idea what came for them, blissfully unaware that they were alive just long enough for the perfect moment to arise.

With the thought, a new pang of hunger kicked me in the stomach. It felt like fire crawled up my throat. God, how long had it been since I'd last fed? Surely, the lack of sustenance caused me a handicap, slowing my progress. The idea of sinking my fangs into the neck of someone warm filled my thoughts. Their veins would be visible, just below the skin, protruding from the furious pounding of their heart in response to my breath on their flesh. Hair rising instinctually at the danger. By the time the flight response told them to run, it was already too late.

The feeling of a successful hunt provided my soul with a sensation that made me feel whole. Their blood compares to an evening with a beautiful woman. The release of energy and the strength that it gave me— addictive, no, essential, to my existence. My mouth filled with saliva in response to the vivid images dancing across my thoughts. A growl formed deep in my chest and blew out through my nose. My limbs started thrashing wildly. Clawing with my hands, kicking with my feet, shaking my head. The space created from my relentless clawing felt more claustrophobic than before my excavating efforts, which drove me to convulse even more uncontrollably. No one heard my wails of frustration.

Stop it! A shallow hiss festered in my throat. You are a gentleman and your actions are no better than an animal! You are losing your grip.

One by one, my muscles obeyed and let go of the tautness that bound them. My jaw slackened last. The episode built up a reservoir of venom that accumulated around my tongue. Some of it dribbled down the sides of my face, while the rest had nowhere else to go but back down my throat, burning the whole way down.

The granular concrete collected into lumpy piles along my backside, sitting annoyingly in places they hadn't been before. Maybe because my body felt heavier than before my tantrum, as though the pressure points were directly connected to my despair. There was no energy left for me to do anything about it, so the feelings festered deep into my muscles and bones. For the first time in a very long time, I just laid there. It used to bring me comfort to focus on the feeling of air entering and exiting my lungs, but that luxury no longer applied. Now, counting brought comfort. Starting at one, then two, three, four, five…

All the way to a million. It took a while and after reaching the seventh digit, whatever demonic impulses took over my body no longer held me hostage. A faint twinge of anger refused to let go, encouraging another marathon count to a million. Instead, my finger retracted as it had so many times before and the familiar sound of a fingernail against rock soon filled the cavern. Thoughts of something pleasant replaced the utilitarian numbers that provided some sort of numbness.

Images of my lovely wife always occupied the forefront of my mind. An angel sent to me from heaven. Her eyelashes fluffed up over green, doe like eyes. Below her button nose were the rosiest lips a man had ever seen. A shiver ran down my spine remembering they tasted like fresh buttercream on a warm summer's day. Oh, her body. Only the Lord would send someone so tantalizing to test me. Her tiny waist accentuated round hips that met in a perfect apple shape. My dead heart clenched at her memory.

What a fool I am! One selfish mistake took her from me prematurely. She would be alive right now if it wasn't for my arrogance. Well, maybe. Her natural life could have ended regardless without having a broad concept of how much time passed since being sent to this hell. It could have been five years, it could have been fifty. Her lifeless body draped across my lap, nestled limply against my chest, as my hands futilely grasped at the last remnants of her life. Her green eyes stared up at the sky without focus before her last breath seeped through her lips as her soul left her body.

That was the last time I saw her. She could have been put to rest, surrounded by strangers who didn't know her favorite color changed from purple to red depending on the time of year or that she only wore white when she knew she didn't need to pick fresh flowers. They probably didn't know that she wanted to stay on our farm, even after death, because it brought her a sense of peace that no other place gave her. Those men never gave me the chance to share this before condemning me to this place.

The same panic from before built up and climbed its way out again. The growl started low and sizzled out of my clenched jaw. With fists balled up so tight the fingernails cut into my palms, blows of immense force pounded the top and bottom of the space while my upper body jerked from side to side and feet kicked out in similar fashion to a toddler who didn't get their way.

A crack reverberated through the concrete. I stopped, listening to see if the noise truly happened or it resonated in a wishful thought. Remaining still, my attention honed onto anything that could be considered different. The buzzing that accompanied a silent space became apparent without the slightest hint of the walls breaking down around me. Perhaps a vain attempt to leverage the rocks apart would be a waste of energy, but it felt like the right thing to do. With my elbows propped up as the leverage point, the broad part of my chest strained against the roof, gradually compressing. The bony points of my elbows protested loudly when a microscopic creak caused me to pause. The noise dispersed with the flopping of my limp body. More than the noise, something shifted.

In its current state, it would require the strength of twice the man to get out of this predicament, but that luxury could not be awarded to me, and my patience had expired. The thrashing worked before, so it would have to do again. My rage lurked skin deep, and it wasn't hard to summon the face of my deceased wife and channel it into my body. With her guiding me, she helped kick and punch whatever surface came closest. Another crack, but this time, something assuredly changed.

It felt as though I pissed myself. Impossible, since my kind doesn't do that sort of thing, but the sensation took me back to a time where four pitchers of beer and a good band led to waking up in a bush, embarrassed to be seen. Water pooled on my backside, soaking my pants and endangering my pocket watch. The smell of salt water and decaying fish filled the gaps where the water hadn't yet reached. Steadily, the stream found its way through the particles of concrete, the broken-down fibers of cotton, and pockets of stale air, tickling the hair on my arms as it made its way closer to my head, leaving a shiver in its wake.

It made perfect sense why the concrete remained stubborn to move. The weight of the ocean rested on top of me with no way of knowing the depth. With the same leverage as before, the top of the structure ground against itself as it moved a fraction of a centimeter. Little by little, it snaked further down until a gap formed over my head.

There was little to see. Darkness consumed everything in the immediate area except for occasional glimmers of seaweed that caught what little light that penetrated this deep. Sparkles of the sea floor danced in reaction to the movement of my head. Not enough room formed to swim the rest of the way out, leaving no other choice but to keep working the lid further down until it exposed my chest. From here, the molds that originally kept me trapped could no longer maintain their hold, giving way to the freedom that presented itself now. I kicked my way out from the confines of my prison and fought the overwhelming feeling of emptiness as my feet gently settled on the ocean floor. The commotion unsettled the dirt, filling the immediate area in a cloud.

The sensation felt odd. Could this feeling be what it felt like to have blood rush out of your head and cascade deeper down in your body? The longer I stood, the feeling settled just like in the surrounding sand. Each muscle group responded stiffly and slowly, gingerly flexing them one by one to test their responsiveness. Overall, it would have to do, but it felt awkward to be upright after so long. The current picked up bits of sediment and tickled it across the tops of my feet. It brought a smile across my face, something foreign to me, as well. The stretch of muscle across bone felt good when my arms raised above my head.

In the immediate area, little stood out as inspiration. Standing in the darkness invited a claustrophobia almost as oppressive as the prison that now sat vacant at my feet. The depths of the water swallowed any bit of light, even with my brilliant eyesight. There were many choices in front of me and a decision needed to be made. Muddling through the subtle hills of the seabed, or ocean floor, came to mind, but so did swimming up to the surface.

Contemplating the next move seemed monumental until a noise derailed my train of thought. *Thump thump, thump thump*. My instincts overwhelmed the rational part of my brain and the animal within took over. The landscape blurred into various bluish-black blobs, making the fervent search for any sign of where the heartbeat had come from nearly pointless. My ears tried to pinpoint its direction. The blobs only held a form for a couple of meters before they disappeared into the ether. Hunting in the water magnified everything, echoing the sound from all directions. The thumping grew louder, softer, then louder, then softer until it became undetectable. Just when I'd given up, the sound showed up again. Swirls of sand followed my unsure, choppy attempts at following the creature, leading me in circles.

My feet kicked up and started swimming in the direction I thought the sound came from. The motion came naturally, pumping through the water with terrifying efficiency. My wake barely disturbed the water as if it were an eel and not a man. When the heartbeat appeared again, the doubt that clouded my pursuit from before stayed with the coffin. The beats grew louder, ebbing me to swim faster, until the sound multiplied. A school of fish then. Venom moistened my tongue in response to the vicinity of my prey. A little further, and the searing pain in my throat and stomach would ease.

In the distance, the glint of their scales caught the light. Ghosts in the darkness, but their beating hearts gave them away like a lighthouse on the shore. Well-worn fingernails clawed at the rock below me and used them to propel faster through the water. Once infiltrated, the predator took over. Bits of flesh floated through the watery grave. Each fish provided just a sip of nutrition and as a result, my stomach bloated with as much salt water as blood. The sensation made my insides cramp, but it didn't stop me.

It took only a few minutes to claw and bite my way through the hundred or so fish before there were none left. With my thirst only partially quenched, my interest moved onto the next kill. Crimson swirled through the water, tempting me to filter it as if I had gills. The urge passed and the idea of something else to drink kissed the edge of consciousness, sending me on my way. My time without nutrition left a pit so deep, it would take another thousand fish to saturate it. Or a human.

The frenzy attracted a different kind of predator. Its fin brushed against my arm while the familiar, lower thumping of its heart caught my full attention. Even on a good day, this kind of temptation would be hard to pass up, and that wasn't today. Fingers sunk into its rubbery flesh, hooking it into an inescapable fate, while the mass of flesh and muscle wriggled in panic, trying to dislodge the uncanny threat.

Its heart beat a mere two times before the blood that gave it life drained away through the bite wound inflicted behind its gills. The shark thrashed a couple of times at the unexpected turn of events, but it did not last. The body relaxed and started to sink. The flow of warm, red liquid slowed until it altogether stopped, prompting me to release the iron-like hold on its fins. Not a drop wasted. The body melted into darker shades of blue until it disappeared into the void.

The weight of the blood mixed with salt water added a buoyancy that didn't fully satisfy the burning hunger. My mind returned to a semblance of discipline, but a long way from absolute control. Red pushed at the edge of my sight and one thought lingered above all else. I needed human blood.

My feet kicked out like an oar without regard to a particular direction. It didn't matter. Humans could be found just about anywhere, well, except for the bottom of the ocean. My trajectory adjusted accordingly and as the surface of the water got closer, more animals started to appear. They didn't have a chance to notice the misplaced creature among them as my arms pumped in terrifying efficiency. Slipping through the water barely left a wake. They did not interest me anymore.

Something about human blood fulfilled my never-ending thirst unlike anything else on the planet. It filled an abyss that my kind lost when we converted. It drove us to the ends of the earth, only relenting when we got what we wanted. Even now, it prodded me to keep swimming to a place that didn't matter, as long as it had blood. The water grew unsettled and more tumultuous closer to the surface, fighting every breaststroke. The landscape became clearer, brighter, making the finer details of the fish harder to see. Brilliant rays of sun penetrated the water, reflecting harshly against the darkness deeper down.

A pang of emotion swelled in my chest at the idea of seeing something so rare for the first time in such a long while. I stopped my pursuit and bobbed under the surface. About a kilometer distanced me from the daylight, giving the water plenty of space to absorb the danger of the sun's harmful rays, but close enough to admire the beauty from a conservative depth. It danced like a ballerina and kissed my face. My cheeks warmed at the sight of something so dangerously beautiful.

In fact, the sight held me captive as it moved across the sky and dipped under the horizon. When the last of the orange and pink streaks faded from view, a bubble of water popped over my head as it broke the surface. The crispness of fresh air tickled the droplets of water on my cheeks. A shiver ran down my spine, not because of the foreign sensation, but because water filled the horizon as far as the eye could see in every direction.

The full moon filled the eastern horizon and without knowing which ocean this was, it could be pointing home, or it could leave me swimming to something entirely new. I may know sailors, but my feet had remained firmly on hard ground my entire life and therefore had no reason to learn how to read stars. It seemed as good of a choice as any and swam toward the moon in the blanket of night.

The sun rose and fell two more times before anything changed. For two days, the fish were my only company and the single line of blood thirsty thoughts. The very thought of biting a human was enough to cause my body to go into a predatory mode. An excess of venom continuously accumulated in my mouth and instead of letting it burn by throat, discharged it into the water. The allure of getting it rose above all other needs. More than life, more than my wife.

A peculiar shadow appeared in the far distance, cutting a large swath of darkness on the water's surface. It bobbed along the top of the water like a mirage. The shape came close to a whale's in the same grayish blob, meandering along the surface, but this thing couldn't be organic. Unwavering in its long, smooth shape, it pounded the water with forward progress. Doubtful it could be anything but a boat, however, it couldn't have been made from wood.

Caught up in my curious quest, the sun's rays penetrating the water caught up with me, searing the exposed parts of my hands and neck, forcing a retreat deeper into the water. It took the better part of the afternoon to snake my way closer and, about a kilometer away, the water turned putrid. Overwhelming the taste of salt was something metallic, almost like gunpowder, but not quite. The toxicity of it encouraged me to find a different path, however, as if it were an underlying note in a fine wine, existed the faint note of human. Seamen often smelled of body odor and drink. This group had traces of soap mingled with something sweet, but not alcohol, pulling me to their boat as if a fishing line pulled us together.

The vastness of the floating object filled the horizon until its hull blotted out the late day sun, casting a shadow along the port side. Never had I seen a creation as large as this. From tip to tail, the boat could have been close to a kilometer in length. Below the water, three large fins churned the water so aggressively, bubbles exuded off the end for another kilometer.

It took every bit of my discipline not to clamber up the side as soon as I reached the hull, but years of experience dampened a potentially stupid mistake. It would be fair game after the sunset, however. When the clouds blazed yellow and orange, the shadow of the boat provided ample cover to investigate the easiest way onto the deck. My head broke the surface and searched for a cannon hole to latch onto. Alas, the sides of the vessel were completely smooth, apart from the railing that lined the top deck at least six stories above my head.

After swimming a lap around the vessel, climbing the side wouldn't be an option. Water closed over my head as I dipped down to wait out the rest of the day and contemplate the next move. When night fully encased the ship, a stirring of bubbles engulfed my legs as they kicked voraciously to get the necessary speed before breaking the surface. A spray of water danced behind my quickly ascending body, the sound lost among the slapping of the ocean against the hull. The railing proved to be the perfect place to latch onto and held the unexpected weight effortlessly. With a little hop, my feet landed on the deck with a squelch of the remainder of my oxfords. To human ears, it wouldn't have made a sound, but to my sensitive hearing, the salt water tinged every time it dripped onto the ground. The patchy remnants of my leather shoes shifted precariously with every step, making the decision to yank them off and throw overboard an easy one. The drips coming from my clothing slowed as well, silencing the positive progress through the top deck of the ship.

The vessel had no personality. Gray paint covered every surface. Hints of rust poked through the worn paths where men trod through the years. The silver railing lacked luster, blotched with irreparable scuffs. Yet, this place felt like a floating island. A feat of human engineering. Waves attacked the sides of the ship and yet nothing moved because of it.

A human's breath hitched somewhere behind me, accompanied by an increase in their heartbeat. Their eyes could be felt boring into my backside, not daring to look away for even a second. Seeing me on their boat would be quite the specter, dressed in tattered clothes, with overgrown and matted hair, and deathly pale skin.

He locked eyes with me. About 25 meters stood between the two of us and even so, he looked on dubiously. His weight shifted from one foot to the other, not bothering to close his hanging jaw. He managed to take a single step backwards before I assaulted him with the entire weight of my body. A muted huff grunted out of his lips from the force as we collapsed to the ground. In the confusion, he didn't have time to call out for help before my hand clamped over his mouth and my teeth sunk deep into his jugular.

The reward of receiving human blood far exceeded whatever expectation my brain conjured up. It would have been nice to enjoy this first sip, but as soon as the liquid touched my tongue, desire overwhelmed me. Gulps of blood clogged in my throat as I tried to consume the liquid faster than my body could handle. The ordeal lasted no more than twenty seconds, but even so, it wasn't fast enough.

The spark of life reignited in me. It started deep in my stomach and, like warm brandy, spread through my veins like fire, settling in every recess of my body. It pulsated through my veins and brought strength to my debilitated muscles. The sensation started in my fingers, up the arm, through the chest, down my legs, and finally groped my tired thoughts and cleared away the fog that consumed me, but I wanted more.

My fingers loosened their hold and, with nothing to support it, the corpse flopped to the ground. Not a drop of blood wasted. It surprised me. For how animalistic this kill had been, there should have been some splash back, but upon thorough inspection, the only sign of the struggle was the smear of blood on my cuff from using it to wipe my lips.

It would be easy to leave the body there, but inevitably someone would find it, giving away the element of anonymity. The man's shirt creased between my fingers and held strong as it carried the weight of the man being drug to the side of the boat. It ripped slightly when it gathered under his armpits, supporting the rest of the body from being hoisted up and dumped overboard. Several long seconds passed before he splashed into the water.

Pools of light illuminated the ship's deck, although there weren't any torches. The light caused me no discomfort, even after sticking a curious hand into its rays. The sailors, oblivious to the uninvited guest, continued their work, and it would be wise of me to maintain the ruse as long as possible, doubtful they would be receptive to my presence.

Sneaking along the top deck required a weaving technique that avoided the dots of light that nearly overlapped. Surrendered to the shadows, the path led me along a path of brightly colored boxes stacked high above my head. Each box was a man and a half tall, making the overall enormity of the scale humbling. Organized in rows, it forced me along the length of the ship before stopping at what looked to be the living quarters.

Above it all, a brightly lit room with large windows overlooked the boxes. From this low angle, the captain's head barely poked out above the edge of his room, staring lazily downward. Sitting next to him were two others, talking amongst themselves. My tongue traced the outline of my lips at the thought of getting more sweet sustenance. The temptation to keep gorging myself enticed me to climb the exterior of the cabin and sabotage them, but the one human did for me that three dozen fish could not. Who knew how long this journey would be and I would need something for later. They lived, for now.

A boat this size would have a sizable crew and at this early night hour, groups of muffled voices sounded somewhere on a lower deck. Their feet scurried along the corridors like ants. Though it seemed like the noise originated from the lowest possible deck, its drumming caused the hull to vibrate on a minute level. There were no sails to attend to, only the props at the rear of the ship, making me think that whatever powered those would be powerful enough to reverberate through the walls. Something like that would require a lot of attention, human attention.

The noise lured me toward a door at the back of the ship. Each ping, tap, clunk, thud caused me to stop and listen for anything that would give me away, yet each noise proved to be nothing of consequence. The corridor groaned in sync with the subtle swaying of the ship and each room along the hallway held various recognizable items, like chairs, desks, tools, cups, and other things. The passage ended in a double stairwell that went up or down.

A dozen or so heartbeats scattered across the different levels, but none of them worked close enough to interrupt my exploration. This proved the same with each lower deck, consumed by the tasks that kept them busy. By the third level, the drumming grew to such viciousness, it became unbearable, making this the lowest level I could go. It thudded in rhythm like a monstrous metal waterwheel. In such a short amount of time, it ate away at my patience. A long hallway led away from the sound, and fortunately, to a place no one else bothered to be.

It passed another stairwell and ended at the bow, obvious by the sharp angle where the hull of the ship joined. The room hosted a variety of forgotten tools and moldy boxes. Cobwebs decorated the corners and only the faintest smell of human lingered, making it the perfect spot to hide. A cubby at the back of the room formed a perfect shelter from anyone who pried into the room, leaving whoever sat there shielded from view. The door into the room whined when it moved, and I felt instant relief when the thing clicked shut. Light peeked around the edges, leaving a little circle illuminated in the otherwise pitch-black room.

It would have been nice to have a chair, but the ground would do. My legs splayed out in front of me, while my back slouched against the cold metal of the wall. I let out an emblematic sigh, taking in my appearance for the first time since escaping the prison. My once crisp pinstripe trousers now looked like they would dissolve in a gentle breeze. Patches of the fabric frayed where there had been the most friction, notably my thighs, calves, elbows, and across my shoulders. It hung off me in strings. The cuffs of my once white shirt were stained with cement dust and tired too. Splotches of the concrete clung to the fabric like urchins. My downward gaze caused clumps of my brown hair to fall over my shoulders in mats. Bits of ocean debris clung to the snarls. The overgrown mop attached to my chin itched with irritation. The oxfords that once adorned my feet sunk somewhere at the bottom of the ocean, unable to hide the imbedded concrete under chipped toenails. My fingernails held the same hardened material.

The lot of it disgusted me.

Absent-mindedly, I picked at the debris under my nails while my mind wandered to the pocket watch tethered to my trousers by a gold chain. The round lump brought comfort despite creating an uneven bulge to sit on, reassuring me of its presence. My weight shifted, allowing my grubby fingers to ease it from the pocket where it had sat since before this mess started. Admiring the pristine condition of the watch, my finger traced the delicate details of the engraving on the gold face. It shouldn't have been a surprise since the watch had been tucked away between two layers of fabric. Seeing it now, it felt ridiculous spending so much time worrying about crushing it with my struggles to escape. Water dribbled out of the bottom when it opened and pooled on the floor between my legs.

The hands were stuck on 10:26, December 28th, 1851. The last newspaper delivered to my house, before everything fell apart, was November 9th, 1850. My assumption that the watch lasted a year before giving up turned out to be true and a glimmer of a smirk dared to smear my face. It troubled me not knowing the current date, however.

The value of the watch could not be measured in dollars. Despite the quality of the gold and the intricacies of the engravings, the picture inside made it invaluable. She dressed in her finest clothes for the photo and done up her hair for hours to make sure it was perfect. She required us to take the covered wagon to town, so as not to undo the work she put into her appearance. The journey took several more hours just to take the smoother roads. The photo turned out divine. Her delicate smile always greeted me from her side of the pocket watch, but now, the pasty remains of my wife's only picture smeared the inside.

A pang of remorse murmured deep in my chest. She'd been my constant companion through this hell, and now she existed in memory. The growl built and spread down my arms and suddenly, fists met metal as they pounded against the wall with a rage that made the structure yield. Every blow bowed the hull a little more until it gave way. The force of the water scooped me up and slammed me against the far wall, along with the broken remains of the crates and their contents. The smooth floor provided little traction as feet and hands scrambled to get whatever purchase they could. The little room quickly filled with water, tossing the contents around like a whirlpool.

My fingers caught the edge of the door frame and then fumbled around for the handle. The pressure against it made pulling the door inward difficult, but a little success meant a torrent of water pushed its way into the hallway, sweeping me along with it. The surge carried me to the stairs, where the railing provided enough support to stop me from being pushed further down the corridor. The tumultuous current threatened to pull me off my feet, and with each passing second, the pool got deeper. Over the roar of invading water, a group of bellowing men thudded their way down the stairs. It would be a matter of seconds before they discovered their stowaway. With both hands firmly attached to the railing, the rest of my body retreated below the waterline. Dark brown hair floated on the surface like seaweed while my eyes watched from below.

Then they did something unexpected. Instead of submerging themselves into the rising water to bucket out the intrusion, four men struggled with a heavy iron door. The structure reminded me of something out of a bank vault. In unison, they tugged at the door until it thundered closed above me. The light from the stairwell above dimmed until there was nothing but darkness. A feeling of familiarity crept up my spine and threatened to overwhelm me. All the fear, anxiety, and claustrophobia of being trapped in a cage rushed to the forefront of my mind. The idea of being stuck down here for any length of time terrified me.

A couple of steps remained between the top of the water and the door. It wouldn't be long before it touched the bottom of the frame. The sailors knew this and fumbled with what sounded like a latch. Before they could seal me down here for good, I charged up the few steps between us and used the momentum to ram into the door, shoulder first. A gap formed with the accompaniment of scrambling feet, but the success didn't last. A thunderous noise echoed around the space when it clattered against the frame, propelled by the weight of the reorganized men.

Water leaked through the seams around the lower half of the door. With every second, the line made its way higher up the frame. Even with four strong men bracing against it, the rising water forced the door further from its frame, widening the gap with every additional centimeter.

"Push harder!" huffed the one on the right.

What they did not see were the hinges damaged by my impact. The pins bent just enough so they would no longer fully close without a superhuman amount of strength. The sailor on the left shook his head after observing those same hinges and yelled instructions over the raging sound of the water, "Let's go to the next door, lads, this one isn't budging."

They turned to race up the stairs, but stopped just as quickly, rooted to their spot in shock. I suppose seeing a grown man balancing on a railing only 5 centimeters wide would be a sight to see, but more so, my lips pulled back, exposing my fangs. The peripherals of my vision smoldered in crimson from the sound of their hearts pounding against their rib cages, elevated with excitement and flowing with adrenaline.

The man who stood closest to me struggled to maintain his balance and thudded against the wall, taken completely off-guard by the speed at which he got jumped. While taking a hold of his shoulders, my teeth sunk into his neck. It took a matter of seconds before his comrades realized he was being attacked. One man started clawing at my face. Without letting go with my teeth, I grabbed a fistful of his shirt and held him at arm's length, unperturbed by the punches he landed on my head. Another man managed to snake his arm around my neck and fervently tried to block my airway. There were many reasons why this wouldn't deter me, but most of all, this move required someone who needed air to function in the first place, which I did not. He hung from my neck as the first body slumped to the floor and remained there when the man caught by the scruff of his shirt got pulled in closer to my face. Fangs sunk into his shoulder.

The remaining two men beat on me like a sandbag. The one wrapped around my throat laid down his best efforts against my ribs while the other one kicked at my legs in an effort to sweep them out from under me. Normally, their feeble attempts would make me laugh, but my mind focused entirely on their blood. The gross quantity of it swelled my stomach, yet somehow only left me craving more.

The second body splashed to the ground and bobbed face down in the rising water. The fourth man disappeared up the stairs, taking them two at a time. I grabbed the wrist of the arm still wrapped around my neck and casually uncoiled it while the man grunted, straining to maintain his upper hand. The blue veins in his wrist pumped vividly just under the skin. A faded tattoo barely caught my attention before teeth hooked onto his forearm. He wouldn't stop grunting, and the noise irritated me. A yank of his arm flung him into the wall in front of us and he went limp onto the floor. While sucking, the fourth man thundered back down the stairs, stopping a few steps away. The air sizzled with the sound of an instrument whooshing through the air before bouncing off the back of my head. I finished with the third man before turning to see what he hit me with.

In his hands, he held a wrench so big you'd normally only see one in an iron mill. He struggled to hold it even with two hands. He threw his weight into swinging it at my mid-section. My left hand caught it before making contact and yanked it from his grasp. He stared at me with wide, petrified eyes as the weapon kerplunked into the water below us. The last thing he saw were my lips receding from over my teeth into a grotesque sneer before the opening between us closed with a leap. Our combined weight threw him to the floor.

The pressure of my stomach bloating past capacity almost made me quit, but the esurient side of me saw his blood drained to completion. With my desire for blood saturated, it was as if the damp, suffocating veil over my eyes lifted, revealing a world that didn't seem so limited. It had been a long time since my body needed oxygen to survive, but the feeling reminded me of someone surfacing the water after holding their breath for several minutes. The sensation made me feel euphoric.

It took a matter of seconds to strip the man of his clothes and replace them on my own body. The relief of ridding myself of the rags that hung off me brought another layer of normality, yet not ideal. They stank of someone who long required a bath and scratched cheaply against my skin. The cotton shirt didn't rub nearly as harshly as the stiff pants and nothing like what sailors usually wore. The man's jacket dwarfed me, and instead of buttons, it had two strips of metal that seemed impossible to fasten, so it flapped against my chest as I made my way up the stairwell, my gold watch tucked securely into my front pocket.

The boat had a definitive lilt to it. Sailors stumbled across the top deck, grasping onto the railing to keep from losing their footing. The stacked boxes whined against their bindings, threatening to give way at any moment, prompting me to stick to the outermost railings, ready to jump. The men running around didn't give me any mind as they fervently yelled instructions to one another. The sound of grinding metal reached me before the sailors, but the inevitable became obvious to us all in a heartbeat. On the far end of the ship, a deafening snap pulled everyone's attention to the top container tipping, pulling the ones below it over the side and into the water. The sudden loss of weight lurched us violently. More of the cargo became unsettled and fell, causing the boat to rock from side to side. Water slithered across the deck, lubricating any point of purchase. Quite a few men lost their grip and slid helplessly toward the ocean. They worked together to grapple any outstretched hands as they slid by.

The men made their way to the dinghies, which dangled and thudded against the side of the ship. They stumbled into the rafts one by one. Someone grasped onto my shoulder before shouting over the turmoil, "What are you doing, man? Get in the boat!"

He pushed my shoulder forward and used it as a guide toward the rest of the crew. He didn't have the smell of manual labor about him and shouted orders at several others from behind me, making it obvious that he was the captain. My appearance alone should have given him pause, suspecting he hadn't looked too closely at whom he was helping. My recent gluttony had undoubtedly left a profound effect on my skin. It wouldn't last, but for the moment, my skin had a puffy fullness, as if it were alive, complete with a rosy, warm glow. A stark contrast to its usually chalky texture.

He let go when we arrived at the life rafts, leaving me to climb into one while he stomped his way to the other directly behind it, never having really absorbed who he helped. Half a dozen warm bodies packed into the dingy before it lowered into the water. The lurching of the ship sent out ripples of waves, tossing us around like rag dolls. A tiny version of the turbine whirred to life and propelled us away from the wreckage.

Only the tallest part, at the back of the ship, remained above the surface. Everyone watched in silence as it slowly dipped under the waves and the top of the water smoothed out to an almost mirrorlike reflection. Only two dinghies bobbed on the water with no evidence of their ever being a bigger boat. All around us, the dark blue of the water created a horizon against the lighter blue of the sky.

My next problem prickled the back of my neck. The inconvenience of being discovered as inhuman by the smoke curling off my skin unsettled me more than the incoming pain. Falling back into the water and swimming down far enough so the sun's rays could no longer burn my skin tempted me. However, without a doubt, this resulted in unwanted attention and an ensuing rescue attempt. The remaining men needed to stay alive and aloof for a couple of reasons. Experienced sailors, like this group, knew to head toward more civilization. As long as I kept my thirst in check, there wouldn't be a problem in staying with them a little while longer. Plus, six bodies of preserved blood waited for whenever they were required. A supply good enough to last weeks.

With my mind made up, my fingers found the edges of my new jacket and pulled the hood over my head. It covered my ears, scalp, and a bit of my forehead, leaving my brows, nose, and lips exposed. Turning helped. The sun now blazed against my back, unable to penetrate the layers of the clothing, though it still felt as though a campfire crackled behind me. I welcomed the rare opportunity to warm myself.

With both hands tucked into the jacket, weary thoughts lurked uncomfortably close to the forefront of my mind, ready to follow me for the rest of this lengthy journey. My temper landed me in this situation in the first place, so my best bet of getting to shore would be to concentrate on a neutral train of thought, like counting. One, two, three.

By the count of ten, the humans began exchanging unpleasantries, making it impossible to concentrate. My eyes squeezed shut, trying to block them out, and traced the outline of each numeral to fill any wayward ideas.

"What the hell happened?"

"Dunno. I heard yelling from the aft part of the

ship, but by the time we got over there, the alarms were going off."

"Did we hit something? I didn't feel a thing!"

"No, nothing. I'm telling you, it's the rushed inspections. This old rust bucket was bound to break in half!"

"Don't be dumb, Pete. We definitely hit something for it to go down so fast."

"Then why didn't we feel anything?"

"Whatever happened, we lost good men today."

"So, who are we missing?"

The guy named Pete sounded like he was counting. He stopped at six before yelling across to the other raft, "Oy! How many do you have over there?"

"Twelve!"

"So, who is missing?"

"Do you have Quill?"

"Right here!"

"Jordan? Jordan?"

"Dammit. What about Porter?"

"I haven't seen him since breakfast."

They went back and forth until they named all five missing men, which happened to be the same number of men who'd crossed my path. My fingers grasped the edge of the jacket as I clutched it tighter around my body, while the rest of me nestled deeper into my seat, hoping to be forgotten in their exchange.

"Who are you?" The voice belonged to the man named Pete. His fishy breath curled around the edge of the hood and invaded my nose, making me think the question concerned me. When no one spoke after several breaths, the guy to my right elbowed me in the back.

"Phil," my voice cracked. The word came out heavy, and it felt as though cotton stuffed my mouth. No wonder, since it had been at least a year since speaking. My name sounded odd coming out of my mouth.

"No, I mean, who the fuck are you? How did you get on our ship?"

The dingy suddenly felt very small. Their bodies released more adrenaline and their hearts sped up in anticipation. A dozen eyes bored into the depths of my jacket. The sun illuminated from behind me like a beacon, leaving the fine features of my face swathed in shadow. Through my eyelashes and the edge of the jacket, the others were shifting their weight to rise easily to their feet. Every one of them flexed their hands into fists.

"Did you do this?" Pete gestured to the two rafts. "Did you fucking sabotage our boat?"

His yelling piqued the interest of the other boat, and the twelve men turned to see what the commotion was all about. Their navigator turned their boat to meet up with ours. My lips curled at the thought of dealing with a dozen or so angry humans. It would be such a waste to let their lives end for naught. Their bodies would spoil quickly under the unsheltered sun and as such, were much more useful to me alive.

"I wouldn't dare."

"I wood-ent dehr?" Pete mocked. "What is that? Are you a tea sucking terrorist or something? Trying to start World War Three?"

"What?"

"Uh, uh, whut? Come here, dumbass. I'm going to kill you for what you did to my friends!"

Pete made his way across the dinghy as only someone who lived on the seas could do. At least two others joined him by the time he reached me, while the men sitting next to my right and left latched onto my jacket, pummeling my face and neck.

Their efforts only worked them up more. Hearts raced while sweat beaded on their skin. Venom swelled in my mouth, but losing control wasn't an option. There could be no witnesses to retell what happened here. Resigned, I let them wail on me with my head tilted toward the floor.

My wife called me a patient man, but even a saint has his limits. It felt like being stuck in a barn with a thousand flies. They couldn't hurt me, but their incessant buzzing, while bouncing off my skin, chipped away at my tolerance, little by little, until it reached a crescendo. I simply stood up, taking the two men attached to my jacket with me. They stopped punching in confusion, shocked that they didn't have near the control they assumed they had. Pete looked up at me, poised to land another blow, but resorted to kicking my shins.

The two sailors on either side of me flopped like fish when my hands caught hold of their chins, lifting them, and then tossed into the space between our two dinghies. They were greeted with a chorus of yelps when they splashed into the water twenty meters from where they had started. The rest of them halted their assault and backed up as much as the space allowed. No one dared to move, not even breathe too heavily and attract the attention of the intruder. The propeller whirred dutifully behind me, breaking up the silence of the otherwise peaceful boat. The stillness gave me the mind to refocus, despite the yelling coming from the other boat.

The tension from the fight relaxed my muscles and gave me the confidence to address the situation. Pete stood right in front of me. Realization flooded his face and his skin paled. My lips pulled back over my teeth, exposing my jagged smile. He took a step back, but I grabbed him by the shirt and pulled him within centimeters of my face.

"Not so tough now, are you?" I growled.

"Wha-what are you?" he stammered.

"Your legends call us vampires."

Pete struggled and slapped at whatever he could reach, trying to get out of my grasp, but his feeble attempts quickly grew tiresome. A stern shake settled him.

"I single-handedly punched a hole in your ship and took a beating as if you were flies. There is nothing you can do to kill me, so if you breathe a word of me to anyone—I will kill you. All of you."

That's when one of them tried to shank me. The blade ripped into my shirt, but when it met my skin, it slid off and caught in the fabric. He flew over the other men and landed belly first beyond the edge of the boat. The rest of them lost their minds. Some screamed, while others yelled, trying to organize their attack. Pete was the smart one. He clambered over everyone to get as far from me as possible.

"Wrong choice."

There was little thought of who came next, but one after the other, their flesh tore and their bones broke under the unrelenting slaughter through their ranks. Some fell quickly, while others were more willey, rocking the boat as they tried to squirm away on their hands and knees from the foray. Pete dove into the water and swam desperately toward the other boat. He barely made it halfway between the two vessels before the remaining crew reached out for him, encouraging him on. The water swallowed me like a rock when I side-stepped off the edge and disappeared seamlessly into the void.

The propeller from the other boat churned the water into a vortex of bubbles, making it hard to pinpoint the exact location of the dinghy's hull. My fingers found it when they jammed into the revolving fin, causing the rest of the boat to buck once before settling. The propeller stopped under the iron grip that now held onto one of the three props, but my left hand recoiled in surprise. A thin line of blood floated out of my palm where it bit into me. Lips wrapped around the tiny wound and sucked what little came out. The bleeding slowed after a few seconds and, with further inspection, the wound had already healed.

With two hands on the propeller, my feet found their way to the shell of the boat and used the leverage to pull as hard as possible. It popped off, along with a sizable chunk of the metal exterior, opening the hull for water to rush in. One man stood near the hole, so he got yanked through the opening by the ankle and screamed as the sharp edges cut through his clothing. Blood swirled in the water. My teeth clamped down on one of these wounds and sucked the rest of it out.

The boat sank quickly. One by one, plops of bubbles entered the water as man after man abandoned their island of safety. Their feet churned the water in an irresistible buffet as they kicked toward the other boat.

A large fish brushed against me and we were no longer alone. A great white shark joined the feast. It wasn't long before another, and another, joined the first. Before they could tear the group to complete shreds, it crossed my mind to pick out one last body for myself, so I swam up, grabbed his ankle, and pulled him further down. A pocket of bubbles erupted toward the surface when he got bit in the neck. After just a minute, his body drifted downwards, along with the wreckage of the boat and bits of other sailors.

It seemed obvious to follow the same path as the large boat, even without the knowledge of how far it still had to go to get to its destination. My binge gave me an immense amount of strength to pump effortlessly through the water and, from a safe distance below the surface, made excellent progress by simultaneously using the sun, then the moon, as my compass. A week passed before anything changed.

The water grew unsettled. It encouraged me in a specific direction, where if I swam against it, the current fought back. A tickle of excitement shimmied down my arms when the lightness that came with water being forced up from a receding shoreline tossed me around. Far below, the sandy, jagged bottom of the ocean floor became more visible with every breaststroke. In the distance, another large ship sat anchored. The pull of hard ground made it easy to ignore the souls aboard. Besides, there were two more right behind it if the opportunity presented itself. The closer the shore came, the more boats dotted the water, but nothing could stop me.

A crab scuttled out of the way when my feet contacted the ground. Water sloshed around my busy legs, trying to climb the boulders that made up the seawall. Free of the water, moss caused me to slip several times before reaching the top of the wall and the railing that lined it.

With a little hop over the fence, I stood on solid ground. Water pooled around me and stained the walkway darker. The weight of the new landscape froze me to my spot, and no influence could break the spell that bound me. The rough texture of the stones grated against my skin as my toes gripped into it. The rush of waves climbing up the sides of the wall lulled me into a deep sense of security. This feeling would pass too soon, so my damned soul remained receptive to the feeling for as long as possible.

Admittedly, I was an easy man to anger, but not one to be left speechless. The scene before me squeezed the air from my lungs and trampled whatever expectation my mind had conjured up.

A great, green statue sat on a platform made of marble. Torches illuminated her face in the dark. A tiara graced her head and she held a beacon of carved fire stretched proudly above her. Despite her size, it wasn't the copper woman that impressed me but the scene behind her. A city rose on the other side of the water unlike anything back home in London. Buildings stretched endlessly into the sky. Even in the dark, you could see their silhouettes stacked behind each other for kilometers. As far as the eye could see were these monuments to human progression. Somehow, they efficiently absorbed every trace of light. Millions of candles burned to keep all of it alight. Some glowed from high above in their towers, while others danced in the sky like a beacon to heaven.

It didn't take long to circle the island. A guard wandered in the opposite direction, while his partner waitcd in a building nearby. Otherwise, there were no others here and it would be useless to stay any longer. The ripples where I jumped back into the water dispersed in the waves.

Like the little island before, the shore sat a couple of meters above the waterline. On the top, a footpath separated the inlet from land, lined with mature oak trees that butted up against the start of the buildings. At this time of night, there should have been a few people meandering about, maybe a carriage or two, but instead, dozens occupied the midnight air. All of which walked in a hurry. They breezed by without a second glance, even with my clothes dripping with water. One of them bounced off my shoulder. I turned to growl at him, but he was well down the street.

The city begged me to come closer and guided me further into its belly. Something loud blared as it approached. A carriage lurched to a stop centimeters from my legs. Shocked that there wasn't a horse hitched to the front, or really, anywhere, the thing seemed to move on its own volition. While marveling at the ingenuity before me, the man in the carriage-like object leaned out the window yelling profanities. Though he spoke English, the accent came as a surprise. The words were crisper and unlike anything spoken back home. Intrigued with his pronunciation, I remained in the middle of the road and listened. He kept on with the string of profanities until eventually he'd had enough and opened the door. He stepped out and started toward me. Once he leaned right up in my face, my hands grabbed fistfuls of his shirt and shoved him against the side of his carriage. The glass shattered under the weight. With my mouth a breath away from his neck, peculiar red and blue lights flicked across his face. A glob of venom dripped down and soaked into his shirt before curiosity turned my head to see what produced the lights. The intensity made it hard to distinguish anything in their direction. The outline of a person marched toward us between the red and blue globes, while white lights shone on the back of their legs.

"Step away from the man and put your hands above your head," she belted.

A rather large group of people gathered around us, while others brushed past, trying to get by. My lip curled, and it took a great deal of discipline not to tear into the lot of them. There had to have been a hundred humans in the area, making my chances of fighting them all next to impossible. Memories from my past reminded me of what a ruthless mob could do.

My hands loosened their grip on the driver and he fell heavily on his feet, huffing as he squirmed out from between me and the car. The amount of people watching put me in a place of vulnerability. Shouts of, "Stop! Police!" followed me away from the scene.

Once the humans were well hidden behind me, my discretion evaporated, and my speed became such that their eyes couldn't conceive it. It made it much quicker to find a quiet place to think. A city this size would be easy to disappear in and, with a little luck, one such place came to me in the form of a windowless alley. Unlike so many of the other options, this one didn't have any humans mulling about and it ended in a solid brick wall, leaving no chance of an ambush. Large, square containers overflowed with garbage, spilling out onto the ground and attracted rats just like in London. These boxes created a little nook that hid me from any casual observer. Resigned, my butt landed hard on the ground, while the rest of me sagged with an exhaustion that didn't come from lack of sleep. I leaned my head against the wall and contemplated my new, dire situation. There had to be something to tell me where, and when, this was.

In stark contrast to the dark walls around me, the glint of a white pocket square sat squalled just within reach. After picking it up, I realized it was made of paper instead of cloth. Smudged with lipstick, it attracted particles of dirt, marring its original color. Under the grime, a series of hieroglyphs were printed on its face that meant nothing to me, so it got tossed aside. As the night got deeper and deeper, the sun eventually kissed the horizon, and the little piece of paper teased me as if it held the answers to all my questions.

"Dork for NY"

Chapter 2

The sun crept closer to my hiding spot. It would appear in the gap between the four-story buildings and reach me by noon—maybe an hour from now. My pocket of safety shrank with each passing minute, pressuring me to move on. The curious piece of paper received one last consideration before it totally left my thoughts. Bare feet slapped against the ground, echoing enough to scatter the rats. The diminishing shade pushed me to follow along the edge of the southern building. The mouth of the alley provided no shade at all, keeping me a few feet off the main path where humans passed by regularly. With no commitment to a place to go, I contemplated what to do next.

My cloak would have been very useful right now, but the clothes stolen from the sailor provided enough protection. A ratty, musty shirt clung to my shoulders under a jacket stiff from the salt water. It showed a clear history of the arduous journey through the water. Microscopic particles of sand and dead things embedded into the weave. Not to mention the smell. Old fish and decay wafted from not only the clothing but also my hair and skin. The idea of wearing the ensemble any longer made me itchy, however, not enough to strip down and expose myself to the sun.

The tips of my toes started to tingle. Rays of sun kissed the edges of my body. The warmth absorbed into my skin, raising the hair on my arms. I tilted my chin up so the heat could touch my face and remind me of days that were long gone. The feeling lasted for less than a breath before the woman-like kisses on my skin were replaced by someone stabbing me with a thousand needles directly into my face. Every passing second made the pain worse, but it wasn't enough to make me move.

Survivalism pulled me back a step and just as quickly as the sun had warmed me up, the bitter kiss of the shadows welcomed me back. All the while, throngs of people passed by without a care. Just like the evening before, no one gave me more mind than anyone else who lived there. My clothing alone should have cast me as either a delusional man or as someone who lived on the streets. Hundreds of heartbeats all within a couple meters of me and not one second look. No hesitation at all. Curious.

The horseless carriages—which I discovered are called cars—looked like a solid mass on the road, rushing forward in spurts before stopping again. Many were painted in the most tactless shade of yellow. It reminded me of a sunflower. Each of them had "Taxi" written on their sides. Someone stood on the side of the road and waved purposefully toward one of these carriages to catch a ride. Glad to see something recognizable, this world now didn't feel quite as foreign.

The rest of the pedestrians were a bit of a mystery to me. They weren't paying attention to their surroundings at all. They weren't looking for pocket thieves, watching out for horses, or simply watching their step. As if moving in a queue, everyone stared ahead, bored. Under the murmur of noises coming out of the horseless carriages and the murmur of everyday conversation, faint sounds followed the heads of many of the people. Most of it seemed like insensible dribble, but one woman surrounded herself with Mozart. I'd recognize that piece from anywhere. The sound followed her without an orchestra to accompany it.

Through the chaotic noise of a hundred sets of shoes scuffling down the walkway, one set slowed down until they eventually stopped. The man stood directly in front of me. My eyes narrowed as I watched him from just a few steps away. His dark tinted spectacles studied the ground as his hand dug through the back pocket of an expensive-looking suit. A single row of buttons complimented a subtle pinstripe on dark gray wool. The white undershirt peaked out from under a pressed collar and perfectly matched the pocket square. His soft leather shoes casually pointed toward me, made of a black so deep, you'd normally only see it in Italy. Unlike most of the humans today, he wore a flat cap. The color reminded me of the trousers that accompanied me to my burial; a navy blue with a hint of yellow. He held a leather clutch in his left hand while the right pulled out a couple of bills from its folds.

"God bless," he said as he thrusted his hand toward me.

His emotionless stare became hung up in my own, unable to move away from my piercing gaze. Neither of us moved, but the longer he stood there with his hand extended, the faster his heart pumped. He started to get impatient with the lack of initiative and he shifted his weight. My chin thrusted to the right, encouraging him to move on without breaking eye contact. He let out a little of the breath he'd been holding. It came out on the word, "Whatever."

Hc tossed the money at my feet and walked away, blending into the crowded street. My lip curled involuntarily and another growl formed in my chest. I retreated deep into the alley and out of view of any prying eyes. The brick wall at the end couldn't have been more than three meters tall and it took little effort to jump it flat-footed. On the other side, it led to an alley that paralleled the same path the man headed down while being covered in shadow. It made progress much easier than if the sun beat down on me. The distinct rhythm of his heartbeat and straightforward gate made it unchallenging to track him, even through the buildings. Ahead, a narrow passage cut between the buildings and led back to the street. A trashcan blocked the way, but a quick toss fixed the problem, and it clambered behind me as my body squeezed into the pace. Both shoulders brushed against the sides of the buildings, prompting me to adjust my body's angle to hasten the progress through the passage.

From the safety of the tiny opening, it would be hard to see me waiting for the man to walk by. It took several seconds before he came into view. At first, he kept going, oblivious to my hiding in the shadows, but at the last moment, he glanced over just enough to catch my glare. He stopped, taken aback, clearly not expecting to see me again.

I offered him a humorless smile before snagging him by the back of the neck. He drug his feet and clawed at the walls while being yanked through the narrow path to no avail. We made it back to the roomier alley where the shadows took over and the only eyes to spy on us were his. The sooty brick surrounding us almost reminded me of home. Not only did the area reek of old trash, but rats could be heard scurrying out of the way while the rest of the world's pulse continued. The man stumbled along, trying to keep his balance despite being shoved halfway to the ground. He threw profanities at me, but it didn't change anything.

My attention now turned to potential witnesses. A cool breeze whistled through the cracks of the buildings. Birds tapped their way across roofs. Water streamed somewhere below us. A symphony of sound, yet the only sign of human activities muffled through the walls that enveloped us.

Everything was harder in the daytime. Their eyesight worked better with everything lit up, so naturally, they were more active. All it would take would be one wayward person to wander into the wrong alley at the wrong time. After so long, the lust of accidentally being caught lost its appeal and just became a chore.

The man raised his voice to unbearable levels, and it would soon attract the kind of attention no one wanted, so my hand clamped over his mouth and twisted. He would have collapsed to the ground if my hold on him wasn't so secure. It had already been over a week since my last meal and maintaining control to get this far into the city, without any accidents, didn't come without effort.

That same effort would need to be extended to staging the man's death so as not to look too suspicious. My teeth sunk into his neck and sucked until only a bit of his blood remained. Instead of completely letting go, a chunk of his flesh tore away from his body when my mouth pulled back. The rubbery texture didn't agree with me, so I spat the chunk onto the ground. The result across his throat looked more like an animal ravaged him than something unnatural.

With my right hand gripping him by the neck, I used my left hand to unbutton his overcoat first, then his undershirt, and finally his pants, taking special care to remove them without touching the dirty ground. Once free of his earthly belongings, he collapsed into a fleshy pile.

The fabric of my existing clothes tore easily when ripped from my body. They served as a cleaner surface to stand on while getting into my new ensemble. The suit fit as well as it could. The sleeves ended at my wrists and the trousers did not drag on the ground. If anything, the fabric pulled across the chest, but it would have to do. His shoes squished my toes together, but with any good leather, it would stretch and get more comfortable with time. I grabbed my pocket watch from the old pants and tucked it into the inner pocket of my jacket, looping the chain around the button next to it. My hand pressed against the small lump, bringing it closer to my non-beating heart and for just a moment, fantasized about my wife and let my lost love for her flood me with warmth.

The man's body laid conspicuously out in the open. With a firm grip on his ankle, I dragged him behind me and dumped him into a pile of trash. Disturbing the bags wafted up smells that would make anyone gag. A tuft of hair poked out of the pile, but otherwise, no other part of him could be seen. In a city this size, inevitably, someone would find him, but it didn't matter to me. This wasn't my first time disposing of a body.

The rug of my old clothes peeled off the pavement and landed on the pile of garbage. The last thing to do was make sure nothing else remained.

His wallet materialized a few feet away. The color matched his shoes, almost getting lost in the surrounding grime. The dirt brushed right off when my fingers swept across the surface. Inside, a couple of things stood out to me. He kept quite a bit of cash on hand. Making quick work of fingering through the stack, there were ten bills of a hundred...dollars. American dollars. So, this was the United States. My burial in concrete took place on the shores of Cardiff with their massive, white cliffs set as a backdrop. A humbling distance to have traveled, that is for sure.

He also had a couple of rectangles organized in the folds. The length and width reminded me of a deck of cards, but only a fraction of the width. They weren't made of paper, but their rigidity reminded me more of metal. But it wasn't that either. The thing bowed when squeezed on the ends and returned to its shape when released. A series of numbers engraved the face above the name Miles Cage. In fact, all the rectangles were inscribed with different arrangements of numbers with the same name. The back didn't reveal their purpose any more than the front. My finger tapped the edge in thought before sliding it back into the slot.

The final pocket held a stack of paper business cards. The cardstock had a smooth finish, printed in black ink, with the name Miles Cage in bold font at the top. It appeared that he worked as an investment banker in New York, New York. Somehow, it all made sense. Even from London, everyone knew this city served as a central hub for immigrants, goods, and trades. No wonder it grew so big.

I slid the wallet into an interior pocket and made my way out of the alley. Black leather shoes clicked along the path smartly. The road in front didn't seem so intimidating with proper clothing, and a heavy shadow laid across the path. My body became one of many as the crowd absorbed it into its natural flow, free to observe my new reality in anonymity. That is how the rest of the day flowed. Buildings towered over me for an impossibly vast distance. Kilometers of unchanging, gray masses. Yet, within the maze were neighborhoods as distinct as the people who inhabited them. Chinese, Muslim, Jewish, African American. The city divided itself into subcultures that blended easily from one block to the next. They all coexisted seamlessly.

Like a breath of fresh air, a forest emerged in the middle of the city. Mature trees towered over the road in every shade of red, orange, yellow, and green. Bushes lined the walkway, inviting me further into the garden. The space supplied a welcome relief from the fumes that puffed out of the horseless carriages. The humans spread out in various positions and various states of dress. One in particular caught my eye. He only wore undergarments, but they barely covered his genitals and buttocks. The material was shiny, like the surface of the water or a fresh layer of snow. A robe that looked to be a single thread thick draped over his shoulders, providing little protection from the approaching, brisk night air. Black tracks of ink decorated his skin in various geometric patterns, dancing around several varieties of flora, peeked out from the unfastened belt. What piqued my interest the most were his erratic movements. He convulsed his arms wildly, pumping the air in front of his chest over and over. His hips thrusted in the same horrid movement. All the while, his eyes stayed closed and his jaw was slack. The same rancid sound floated around his head with no obvious point of origin.

Fascinated, I took a seat on a bench tucked under the long reach of the oak above me. Across the walkway, a smelly man took refuge along the length of his makeshift bed, fast asleep. The scene became more bizarre with each new human. No more modestly dressed women or well-appointed gentleman. One handful of women wore skirts, while the rest wore various styled pants. Another group of young adults conversed by an overflowing waste bin. They were matching of a sort, all wearing various shades of black. All of them, even the men, fashioned themselves with white face powder and black-lined eyes, black lipstick, and black hair. A couple of the girls wore fishnets around their legs, contrasting against their pale legs. They all looked to be wearing military boots.

A man trotted past, not terribly urgent, dressed in a flappy shirt and shorts that ended mid-thigh. His breath came out in even huffs in time with his beating heart. The same peculiar noise clouded his head. My instincts told me to follow him and before the thought could reach the reasonable part of my brain, I left the bench and started to stalk the man. It lasted a few strides before practically won out. Nothing good would happen when he got mauled in front of a dozen or so people. Instead, my eyes tracked him from the discretion of the bench. He followed the path along the edges of the garden until he momentarily passed behind some trees and reappeared along the other side. He looped back around and continued on the same path.

It all started to make sense. The oddly dressed people around me, the strange behavior, and the outlandish dancing had to be part of a nearby circus troupe. I casually looked around for the wagon train that would announce their nature, but nothing obvious stuck out. Perhaps they were parked at the end of the garden and out of sight. The corner of my mouth twitched upward at the thought of perhaps going to the show. A welcomed sense of normality.

"I still cannot believe the scene Gina made at the baby shower last night. Did she really have to push Tish's face into the cake? Totally called for, but like, still totally unbelievable," spoke a soft voice from my left. She marched purposefully through the garden.

"Right? Like, what would have happened if Jerald was there? He started all this and he sure as hell would not have been quiet," she continued.

My eyebrows furrowed, trying to understand. She talked to herself and not in the mutterings of a madwoman, but in a concise conversation with an invisible second party. When she got closer, the faint replies of the second person could be heard near her head. A white bar perched in her ear, emitting sounds of the other half of the conversation. The confidence of her speech made it impossible not to picture the second person walking next to her. Her voice carried her out of sight, but others took her place with their own inner ear sound boxes, oblivious to anything else.

"My dearest, I would give anything to tell you about what the world has become," I whispered to myself.

A pang of loneliness threatened to choke me. I

coughed away the feeling, along with the tears that threatened to spill. It would do me no good to succumb to the feeling. She's dead and the grief, though painful, needed to be controlled. My thoughts took a right turn and pictured what it would have been like to have taken this journey with her. Her smile lit up my imagination as she asked me to share the inconsequential details. My hands found their way to the matted hair that hung from my head. It had grown to my waistline. The mass of brown knots reminded me of something a rat would construct, so my fingers became a comb to untangle the mess, one strand at a time. With my eyes closed, it almost felt as though my wife's hair lay in my hands, making it easy to shut out the outside world and complete my task.

The memories carried me until the sky started to match the color of the leaves. With the change of the light, so did the people. The troupe of clowns dispersed, leaving me with the homeless and the stupid. Anyone out after dark existed at my mercy and the energy of it radiated in my bones. No longer did the shadows bind me.

A crown of hair hung straight down my sides by the time the last vestiges of day dissolved. Something to bind it out of the way, or chop it off, would have been nice. As such, I tempered the annoyance it caused by smoothing it on my backside. The grooming did little for the rancid smell of the salt water and brine clinging to my skin, but whatever perfume the dead man was wearing, thickly veiled his stolen clothes, creating an odd vapor around me. It masked enough of the smell to make me presentable to the less sensitive, but not enough to erase the appeal of finding somewhere to bathe.

Time did nothing to improve my mood. Marinating in my memories should have brought me to a happier place, but instead, it pulled me under. So, I set off to fill a craving that blood couldn't. The city consumed all sides of the park, but the crowd seemed livelier to the south. Somehow, the people wore even less formal clothing and instead of business suits; the men dressed more flamboyantly. Buttons undone to the middle of their chests while their hair, heavy with pomade, stood out in exaggerated fashion. Then there were the ladies. Dresses just long enough to cover any sin. The fabrics tightly hugged every curve over legs that plunged for what seemed like forever. Their heeled shoes forced their feet at an unnaturally high angle, accentuating every muscle down their calves.

My curiosity led me in the same direction as the provocatively dressed group. They meandered toward a similarly dressed group of individuals and stopped at the end of a long line of people, organized with a velvet rope. At the front of the line were two muscular men guarding the entrance to what looked like a pub. The smell of liquor and sweat seeped from the doors, which did little to muffle the sounds of excited chatter and intense, rhythmic thudding. Above the doors hung an illuminated sign that was harsh to look at against the deep progression of the night. It blazed in a white halo, with blue lettering that reminded me of a cornflower. The name on the sign said, "Trap Door".

Several people watched me walk on the outside of the skimpy barrier and straight to the door. My hand didn't reach the handle before one of the burly men made a point of stepping in front of me

"You got to wait in line, bro," he said.

He looked at me, completely void of expression. Our eyes met at the same height, but the man must have weighed twice as much. The black suit he wore fit tight against his broad chest, and the single button that held it together looked ready to give up. He was a good choice for such a job, and a copy of him stood less than a meter away. A twin in their body types, the second one stood up from his stool at the front of the line. His accomplice stepped toward me in a way that herded me away from the entrance. They casually applied pressure to the situation, trying to get me to step off their stoop and to the back of the line. Resolutions to this kind of conflict required a certain finesse, so my hand reached into the inner pocket of my jacket and pulled out Miles's wallet. With no idea on conversion rates, a guess would have to do. I slipped a hundred-dollar bill out of the fold and thrust it toward the guard, but a sweet voice behind him interrupted the exchange.

"Let him in. This place could use some more beautiful faces," she said.

The woman leaned against the brick building, tucked in against the far end of the entrance. The blue glow of the sign washed over her face, leaving ominous shadows under her eyes and nose. Her face momentarily lit up red from the end of her glowing cigarette as she inhaled. It sparkled in her brown irises. She lowered the stick as a puff of smoke blew from her pouty lips. She was older than the group of people behind me, but still toying with youth. Her full body provided the perfect form for her dress to drape off her in all the right places. The corner of my lip curled up as her allure pulled me in.

"Keep it," I said to the guard while stuffing the bill into the man's hand. The other guard received the same amount of appreciation. With my attention fully on the woman, my eyes sparkled with interest. "Ma'am."

Her eyes bounced up to my face from under thick eyelashes, enticing me to make my way over to her. She stopped me after just a few steps. "Don't make me regret my decision."

"I would never break the sanctity of kindness from a beautiful woman," I replied, feigning insult.

"Do you have your ID?" she responded.

My eyebrows crunched in misunderstanding.

"Your identification," she enunciated. "Don't play coy with me. No ID, no entry. It's not worth the trouble if you don't have it."

"You've caught me off balance." My hands patted the various pockets located around my clothes.

"You a Londoner?" she asked.

"Indeed, I am. Are you familiar?"

"With their drinking laws? Yes, but this is America. You must have brought your wallet, so take it out! I don't have time for this."

The wallet slid smoothly from the silk lined pocket, but didn't obviously reveal what an ID consisted of. My fingers teased through the various layers of cards, hoping she would clue me into the correct choice. Her breath came out in an impatient sigh and the same hand that clutched her lit cigarette gracefully plucked out one of the cards. She held it close to her face, while her eyes sprung back and forth from the square to me, undecided.

Finally, she offered the card back and, after releasing it from her gentle hold, took another long drag on her cigarette. She looked at me with undecided eyes. When she blew the smoke from her lips, she said, "You should probably get a new picture for your license. You are much more handsome in person. Though, the long, goth hair doesn't suit you."

Taking this as an invitation, I took another step in her direction. She answered my approach by saying, "Have fun." and open palmed, pointed to the entrance, while taking in another puff. Confused, her mixed advances stopped me. This wasn't the usual effect my kind had on women. Normally, they'd recognize the danger and subconsciously shut us out. This woman danced a fine line of allure and indifference.

Occasionally, our appearance attracted a certain kind of affection, well, more of a sinful curiosity. Still, our kind learned the art of seduction in the rare opportunities where a little encouragement sealed the deal. Marriage negated any reason for me to seduce random women, driving me to take my meals in the damp, dark corners of the town where an unfortunate wrong turn led. Yet, the skill never truly went away.

Meanwhile, this woman was oblivious. Her reaction showed that she contained an immunity to my strangeness. She didn't even bother keeping an eye on me, but stared down the length of the queue.

The invitation to enter the pub seemed more appealing than wasting any more time on this woman. Her demure attitude lingered until the cacophony of what went on inside the building derailed all train of thought. Overall, the place was dark. My eyes easily saw through the curtain of mystery the place tried to convey. Lights spotted various key locations, making enough of an impact to know where to go. Bodies packed the space around a recessed center. They attempted to dance. However, it looked more like they were jumping, convulsing, and wiggling to a wretched sound blaring from a central point in front of them. A single woman stood behind the boxes controlling the various sounds coming from the contraption. Resigned, I finally let go of the indignation that the sounds that followed people around and currently filled the room were a loose interpretation of music.

Heightened sounds of their elevated beating hearts overwhelmed the music. Some responded to the exertion of dancing and others fluttered from the allure of the person sitting next to them. Their love muscles spread the smell of hormones throughout the space. The hair on the back of my neck stood up in response when the scent tickled my sinuses. Instinctually, venom flowed into my mouth and the taste rolled across my tongue.

A smattering of standing tables surrounded the dance floor, crowded with people laughing, sipping, or leaning. Natural paths formed between the groups as the occupants tried to navigate the overly filled space. Sticky tabletops supported an assortment of glasses, whether they were half drunk, empty and waiting to be picked up, or abandoned because someone forgot where they set their drink down.

Deep, built in booths lined the outside edge of the establishment. They gave their occupants the illusion of more privacy, but in reality, only gave them a place to sit other than the bar counter. Much like the standing tables, people enjoyed having a place to set their drinks or, in the case of one couple, trying to make out.

At least one thing hadn't changed. The most

crowded part of the place was the bar. People pushed into each other trying to get to the front, leaning over the occupants who had seats, vying for the female bartender's attention. She hustled from one end to the other, occasionally stepping around a second bartender to get to a particular bottle of liquor. They stacked against the wall high above both of their heads, arranged in a cascade. Illuminated from below, each layer accentuated the various colors of the bottles. It looked like they had all the usual options, like scotch, bourbon, vodka, whiskey, rum, and tequila, with some options that were unrecognizable.

I slid through the wall of people easily and found a place to lean against the sticky wood surface. The bartenders worked like machines. A new face would appear at the counter, they would lean in close to the mouth of the customer, have their drink order yelled into their ear, and then they would get to work. Beyond this, no formal queue determined who went next. Some waited longer than others. Frustrated whines came out of more than one person.

The female bartender closest to me pushed up on her tiptoes to reach just the second shelf. When someone ordered a liquor higher up, she slid a crate over and used the extra height to get what she needed. Wildly curly hair bounced when she stepped back onto the floor. A deep purple color shadowed her eyes that ended in a neat point. Just like the other ladies in the pub, she wore a short cut skirt and an exposed mid-section. Jewelry glinted off her neck, ending in a thick puddle between her breasts.

"Excuse me." My voice carried the words sharply through the torrent of sound. My breath carried the words to the woman, knowing what would happen. Like a whistle to a dog, she stopped and looked up at me. Someone leaned over the bar to place their order, but she walked away, evoking the frustration of the patron who thought they were being served. Her eyes snared in my friendly grin and when she leaned in to get closer, her eyes remained locked on mine until my lips tickled her cheek.

"Scotch. Neat. Make it a double," I instructed.

She smelled sweet, like chocolate, making me wonder how she tasted. No doubt it would be just as good. Her breath came out ragged. She looked up at me then, winked, and set off toward the scotch bottles. Hands that poured a thousand times before expertly maneuvered the butterscotch-colored liquid into a glass. But under the confidence, her grip trembled so slightly, human eyes wouldn't be able to notice. The glass thudded down in front of me and her lips were back to my ear.

"Want to start a tab?" she asked.

"Depends. How late do you work?"

"Just started," she answered.

"I'll wait."

"Good," she whispered.

With the wallet once again in my hand, I reached for another bill for her to hold on to.

"No cash," she instructed.

Not sure how else to pay, my eyes searched her face for a clue.

"Allow me," she said as she reached for the wallet. For the second time this evening, a woman pulled a foreign card out of my wallet. She did not go for the 'ID' as the woman outside had. She pulled out one with the numbers along the bottom. From under the counter, she set a little black box in front of me, slid the card into the bottom, and just as quickly removed it.

Her fingers lingered on mine when she handed the curious thing back. She received a wink before dissolving into the crowd. A group vacated a couch near the dance floor and before someone else could take claim, took my place onto the middle cushion while taking the first sip. The familiar sting of the alcohol against my sensitive taste buds made my face pucker, but the feeling wasn't entirely unpleasant. The drink had notes of vanilla under a heavy hue of oak, creating a pleasant taste. The drink brought a nice change to an otherwise monotonous diet, despite having no effect on my kind since our livers technically didn't function. We mostly enjoyed it for the taste and the chance at socialization, while some used it as bait in a highly populated hunting ground. Holding a drink made you more approachable—at least, that was the case back at home.

Home. Not sure what that meant anymore. Nestled in the hills just outside of London, my house probably sat vacant, if someone hadn't already taken over the space. My roses were hopefully still alive, but doubtful. The limestone home was constructed deep in the woods and far from the city, allowing me the privacy to exist without the distraction of humans. Also, where I hoped they buried my dearly beloved. My thoughts went down a dangerous road and if they continued, bad things would inevitably happen in such a crowded place. Looking around for a distraction, it came to my attention several people watched me. If they wanted my couch or something else, they could come up and ask.

"Ready for another?" spoke the woman over the back of the couch.

She leaned over the couch, talking so close into my ear that when I turned to look at her, our noses almost brushed. Her closeness tested my conviction a little too much and my body reacted by widening the gap, not used to the cavalier disregard for personal space. Surely, she recognized that my appearance edged on the side of strange and to stay just far enough away to hold on to the illusion of safety. Any normal human would. Yet, this woman looked at me with the same interest as she did everyone else. When she didn't get an answer right away, she pointed at my mostly empty glass and repeated, "Do you want another Scotch?"

She performed her job so well, it left me wondering if she genuinely held higher expectations than just flirty exchanges. Simply put, she noticed my empty glass of scotch before I did.

"Please." My teeth flashed in her direction.

There had to be a sign that revealed more than hospitality, but she hustled back to the bar without a backwards glance. Her heart rate wasn't elevated, and neither were the other signs of attraction, like hormones. Not knowing how to read the situation put me in a peculiar place. Even when she brought my drink back, she laid her hand on my shoulder, lowered the new drink down for me to grab, then dissolved back into the crowd, only to reappear an hour or so later, repeating the same conversation.

Something changed inside her between the last trip over and now. Her calm, indifferent composure masked the heart beating erratically under her breasts. She leaned over the couch, like every time before, but this time, before she could speak, the full weight of my gaze probed her for answers. A sly grin smothered her face and when she spoke, the words came out breathy. "Come with me."

I eyed her suspiciously, but overcome with curiosity, my glass tinged onto the table beside the couch and reflected the woman holding her hand out to me. She held onto me with butter soft hands and led me through the crowd toward a door that read 'Restrooms'. The door squeaked closed behind us, effectively muffling the droning of everyone outside of it. A person passed us on their way back out, but other than that, the only souls back here were the two of us. She guided me into the room labeled 'Women', closed and locked the door behind us, and pounced on me like her life wasn't in danger.

In the deepest recesses of the building, I forgot myself. Her warm body pressed us against the far wall as she showered eager kisses wherever her lips could reach. Playful nips grazed my neck, but when she grew impatient with this, she wrapped her hand around the back of my head and pulled me down to her level. Our lips met, but the height difference made the affair awkward at best, so my hands found their way around her waist and lifted her onto the sink. She then grabbed my arm in a talon-like grip with her left hand and moved her other hand down to fumble at the front of my pants.

My free hand cradled her delicate neck as if she were a beautiful flower. Her veins pounded under my touch and sweat beaded on her skin. The smell drove me mad. Venom swirled in my mouth as the burning desire to rip into her burned in my throat. For whatever reason, my deadly bite turned into a ravenous kiss. Her skin flushed wherever my lips touched on her neck, jaw, cheeks, nose. She moaned in response and turned to catch me on the lips.

A growl ripped out from deep in my chest and I pulled back. She tried to snatch me closer, but my hands secured any further attempts by binding them against the top of the sink. Something about her trying to touch my lips brought sense back into me. The bathroom smelled of cheap cologne; scribbles covered the walls, and a stranger straddled my torso, grinding their way closer to my face. Loneliness drove me to do something that went against the vows made purely out of love for my wife.

"Don't stop," she whined.

She leaned in and planted her lips against mine in an attempt to get me to continue my explorations, but my mouth remained firmly shut. Her kisses were nothing more than someone making out with a statue for how much I reciprocated. Her enthusiasm waned until she leaned back.

"Please?"

She begged me with her eyes, so my hold softened, and my finger traced her arm, up to her shoulder, along her jugular, and stroked the line of her jaw until my hand propped her chin up so that it pointed at me. The corners of her mouth twitched with excitement. No one could argue this woman held a beauty that raised the standard of everyone around her and anyone with eyes would go to the ends of the earth just to experience the pleasures that followed this kind of encounter, but she held no interest to me for anything other than what came next. My fangs sunk deep into her shoulder and let the red liquid ooze onto my lips. She gasped in surprise, but not in an unpleasant way. Her hand clawed at my backside as she succumbed to the euphoria that flooded her body.

A sliver of my humanity reared its ugly head when her hand became slack and flopped out from under my shirt. Her heart slowed and her body slumped onto the counter, but still very much alive. My tongue licked the red stain from my lips as I pulled away. A line of blood trickled down her collarbone and caught in her elaborate necklace.

"Don't. Stop," she mumbled.

Her eyes closed halfway, and she leaned against the mirror, looking significantly more pale, but horribly satisfied. She reached for me again, even though there were a few steps between us. Blood smeared across her neck and chest, staining the once brilliant jewels a dark shade of red. She had quite the impossible mess to clean up, but at least she had a future to look forward to, unlike so many others who met me.

The smell of her adrenaline stained my nose, and it took an enormous effort to walk out of that bathroom. Experience told me that a second glance meant she wouldn't leave this room alive. Willpower alone kept my feet moving away from her. The lock clicked open and released me from my temptations. A sign lit up at the end of the short hallway with the word 'Exit' illuminated. Once outside, the city welcomed me back into the darkness once again.

Chapter 3

Since escaping from the concrete tomb, blood lust and grief occupied every facet of my existence and for the moment, my world didn't feel like a well of bottomless disconsolation. The liveliness of the city seeped through ingrained instincts and infected me with a feeling of wonder. People bustled around in a cacophony of movement, driven by the same hunger as every animal on this planet. They were getting something done, trying to get something done, or they walked away from getting it done, just to repeat the dance. The only people without purpose were the homeless and myself. My aimless wandering made my lack of direction painfully obvious. With nowhere to go, people to see, or a job to provide me with money, the desire to have a purpose tickled my spine.

A man in my position wanted for very little. In exchange for food, humans gave me their life and could live as an animal in the forest if so, truly desired. Some of my kind chose to exist this way, but that wasn't the life for me. The draw of society pulled me toward tailored clothes and shiny horses, which accounted for very little of my spending. The rest went to our house and adorning the inside to create a space we could live in comfortably. Without my beautiful bride, living in the woods as a monster sounded like an option, but an unappealing one. Life needed purpose, but I didn't know what that meant for me without her.

It would be another few days before the need for blood overwhelmed all other sensible thoughts. The temptation of partaking in a casual hunt crossed my mind for the sake of keeping my sanity. For the evening, the woman from the bar satisfied the hunger enough to keep me from looking for another. So, with nothing else to do, my hands tucked into my pant pockets and followed my feet, which carried me in no particular direction. Without the need for sleep, it left a lot of time to spare, and what better use of it than to explore the city? More than anything, I wanted to experience something new. The answer sat in the distance, touching the sky.

My toes pointed to the base of one building. A series of steps led to an entrance made of glass and above it, the building reached upwards for an impossible distance. My count reached forty before the windows blended the stories together and into the clouds. Copies of the same design clustered around it, separated by the roads dwarfed by their size. The people milling about looked like ants in a canyon for how little space they took up.

There were many choices, but this building looked the easiest to climb. Brick handholds dotted the side every meter and held securely when my fingers gripped onto an edge just above my head. All my weight hung from those four fingers, testing to see if it would crumble. Nothing shifted. Grinning, I started climbing. Story after story blurred by, revealing snippets of the everyday lives of the people who existed here. Each floor showed a different scene that catered to its purpose. Most of them dark for the night, dowsed in sleepiness. Fascinatingly, there was an overwhelming theme to it all: rows of desks and chairs crowded the space in varying shades of beige and gray, stripping what little personality the building had. They were devoid of life in more than one sense.

Then, every tenth floor or so, there would be a single occupant, sitting behind a desk, staring at the illuminated rectangle in front of them. The rectangle reminded me of a typewriter, if not more advanced. The concentration of light repelled my eyes from looking at it for no longer than a brief glance, making me ponder the appeal of staring at something so hurtful. Almost every one of the desks hosted the contraption, but if no one sat in front of it, no light emitted from the front. It piqued my curiosity enough to want to examine it further but decided against it and continued.

The air at the top had to have been ten degrees cooler than the street below. Cleaner too. Human scent didn't stifle the air, nor the heavy stink that persisted everywhere else. The top of the building ended with a lip that circled the cone that extended up several more meters. One foot stepped directly in front of the other. Decidedly, the best seat faced south, toward the mouth of the river and the green statue who originally welcomed me here. Other buildings came close to the height of the one under me, but all fell short, leaving an unobstructed view. My legs hung off the edge and my hands settled on top of the navy-blue pants.

A thin layer of clouds hung heavy over the city, blurring the lights like stars reflecting on the ocean. Behind me, the city folded around the large garden where I watched the sunset just a few hours before. Water split the wall of buildings like fingers and hosted an array of diverse ships. Beyond the rivers though, the city extended further than the horizon, making me wonder if it ever ended.

The view kept me enthralled until the eastern sky started to brighten, begrudgingly encouraging me to relocate or else get caught in the morning sun. The clouds thickened overnight, completely concealing the street below me. More noise filled the air as people began to wake up and start their day. The window to get down unnoticed narrowed with each new commuter. I grinned to myself, wondering how it felt to fly, and flicked myself off the edge.

Air whistled in my ears and the suit jacket flapped above my head, holding on by the armholes. The low laying clouds briefly swallowed me and any sense of space. Dew moistened the underside of my clothing. It spat me out twenty or so meters above the ground. All too soon, my loafers touched down on the sidewalk and the air that followed me down whooshed out, stirring up a cloud of dust. A lady jumped back in surprise at the sudden appearance of another person. She stuffed the little rectangle in her hand into her purse and hurried along. The only other beings to see me survive my high jump were a couple of pigeons and a rat.

My perch among the stars gave me a new perspective on the city and a better sense of the place, even if the view from the street now felt claustrophobic between the behemoth buildings. Last night presented a temporary source of entertainment, but it didn't solve the bigger question: what next? As such, my feet remained frozen to where they landed. The construct of time passed differently to me. After living so long, seconds to a human could be hours to me. Only when a man walked up to me and asked, "You okay?" did I realize how much time passed. Pulled out of my thoughts, a lot changed since checking out. Life buzzed in the streets and the sky glistened blue.

"Yeah, it's all good, mate," I said dismissively.

With no real destination in mind, the shadows on the ground were the only thing to dictate my wanderings. Half a block later, an idea came to mind. Now it seemed so obvious; a chuckle rumbled in my chest while fishing around for Miles's wallet. His business card had an address listed that would no doubt lead me to his place of work, but the place held little interest to me at present. His identification card listed a different address. With nothing but time on my hands, I set out, hoping to discover that this location was his home.

The numbering system of the streets made logical sense, starting with one and ascending from there. Some were odd, some even, but ultimately, they guided me directly to the address in question. The trek would have been straightforward if not for the early morning sun flooding certain roads in light. Everything running east to west was basically impassible, forcing me to make my way north by zigzagging through sheltered streets or alleys that would be good to hunt from. Finally, bold numbers hung above the entrance to a residential building that matched the ones written on his identification.

Huge potted plants created a warm welcome in front of two ornate marble columns, matching the sand-colored stone of the wall behind them. Windows stretched up nearly two stories, letting in copious amounts of light. Waiting above the sidewalk by just two steps, the doorman acknowledged my entrance to the building by nodding his head. Polished marble floors made me self-conscious of the trail of footprints behind me. He discreetly called for a mop after a dozen more steps, assuming his guest could no longer hear the request.

A blonde woman sat behind the receptionist's desk, staring at her illuminated rectangle. My intent was to slip through unnoticed, but when my shadow fell over her, she jumped her eyes upward to see who entered the lobby. She took a double take before spitting out, "Hello. Welcome in."

"Thank you," came out in a polite intonation.

"Can I help you with something?" she asked while removing herself from the chair, looking as though she didn't recognize me. A friendly, but curious, smile touched her face, while her eyes urged me to come over.

Not to be rude, my response left little room for interpretation. "Just heading home."

"You must be new here." She blushed. "I would have remembered you."

"Brand new."

"I must have been off when you signed the lease agreement. Maple never shares when new residences move in! Regardless, that isn't your problem. My name is Lacey and happy you're here. Let me know if you need anything." She smiled sweetly.

At the back of the lobby, a nondescript sign hung from the wall with a picture of a stick figure descending stairs. The delicate details paid to the foyer forgotten in this barren space. The stairwell climbed upwards in a utilitarian design. Painted white steps sat under metal railings bolted to a drab colored wall. A large corresponding number adorned each landing to the current floor. Miles's address listed the suite number 2407, making it logical that the 24th floor would be a good place to start. My steps scaled the stairs two at a time, negligent to discretion regarding my speed, since no one else occupied the area. A matter of seconds passed before the number twenty-four greeted me on the landing. Upon exiting, the flowery wallpaper and marble floors returned. The room copied the lobby, but on a much more intimate scale. Despite the color and the attention to details, the space felt cold and very unwelcoming. Perhaps the smell threw me off, or the lack thereof. Every building had a luster to it, but this one smelled like industry with very little trace of human.

With just one direction to go, the hallway led me past six white doors labeled numerically. Bronze plaques displayed engraved numbers, screwed into the right side of the wall. The seventh door would have blended in with the rest of them if it wasn't for the tape crisscrossed in front of it. There were words printed across the face that repeated 'Police Investigation–Do not cross'. The ribbon came off the frame like tissue paper and tangled around my hand. I ripped it off and tested the door handle. It was locked. My wrist applied a little more pressure, and the feeble mechanism broke immediately. I nudged the door with my foot, and it swung open, revealing a nice, but scarcely decorated, home.

Windows lined the backside from floor to ceiling, making it the most attractive part of his house. Even though it looked out over another building, the view demanded respect. In the near distance, slits of the river appeared between the man-made marvels. Despite the thousands of people around me, the home felt isolated, like the scene outside existed only for whoever looked through the glass. Depending on how close you stood to the lip, determined how much of the stranger's lives you witnessed, including the carriages on the street below and the people who lived in the adjacent buildings. The scenery extended all the way to the harbor and the boats that docked there, if you pressed your head against the glass.

Everything in the home was too bright, however. The floor, walls, and furniture were all white. The kitchen cabinets furnished the only repose from the brightness. They contrasted the overall theme with a dark chocolate finish with silver pulls. The man even owned white bedding. I admired the consistency, but the color grabbed every bit of light that flooded into the room and reflected it back in a flame-like glow. There had to be something in this house that would provide protection from the outside. The bedding could work, but no way to attach it to the wall and cover the vastness of the space. Upon further investigation, the sides of the window hosted hidden curtains. After a little yank, they yielded to the strained whirring of something that they connected to. The darkness didn't blanket the room in complete totality, but it allowed me to freely roam throughout the house.

The bedroom offered the same kind of curtains and, just like in the main living area, transformed the room into a space that could be explored. A separate room stored his clothes large enough to walk into and appointed at least a dozen complete suits. The man's taste earned my respect. The patterns were everything from a subtle black plaid, a light gray herringbone, to an especially crisp woolen pinstripe that begged me to wear next. The rest of the room laid out his other appointments just as neatly. Socks sat folded in their designated drawer, the ties hung carefully so that they could all be seen, polished shoes filled racks that tilted them at a slight angle, while his lounge clothes defined their own section. From the wardrobe alone, envisioning myself taking refuge in this place for the foreseeable future was easy.

His home had a severe flaw that radiated out into the bedroom from somewhere close. The stench originated from under a door at the back of the room, worrying me that it acted like a floodgate for something more disturbing. Through the door connected a room that smelled like shit. Literally. A latrine and a washbasin stank up the space mere feet from where he slept. My nose wrinkled in disgust.

The room complimented the rest of the house in its design aesthetic, but a distinct attempt at masking the less-than-ideal smell with something citrusy created an unwelcoming environment. Continued exposure to the room lessened the effect and it wasn't long before my mind could wander past the smell. A porcelain washbasin rested on the top of a cabinet, but no pitcher. A silver spigot hung over the bowl with two adjacent levers. A curious finger twisted one of them and water cascaded into the basin, only to then disappear down a hole in the bottom. Behind a cabinet door under the contraption revealed the water hadn't run into a hidden bucket or onto the floor, but into a pipe that whisked away the drainage through the wall.

While turning the lever to stop the flow, my eye caught what looked like a built-in shower nestled into the corner. The setup very much mimicked a version from home but updated to be more streamlined. Two valves poked out of the wall beneath the plate like head positioned at the perfect angle. A steady stream of water rained onto my hand and dripped down the drain. It moistened the cuff of my suit, but it didn't bother me since it would soon be fodder for the other choices ahead of me.

Excited to cleanse the years of built of filth, the clothes practically tore under my haste to get out of them and fell into a pile just outside of the glass walls surrounding the shower. To my utter surprise, the water blazed onto my skin when I stepped under the waterfall. The temperature brought on memories of home and what it felt like to be completely surrendered to the one you love, but instead of an internal warmth, it enveloped my body in an embrace. Water splashed over my closed eyes and ran down various grooves, cleansing accumulated grievances along with it. Steam curled around me and filled the space in a fog. In an alcove built into the room, he possessed a couple of bottles of things that were unrecognizable. They had gibberish names and the pep-talks printed on the labels, though entertaining, didn't clear up their purpose. After sifting through a dictionary of useless information, the items amounted to being useless to me, so my hand curled around the only familiar thing and set to work scrubbing with the bar of soap that smelled like pine. Brown suds made their way down the drain along with the weight of the last few…years? Decades?

A swirl of fog joined me as I stepped out of the

shower and into crisper air, feeling more reinvigorated than when all those sailors sacrificed their lives for me. A stack of clean towels rested on a shelf near the shower, so my fingers snatched one from the top and used it to mop up the droplets around my skin. My hair acted like a sponge and slowly released a stream of water onto the floor around my feet, creating a puddle. In all my years, I'd never had hair this long. Many of my kind did, not bothered by the extra length, but to me, it seemed excessive and unruly. My wife liked it best when it barely brushed my shoulders, so that is where it remained. Having it down to my waist intrigued me and created a profile that could possibly work with the right attention to detail. Surely, this man would have something to bind it back. Nothing obvious stuck out in the confines of the room, so my search extended into the bedroom.

The towel lay abandoned on top of the bed while my nakedness made its way back to the clothing room. The hanger holding the wool suit paused midair when an outfit much more my style glimmered from another part of the crowded wardrobe. A matte-black suit jacket and pants complimented the delicate dark blue pinstripes that ran lengthwise down the ensemble. Miles had well-appointed taste regarding the details, making it easy to achieve a coordinated look. My arms slipped through dark-colored undergarments before slipping into the suit. His ties were much too thin and something thicker would have been preferable, but one found its way around my neck regardless. Miles had an insultingly low amount of pocket squares, but I found one that would work. The shade reminded me of a bar of gold and contrasted nicely against the dark threads of the suit from its place in the breast pocket.

His wardrobe fit me quite comfortably, down to his shoes. The black ones from his corpse were a bit scuffed from my nighttime activities and lost their pristine. Luckily, he retained a fresh pair that looked almost identical to the first. To my utter joy, hidden in the recesses of his closet was just the thing I needed the most. A grin crept across my face while holding the item out in front of me. The black wool coat felt like butter under my caressing fingertips, the fabric fell away in a supple drape. Slipping my arms through the silk lining elicited a shiver until the weighted material rested securely over my shoulders. With the collar popped, it brushed the middle of my ears, creating a tent of protection my chin could tuck into. The coat's hem ended mid-calf, seemingly in line with modern men's fashion. The only thing left to make the outfit perfect sat lovingly in my hand. The gold pocket watch settled nicely into the inside of the jacket and closer to my heart.

The *ting* of a pebble bouncing on the floor in the living room made me hyper aware of the sound of feet stepping into the home. Two sets, actually. My ears trained onto their movement to see where they went. One of them stepped lightly toward the seating area, while the other one glided into the kitchen. They were nervous, made evident by the shallowness of their breath. A door squeaked when the man in the kitchen investigated a room adjacent to the bedroom, which logically, he'd explore next, making me anxious about finding a place to hide. His partner wandered from the far side of the home and straight for the bedroom. The wood floor just outside of the room creaked from his weight, spurring me to surrender further into the room. I pressed myself into the wall behind the longer jackets, so that only my feet stuck out. It was stupid and they'd see me immediately, but it would give me a few seconds to think.

His shoes squeaked with every step into the latrine. He paused, and then shot out a short, piercing whistle. His partner quietly, but quickly, joined him in the bedroom.

In a whisper, the first man said, "Steam on the mirror. Can't be far."

With a rustle of fabric, the two exited the bathroom and started searching the bedroom. At this point, neither of them could be seen. From my vantage point through the hangers, a sliver of the bed and a corner of the nightstand were visible. The tip of one man's muzzle appeared first, then his hand, then the sleeve of his blue jacket, and finally the globe of a wary eye. It darted back and forth in time with his hand-held torch. The light brushed across my face twice, searing into my irises like a tiny sun. He retreated a single step before focusing his attention straight ahead.

"Police! Come out with your hands up!" cried the man.

Well, dammit.

"Let me see your hands!" he repeated.

His partner had his gun out, and his body pressed against the other side of the door frame by this point, yelling the same commands at me. My body straightened to its full height while releasing the sigh that had built up since the two first made entry. This was not ideal. The two watched with intense purpose as my eyes considered them, then the window. Jumping through it seemed like a justifiable reaction in this situation, but not without consequences. From this height, they would need to see a body splattered on the street to believe the danger neutralized. It would only prompt more involvement and that fell into the category of things I wasn't willing to commit to, even though playing a convincing dead guy came naturally to me. Not surprisingly, my to-do list didn't include digging myself out of another grave today, tomorrow, or in the next decade. On the other side of the coin, if they didn't find a body, it would raise attention and, although my kind didn't have many rules, attracting a police investigation would be a big no-no. I'd be fighting off more than just the human police.

Logic won out. The jackets parted between my hands, revealing the mass barely hidden behind the facade. It took one step to clear the wardrobe, and my feet pointed squarely at the officers. Both men readjusted their grips on their guns and raised them to match the height they weren't expecting. One of them aimed at my head, while the other aimed lower, ready to shoot me in the heart.

"Let me see your hands!" they yelled.

As instructed, they raised even with my shoulders, palms facing forward, and free of any potential weapons.

"Turn around!"

As you wish. My gaze focused on the rows of clothing I'd never get to enjoy. The flap of his gun holster grated against his hand as he flipped it open and replaced the weapon inside. A click of another flap and the jingle of metal told me everything without seeing a thing. Maybe laughing was not the correct response.

"This isn't funny. You are under arrest on the suspicion of the murder of Miles Cage and trespassing on an active police investigation," he barked as he grabbed my upturned hands and wrenched them toward my back.

So, I repeated to him the last thing Miles ever said, "Whatever."

My arm came loose from his grip as if he were a toddler and elbowed him in the side. The bone gave way, and an audible crack reverberated through his body in a wave of pain. A blow of air came out with the force of the impact, inclining his face into my upturned palm. His nose landed straight against my hand and stood no chance, popping instantly. He dropped to the floor. The other guy managed to pull the trigger while his partner received all the attention. The echo of the gunshot ran throughout the room, rattling the windows. The pesky thing embedded itself in my brand-new jacket just below the shoulder blade.

"My jacket!" The words came out in more of a rolling growl.

I cradled the man's head in my hand and slammed it against the doorsill. He fell motionless to the floor. They were nothing but two logs on the ground and didn't notice when their suspect picked their way over them, through the bedroom, and straight out of the apartment. The front door complained loudly when slammed a little too hard, but the latch wouldn't catch even after multiple attempts. It needed to stay shut to deter anyone from immediately finding the two people inside. With an upward tug on the handle, the latch finally clicked into place and the door remained closed even after letting go.

The hall felt so much longer now. The fear of being caught tickled the back of my neck and wouldn't ease unless there were a couple of kilometers between me and the house. Long strides carried me through the building in a blur. As the stairwell approached, a couple emerged through the door. They complained when my body wedged between them and into what was supposed to be the stairwell. Instead, an infinite number of exact replicas of myself stared back at me from mirrors that covered a room no larger than Miles's closet. Confused, I turned to exit, only to see the doors slide closed. A swell of panic itched in my stomach. My fingers clawed at the seam between the shiny metal plates, leaving curls of the material behind in my desperation to get out. This created enough purchase to get a better hold and pull them apart. The tiny gap revealed a wall moving upward at a high rate of speed. To my right, a board lit up the wall with a series of numbers from one to thirty. A red dot flashed on the number fifteen, then fourteen, then twelve. It continued to go down until the dot reached ten. Something in the room dinged and the two halves of the door pulled away from my grip, receding into the walls. An older man shuffled in the space next to me, pressed the '1' button and crossed his arms in front of him. Silently, we both waited for something to happen.

With the countdown complete, the doors opened to reveal the main lobby. The receptionist remained in the same spot, looking expectantly at who would come out of the elevator. The old man shouldered his way past me and beelined it for the door, looking like everything inconvenienced him.

Half a block from the entrance, a herd of horseless

carriages passed by with red and blue spinning lights twirling from their roofs. They emitted the most obnoxious sound, but it worked, since all the pedestrians slowed down to look. I sank lower into my jacket and kept going, even though inquisitiveness urged me to turn around and watch where they went. Their destination didn't remain a mystery for long. They slowed down and stopped in front of Miles's apartment. The police made a ruckus as they piled out and made their way inside. Temptation to watch where they went fought the desire to get out of the area. As a compromise, my eyes looked over my shoulder while my feet kept moving forward and unsurprisingly, bumped into a couple who had also turned around to see what the commotion was about.

"Watch it, asshole," commanded the man, but his words dissolved into my back. My stride didn't break until a couple of kilometers stood between me and the scene.

*****

The city extended out in front of me like a maze, made more difficult to navigate from the bombardment of relentless sounds, smells, and walking temptations called humans. Perhaps it wouldn't be so bad with a place to be or someone to go home to. The resulting fatigue on my mind made it harder to concentrate on the next step. So, all my focus bored into the sidewalk in front of my feet, one city block at a time. An inkling stressed the back of my mind. If your job consisted of paying attention to everyone who came into your building and eventually exited, wouldn't it be peculiar if a stranger returned home, presumably for the day, but left in a rush less than an hour later? No doubt the receptionist told the uniformed officers about me, sending them all in my direction.

Paranoia guided my next steps and when one of the carriages marked with "Police" came into view, my coat tail swung out from the sudden change of direction into the alley. My eyes flitted downward and watched the ground while the thing went by. He continued down the street and gave no indication of recognition.

The second time it happened, a bakery provided ample cover. A bell jingled when the door opened and a breeze sent tiny grains of flour floating through the air, teasing my sinuses. Rows of freshly baked bread reminded me of a time long ago when breaking into one of these loaves was the best part of my day. Hints of rosemary, garlic, butter, and lemon saturated the different parts of the shop, depending on where you stood. The most alluring of all couldn't be bought and stood in line a few steps away. My tongue tested the sharpness of my fang, so I softly bit down to remind myself what got me into this situation in the first place.

My eyes remained vigilant while standing on the street corner, waiting for the traffic to break, when yet another patrol came into view. It would have been easy to simply turn around, but they had already followed me for the past couple of blocks. To my right, the sun blazed down the road, making it the least desirable route. The last remaining option had me going left, but my indecision gave time for the cross-traffic to start moving, inviting both peelers to my location. A mass of people flowed with the movement of the carriages and interrupted the view between us. With hope that they wouldn't see me, a quick glance in their direction made up my mind that the risk didn't seem worth it.

My jaw clenched and I endured the pain that followed. The coat covered most of my body. It provided deep pockets for my hands and a high collar for my neck and cheeks. My hair curtained the rest of my face, leaving a narrow gap from hairline to chin. The temperature this afternoon created the perfect excuse to burrow deeper into the coat as if the cool breeze whipping through the lane caused discomfort and not the sun. With no more time to fuss, I turned into the light and accepted the thousand knives that pricked my face. So much for my hair acting as a shield.

Halfway down the block, it occurred to me my walk was a bit too fast for any normal human. After slowing down, it wouldn't look out of place for someone running late. This section of road happened to be a wall of residential buildings with no outlet or nooks to take refuge in. Door after door created a silent wall of discomfort as my eyes desperately scanned the surface for the bare amount of shelter, even for a minute, to itch the burning on my nose and cheeks.

The homes pushed me along until another road ended the block and into the welcoming embrace of a shadow. The corner of the building formed a solid line separating day from night and my body perched firmly on the correct side to figuratively catch my breath. A scan of the area revealed no policemen, so my muscles relaxed even further under the coat. One finger smoothed the hair out of my face as I waited for the next cycle of people to walk into the road. Once the mob started moving, I stepped out of the shadow and quickly made my way across to get into the safety of darkness once again.

The group quickly became a crowd and soon swept

me into the current like a man floating down the rapids. Attempts at cutting across were met with resistance until my direction matched theirs. At one road crossing, two uniformed officers casually observed the crowd from atop horses. The animals were big-boned and clearly okay with the chaos that surrounded them. A welcome sight, but it didn't mean anything had changed, so my head ducked down in a way that wouldn't attract attention in the shoulder-to-shoulder horde that invaded the area. Surely, they wouldn't notice me among this mass.

The foot traffic dwarfed any crowd my long life already experienced. Unlike the rest of the people in this city, this group acted much more aloof. Straw hats and gaudy shirts adorned a fair majority, but their lack of attention to their surroundings threatened to send me over the edge. Every third person bumped into me, pushing my body further and further down the figurative river. My patience shaved down to a single thread, and it took a wrinkled old man to cross the line. He stepped on my foot. That was it. Both of my hands seized his flowery shirt and shoved him to the ground. Leaning over his prone body, my lips parted, and a hiss seethed through my teeth. A gasp from the crowd momentarily cleared the space around us, breaking my concentration long enough to have visions of my past remind me not to do anything dumb. Swiftly, my hands released their hold on his shirt. Straightening, my goal was to slither hastily from the street. People bounced off my rigid shoulders, but it didn't deter me. My departure incurred quite a lot of complaints, but if I stopped, I would, without a doubt, kill one of these vermin.

Respite arrived in the form of a stairway that led to a lower story below the streets. The entrance connected to the busy road, but it didn't lead anywhere other than a deadlocked door. Years of grime and newspapers built up along the bottom. People didn't care to even look down the stairwell. Cloaked in the shadows, my eyelids drooped. It felt like an out of tune orchestra played in my head and the whole audience cheered them on, regardless. Habits carried me to a familiar place and numbers pushed their way to the forefront of my brain. One, two, three, four hundred, five hundred, six thousand.

The crowd's shrewd noise lessened over the course of the last couple thousand numbers. Fewer heartbeats occupied the sidewalks, and the street grew quieter with fewer carriages trying to pack themselves into the restricted space. After opening my eyes, dusk greeted me. Or not, my eyebrow raised. Night blanketed the sky above the buildings, but the intersection danced in colors that changed from moment to moment. The source of the light wasn't immediately obvious, but when I located it, the sense of security I once knew slipped away like sand through fingers.

A rare, diagonal road jutted off to the left, leaving a space for a wedge-shaped building to crowd the otherwise limited space. Like all the other buildings in this city, it reached for the sky, but a single detail made it different from all the others. The front facade supported a vertical panel that almost reached the roof. Within this panel was a picture. Giants, in comparison to their actual size, suspended on the surface, *moving*. Two people gyrated happily in bright colors before lifting the cup to their lips and drinking the contents with unnatural enthusiasm. The next scene started after a brief pause and this time; a horseless carriage drove erratically. The wheels threw up dirt onto the perspective of the viewer and then transitioned into various angles of the carriage before once again ending on the logo.

For hours, the panel imprisoned my attention. It showed me many things from food, carriages, beverages, clothing. The meaning behind the perfume ads was elusive, though the rest made much more sense. Some ads completely went over my head. The rectangles people seemed to be reliant on flouting different positions while text flashed across the picture boasting about their camera size and computing speeds? By the end of the night, it became predictable which play would start next, how the actors interacted with one another, and how much it cost to purchase a homestead of different objects. It felt like I peeled my eyes from the screen when the allure of the object finally waned. It snuck up on me, but the sky grew lighter above me. The ghost of the panel followed my eyesight for a couple of blinks, not initially realizing the intensity of the light.

A handful of employees making noise inside various shops indicated that the town started to wake up. Mostly, the ones who supplied food. Chairs scraped along tabletops as they were unloaded on the floor. An oven poured newborn smoke through a vent that carried the crispy remains of yesterday's roasted meats. A courier brushed against the railing of my hiding spot, struggling with a load of fresh newspapers, inspiring an idea. No one seemed to notice me when coming out of the musty stairwell or didn't care enough to watch me stalk the paperboy.

He didn't travel much further down the block before stopping at a hut sitting in the middle of the sidewalk. An older man greeted him and took the stack of papers from the paperboy and dropped them at his feet. The exchange ended quickly, and the courier went on his way. I walked over to the sleepy hut and when the man didn't shoo me off, started browsing while he continued to straighten the papers on one of many shelves. His shop sold a wide assortment of choices beyond the black and white printed paper. Catalogues advertised everything from cooking to fashion to sex. My cheeks reddened at the gravitas. A small section appeared to cater toward the unexplainable. Seeing this section brought a sense of relief knowing the legends still existed, but remained safely tucked behind the crazy people who, coincidentally, were right about my kind.

One newspaper caught my attention with a familiar word printed in bold across the top. "Vampire Killer? Is a blood sucker loose on the streets of New York?" Their picture under the headline barely showed a silhouette of what could be a person menacing in the corner. A chuckle blew out through my nose. At least a mob of people weren't heading down the road with pitchforks yet. Those were the days; getting chased out of town by an angry village. It wasn't so much the pitchforks that bothered me as much as their torches did. Nasty burns those caused. Not worth the trouble.

Knickknacks crowded the space around the papers. Some hung from the roof like fringe, while others overflowed in their bins. The shop owner sat behind his cash register now, watching me inspect a cactus planted into a terracotta pot no bigger than the palm of my hand. My index finger bopped one of the spikes out of curiosity before setting it down. This vendor also sold a gamut of colorful shirts. One option had the same symbol as the tissue paper from the first night on land.

"Excuse me, sir. What does this mean?" My finger pointed to the pile.

"Dork for New York," he said in an eccentric accent.

"Glad to hear it, but not really what I needed."

"Dork for New York!" He pointed at other examples of the same symbol. While shrugging, my brow furrowed in frustration. His hand cut through the air dismissively and he stopped answering. He held a wary eye on me after that.

My fingers brushed along the top of his offerings, but as interesting as the different options were, I had always been a sucker for the basics. The shop owner unloaded the stack dropped off from the courier and it turned out to be the daily newspaper. Snatching one off the top, my eyes quickly scanned the cover. The main headline read "Successful Wall-Streeter found dead. Dog attack?" Interesting, but not useful. It should be here, right on top. My stomach dropped. The information that had dodged me since arriving on this foreign land sat between my fingers, written just below the name of the paper. September 23, 2024.

Two thousand and twenty-four.

Panic poured into my chest. My thoughts turned to vapor, and it became impossible to grasp onto the amount of time that passed. That single line of information took me straight back into my black hole. The weight of the concrete pressing against my chest and keeping me from getting any leverage, any hope, of understanding how long it held me captive. Yet, this wasn't a physical sensation. All of it rested in my head and my memories, leaving me with nothing to hold on to. The newspaper slipped from my slack fingers, and it fell to the ground in a waterfall of pages. They settled around my feet at the same time the cashier started cursing at me.

"You better pay for that! It's ruined. All wet. No use. Give me money for it now!" He repeated the words *at me*, but truthfully, nothing he said absorbed. He made his way around the front of his stand and tried to block my path. His head came up to my collarbone, but his finger pointed at me from a couple of centimeters in front of my nose.

"You pay!" he spat.

His words sounded muffled as they entered my thoughts through a bombardment of more important information. It was not necessary to smack him away as hard as I did, but his body crashed into a pile of trash cans a few feet away. Like an apparition, my body floated away from the scene in an air of urgency.

The date kept replaying in my head, stuck in some sort of nightmare loop. Twenty twenty-four. Twenty twenty-four. Twenty twenty-four. One hundred seventy-three years. Total darkness. Alone. I am alone.

I am alone.

The familiar ache for my lovely wife followed up my initial dread, flooding what little space remained innocent from this wretched reality. She'd now been gone longer than the scope of our entire relationship, several times over. The feeling wrapped its gristly fingers around my soul and choked me with my own fears, leaving me crippled in sorrow.

What of the world around me? It was astoundingly clear how much had changed since my time. Horseless carriages, moving pictures, ships larger than entire cities. I had only been on the surface for a couple days and seen so much, but it now felt infinitesimal compared to the span of what I missed. Where would one go to catch up on a hundred and seventy-three years of history? Not just conflicts, but inventions, lineage, migration, science, medicine, and the things that my consciousness couldn't even comprehend! Whenever a glimmer of comprehension came within my grasp, it slipped further away into the void. My mind raced in a thousand directions at once, unable to settle on just one thought, making the rest of me feel as though it were in danger. My arms tingled and my chest tightened. The brick exterior to my right grabbed a hold of me and lowered me to the ground. It would have been nice to be able to breathe right now and use the action as a calming exercise. Alas, the only way to deal with the void was to go through it. With my back against the wall, the cold bricks supported my heavy head while the rest of me tried to shut out the rest of the world.

Is this what drowning felt like? All my energy focused on coming up for air, but the surface never came. All it would take is one foothold, one lifeline of one subject to feel the ground under my feet. Tumultuous thoughts deprived me of something essential, like oxygen to a human. Nothing made sense, and I didn't know how to fix it. Then again, what needed to be fixed? Time marched on without me, but even with my peculiar second life, this wasn't how it was supposed to go.

It all became too much. The scent of people, the sound of their perpetual movement, the allure of their blood, the honking, the buzzing of the lights, the grimy sidewalk beneath me. This place burned into me as badly as the sun. My hands locked into fists and my muscles pulled taut. A single pluck of my figurative string would surely break me. I needed to get out. Out of this nightmare, whatever that meant. Just *out*.

A walk turned into a jog, until finally my legs pumped in a full out sprint, cutting neatly through the other early risers. Black coat tails flapped behind me like a sail. Though my pace remained possible for a human to achieve, it didn't stop people from looking. The balls of my feet tapped down so lightly, it felt like flying, and if my mind concentrated hard enough on that sound, perhaps the darker corners could be kept away. My strategy left a lot of room for emotion to creep in, so I sought a more private path. The alleys rarely hosted anyone of importance and quickly became my haven. Humanity tethered me to the laws of the natural world, but without its prying eyes; no one could be there to hold the leash.

From the depths of the secluded runway, my legs sped up to a more comfortable speed. The rest of the city blurred by until the buildings became shorter, then further apart, until eventually, the welcoming embrace of the forest replaced them. Carriages still blundered in the near distance, but were muffled so harshly that they barely disturbed the solitude. Even here, the bugs returned. Instead of the never-ending attack of human noises, a mouse scraped at some dirt, a bee took flight, and a dried leaf crackled as it settled on the ground. Only the barest of human allure reached me here.

Mostly, it smelled like wet dirt.

My body's reaction to my circumstances crippled me and lasted for a full twenty-four hours. I sobbed in total hopelessness, unable to move past my current circumstances, mourning what was, what is, and what will be. The gravity of the past century and a half pulled down on my shoulders. Just when one problem resolved, another would crash down into the newly vacant space.

In my time spent lying in the dirt in the middle of the forest, one conclusion became absolutely clear to me: I needed to get home and to see that my past life really happened, even if my house was a pile of rubble where it used to be. It would be a quick swim across the Atlantic and a short jaunt through Wales. The decision aligned my body and brain in a way that didn't peg the two of them against one another. My internal compass found its north and sprung life into what felt like a corpse. Scraping myself off the grass turned out to be easy, with a renewed sense of direction.

Dusk descended over the city by the time my leather shoes stopped at the edge of the seawall. Beyond jumping in, the plan to get to London remained loose, but starting the journey at the beginning of the night would work in my favor for a couple of reasons. The sun wouldn't be trying to kill me, and the moon could act as a guide.

Coincidentally, this is where my first steps happened on this new continent, well, other than the green statue island. It all seemed so innocent a mere couple of days ago. This new world seemed fresh and exciting, as if there still stood a chance of starting over. Now it just felt like a shackle in the chain that held me to the awful truth of my situation. Dwelling on it would only hold me here longer, so my fingers found the buttons on my wool coat and started to release them. The movement jostled my suit jacket and the small, round timepiece bounced against my chest like an artificial heart. It roped my thoughts inward with what it represented. My hand pressed it through the fabric as my eyes looked ahead at the giant, green statue on her little island and with her back turned, grinned at her discretion.

"'Ello, Phillip," announced a voice from behind me.

My fingers froze. It was so perfectly recognizable that I assumed my broken memories conjured it up in a cruel punishment. Time had not altered his voice; it remained unchanged.

The rest of me tingled with an icy anticipation that he might actually be standing behind me. I peeked over my shoulder and sure enough, it wasn't a bad memory. Two dark figures stood at the edge of the walkway. One of them dressed much like myself. Except, he had a vest peeking out from under his suit jacket. The other guy came up to his chin, but no less smug in his appearance. Both of them hid their hands in their pockets and sat back on their heels, totally unperturbed by my presence. The light from the streetlamps glinted off their black irises.

"Enjoy your nap?" he asked.

Chapter 4

The moon split the sky in a sliver on the edge of the world. Its reflection mirrored on the water in a million broken shards as the calm evening waves capped in delicate peaks. The water slapped against the stacked stones, folding back onto itself in metronome-like cadence, just a meter below the railing, beckoning me to take just one step into its suffocating allure. The temptation sung to me. My teeth ground together as my focus shifted unwaveringly to the two figures.

They made absolutely no sound. Hell, I didn't know they were behind me until he spoke. No heartbeat, no rhythmic sound of air going in and out of their lungs. Only when the wind caught the edges of their clothes did the ruffling indicate they stood there, almost indistinguishable from the flags that chimed from the poles that lined the shore. Shadows in the shade. Masters of the darkness. Exactly like me. It was one thing to possess such power, but entirely different to be on the receiving end of it—especially when there were two of them.

My whole body shifted so that it faced them square on. With my decision, the shorter one grinned in a sinister line. The other one remained stony in his appearance.

"You look like shit," he continued.

"Nice to see you too, Joseph. John." My gaze

darted toward the other one.

"I'd say the feeling is mutual, but then I'd be lying." He shrugged. "How's New York treating you?"

"Oh, you know," I replied curtly.

My eyes narrowed, waiting for them to make a move. They looked too relaxed, but experience told me to stay alert. Something more sinister hid underneath their outward composure. This reminded me of our last encounter. Joseph and John had me pinned to the ground while they beat the piss out of me. My only protection was my hands, and they scarcely covered the vulnerable parts of my face. As they rearranged my insides, little snippets of their expressions appeared from around my arms. A crazed smile smeared across Joseph's face, enjoying every minute of my misfortune. John just did his job. There could be no other reason for them to be here other than going for round two. My best bet was to keep them talking while I thought of a way out.

"How did you find me?"

Joseph snorted a laugh. "Like it was hard. You've been having too much fun topside and people are paying attention. Tsk, tsk, Phillip. I'm disappointed in you."

"What does any of that mean?"

"Oh, right. You've missed a few…decades," he smirked. "How all of this must look to you. This world is unrecognizable from where we left you. Did you know the humans have colonized Mars?" His face brightened as if the statement was new to him as well.

"Really?" I exhaled.

"No, dumbass, but they did go to the moon," he said seriously.

My eyebrows creased together before answering him through narrowed eyelids. "It isn't nice to lie about those sorts of things."

"No, truly, you should have seen the celebration! It was quite the race, but those pesky Americans got there first."

"Why are you here?" My inflection aimed at cutting through his jokes.

Joseph once again became serious.

"Don is still mad at you."

The words hung in the air and I considered my reply very carefully.

"It wasn't my fault." The words came out no louder than a whisper.

"As if that matters. Besides, he doesn't see it that way and he is still pissed. Oh boy, you should see him when he thinks of you. Entire villages burn. It was my absolute pleasure to tell Don that you escaped your concrete coffin. He couldn't wait to put me and Lurch here on the first flight to America."

Flight? Lurch? My gaze drifted downward as if the sidewalk held the answers. Joseph continued and pulled my attention back.

"Which brings us to why we are here. You're coming with us, Phil. Someone wants to see you."

I could fill in the blanks. They had no intention of escorting me back to London so we could talk things out, shake hands, and go our separate ways. They weren't going to stuff me into another concrete box, either. Very slowly, my head shook in defiance.

"Come on, Phil, let's go," he ordered.

No part of my existence had any intention of accompanying them. My eyes stared daggers first at

Joseph, then John, then back to Joseph. The seconds ticked by and Joseph shifted his weight impatiently.

"Philip," he warned.

My head shook again, ready for a confrontation, my muscles so tight, they would produce sound if a bow rasped against them.

"I'm surprised you don't remember our last encounter. It didn't work out for you then either. You might as well come quietly."

He was wrong. Our last encounter ruminated on the forefront of my mind like a parasite and it paralyzed me in fear. Yet, if they got a hold of me, my death would be permanent. Hiding under my anguish, grief, loneliness, a feeling reached out and caressed the back of my spine. It wanted me to keep going, keep searching for what came next and that wouldn't happen surrendering to those two. My face went numb with the realization.

Maybe I had the upper hand here. Only a couple days passed since walking onto this very shore, but in that time, my journey took me north of Yonkers, east of Brooklyn, across the river into New Jersey, and the spaces in between. Surely, they didn't know about the shortcuts in Manhattan or the alleys that cut smoothly through the Bronx. Joseph sighed impatiently and stepped toward me. I turned right and ran.

****

A short sprint through the garden that lined the shoreline dropped me off on the road, where a block of carriages waited their turn to go. Just as my foot stepped off the sidewalk, the mass started to move. Instead of going straight through, their positions inspired a zigzag pattern to the accompaniment of

93

complaints. Out of nowhere, one of the carriages going the opposite direction caught me just below the hip and scooped me up. The momentum pushed me over the glass front and squarely into the taxi sign on the roof. It bounced me free of the carriage and deposited me off the side. My hands and feet caught the ground like a cat, and like the aforementioned animal, scrambled a few strides on all fours to the spectacle of several onlookers.

After regaining my balance, I scuttled on two legs into the nearest alley, where it continued for a half a kilometer, crossed another road, where it ended with a wire mesh fence. My coattails neatly cleared the top, but in an effort to lose my pursuers, turned left and continued down a narrower alley. Obstacles of old boxes and trash cans brimming with filth made the path a series of hurdles. An opening to the road invited me to change direction, but this one hosted people. My speed skidded to a walk. Half a block away, a dark path invited me back in. Once again out of the sight of humans, my speed increased until the sounds of my footfalls blended together. This entire time, two sets of boots echoed mere meters behind me, making it clear this plan needed some adjustments.

The alley ended at a T-shaped intersection where carriages zoomed by. The thought crossed my mind to turn and climb either of the buildings adjacent to the road, but instead, lowered myself onto my back and slid smoothly into the storm drain. The roof extended a head over me when my foot splashed into the murky water. The smell squeezed the remaining air out of my lungs and remained vacant so as not to pull in anymore of the putrid air. Tears welled up in my eyes as a drip of snot curled onto my lip.

The tunnels were a labyrinth of unexplored territory. Just a few steps in, the tunnel branched out into three different options. Going to the left seemed like a good choice and my guess ended up being decent since it continued on unbroken for a hundred meters or so. Joseph splashed in behind me and unless John wanted to bash his way in, he'd need to find another entrance.

The tunnels forked and twisted their way silently under the rest of society, leaving me feeling uneasy about which way to go. Coming down here felt like a gamble, but a different tactic was needed. It did the trick, though. Only one of them pursued me and the gap between us grew wider. A fine mist exploded from under my feet as they pounded against the thin layer of water, splashing against the walls and causing a shooshing noise to reverberate along the bricks. In a way, it helped me since the sounds would bounce back at a dead end.

The technique failed me. I had not considered a thick metal grate would stretch across one of the openings. My body bounced off after running into it at full speed, depositing me abruptly on the ground. After hastening upright, an inspection of the grate revealed it took little damage from my collision. My fingers wrapped around the weave of metal and started to push when Joseph's hand clawed at my jacket. He hurled me across the space and into the opposing wall. A shower of pebbles irritated the surface of the water, sending out ripples that bounced against my face. His footsteps splashed markedly and as my feet settled under me, his fist cracked against my jaw. My head bounced against the wall before I could catch myself with my hands.

The air whistled as he came in for another blow, but this attempt deflected off my forearm and the other made bony contact with his eye socket. Someone once told me to picture punching through the object and at the moment, it felt like really great advice. He stumbled back with a shocked look on his face. The corner of his lip twitched in what looked like a grin.

"Phillip! There were rumors about your right hook, but never did-" He didn't get to finish his sentence as my foot made solid contact with his sternum, sending him flying backwards into the metal fence. Both he and the grate clambered to the ground. He didn't get the chance to see which direction his prisoner fled.

I tried my best to retrace my steps, but it was next to impossible. My attention had been behind me, listening for Joseph. A couple wrong turns and my hope of escape evaporated. A spot of light reflected off the water from around the bend. Upon closer inspection, it came from another street side drain. A whiff of salt water derailed my plan to climb out and offered something utterly ridiculous. My nose led me around a kilometer further down the tunnel, filling in the gaps of this crazy idea. Get to the ocean, jump in, and swim for England. They would never be able to track me in the water, and in hindsight, what should have happened in the first place.

The figurative light at the end of the tunnel got closer. The stars twinkled faintly at the pinhead sized hole in the distance. Their numbers grew until the entire night sky laid out in front of me. I popped out of the end of the tunnel like a rat. The water ran off the edge and dispersed into the wrinkled void just a few feet below me. My body leaned out of the opening to dive in, but something grabbed a fistful of my hair by the roots. It yanked me up and slammed me onto the ground. John was never one with words and went straight to the punching. Over and over he landed his fists into my face. My own hands flailed wildly, hoping to make a connection as well. My blows grazed his face, his neck, and at one point, maybe even knocked a tooth loose, but it didn't deter my assailant. Every thump against my head made it harder to concentrate until my reality blurred into one shapeless mass. The world grew dark at the edges until one well-aimed blow blew the candle out completely.

****

I was sort of aware of the ground moving under me. It bobbed up and down in a nauseating way. Gravel lightly crunched with every footfall and it made me realize my body hung limply over John's shoulder. My head bounced against his backside and both arms swung helplessly in rhythm with his steps. Apart from the streetlights that would grow brighter, then dimmer, as they bobbed past, nothing obvious gave away where we headed, or even where we were. Trying to listen for anything obvious invited spikes of pain through my head. Black dots marred my vision and when the pain settled, the ringing in my ears didn't go away. Every so often, snippets of awareness tried to stamp themselves on my thoughts before they faded again. Then it went totally dark, succumbing to unconsciousness.

The floor rose to me quickly when Joseph lobbed me from his shoulder. My body landed with a thump and instinctively curled into a protective ball. The sudden change of position jostled me awake. It seemed like a good idea to try and run, but my leather shoes couldn't get a grip as they slipped on the smooth flooring. Instead, my hands and knees scuttled as quickly as they could.

"Nope," Joseph commented.

He grabbed me by the wrist and twisted it to get me on my back. He then dragged me across the floor. My free hand pried at his iron grip, but a blanket of exhaustion muddled my concentration and motivation melted into temporary complacency. Just as the peak of pain waned, Joseph stopped and descended on me. He grasped my neck and lifted me from the floor. He wasn't gentle when he slammed my body against the wall of wherever we were. The way he held me left little room to get a hold of him and only my fingertips brushed his clothing after having to reach around his arms. Kicking his legs had as much effect as trying to convince a village that the woman at their pyre wasn't a witch. Instead of hurting myself further, my legs wrapped around his midsection and thrashed from side to side.

John showed up then, holding a thick metal rod. One end had a lip, and the other ended at a point. Too slowly, I realized he held a railroad tie. Joseph forced my arm above my head and watched as John lined up the tie into the perfect position. He pierced my hand straight through and pushed the rod securely into the wall behind me. Growls ripped from my chest as my teeth snapped at Joseph's face. He just laughed.

He released my arm and wrenched the second one into the same high position. My legs uncurled from around Joseph and wedged themselves against his hips. The results made it worth the effort as he slid back, but

John saw what happened and swatted my legs away from his accomplice. The soles of my shoes barely touched the ground before they climbed up Joseph's body again. This time, my aim was for a more delicate area. It didn't matter. John slammed the second pin into me the same as before. The pain barely touched my awareness, since my concentration focused on cracking his eggs. The ferocious growling filling the space around us came from me. The two stepped back and out of reach, but my feet still kicked out at them. There was nothing else I could do. Joseph mocked me for a few moments before pulling out his pocket rectangle. It beeped once before he spoke.

"We've got 'im," he announced.

A muffled voice replied, but the words gurgled out incoherently.

"Yeah, no. I hoped he would, but he didn't come quietly. Plane is no good. We'll have to charter 'im," he turned his back and started to walk away to my right and out of sight.

To my surprise, so did John. Joseph's one-sided conversation carried through the space for quite a while before it altogether disappeared. Then the ghosts of their presence moved in. A creak, a buzz of an insect, a fake footstep. Every little noise made me jump and with the little space these shackles allowed me, my eyes would jump from person to person who wasn't there. The seconds turned into minutes, and when an hour passed, I started to pull at my restraints. The angle made it difficult. My hands were secured high above my head, slightly behind as well, and only the balls of my feet touched the floor, taking away my leverage. They crucified me in the most awkward position. With the slightest push of my shoes, the leather soles would slip and leave me hanging from the railroad ties.

Upon further observation, the wall that suspended me was instead a large, round column in the middle of a room. Beyond the immediate area were more of the columns, arranged in pairs throughout the length of a long, straight hallway wide enough to have four carriages pass each other comfortably. Rows of businesses lined the hallway. Glass shop fronts with wide, welcoming entrances. Two sets of stairs were visible: one to my left, then another to my right. They connected to a second layer of shops mirroring the layout of the first story. The second story had a walkway around the outside to connect all the shops, with bridges that crossed the empty space in between. Above it all, a glass roof followed the length of the space. A whole village existed in the interior of this building.

Interestingly, it appeared as though everyone forgot about this place. No signs of life within earshot. It had been this way for a long time by the looks of things. A layer of dust thickly coated all the surfaces of the village. Three sets of footprints marred the otherwise perfectly dirty floor. Around me, construction equipment sat abandoned. Sheets of glass leaned up against walls and saws littered the ground around untouched boards of wood. The place was clearly abandoned, and no one would be coming in here by accident.

A noise echoed awkwardly off the wide space, bouncing around, distorting into something unrecognizable. Then, I realized the sound came from me. Cries of frustration rolled from my furled mouth like a wounded animal until the resentment flowed into my limbs. The tips of the oxfords bit angrily into the flooring in an attempt to gain just a little more leverage. When that didn't work, my feet kicked up as if climbing the pole backwards could work, yet each step resulted in my foot sliding back down. My last-ditch effort consisted of pulling my body up as far as possible. All my weight hung from the railroad ties and when my head sat level with my hands, I released my muscles and flopped downward, but the pins wouldn't budge and neither would the column.

Defeated, my body went limp, and the pins held me up like a shirt on a clothesline. My chin rested against the top button of the shirt while staring at the grime filled spaces between the white tiles. The only thought that crossed my mind was how uncomfortable it felt to have the button pressed into my skin. A contrite laugh blew through my nose at the ridiculousness of having *that* be what bothered me most.

The short break renewed the urge to escape, but instead of flinging my bodyweight against the restraints, I looked around for anything that could be used as a tool. A telling story unfolded in the layer of dust in the room. A dozen or so footprints disturbed the majority of the dirt and, of course, the scuffle in front of the column. There were also splotches where other objects had recently sat, like a vague square, the outline of a hammer, a circle that could have been a roll of rope. All it indicated is that someone took the time to remove anything that could help me escape.

Resolved that the best way out of this situation involved doing something wretched, my mind reassured me this predicament compared very little to what came after the other two came back. Instead of throwing my weight into the railroad ties, I leaned just enough so all my strength could be focused on one side, instead of split between the two. With the strength left in me, my shoulder, my elbow, and my back pulled down hoping to tear the flesh of my palm through the restraint. The grinding of teeth reverberated through my head and a strained groan soiled the otherwise quiet place. That is when a new presence crept up on me like a ghost.

The building fell silent and the railroad ties remained dutiful to their job. To my left, the sun started to peek through the window on the roof. To my horror, glass ran the length of the building from east to west. Those bastards knew. They left me here to fry in the sun all day. The calculated and focused efforts to meticulously get out turned into an all-out seizure of movement to escape.

The burning started on the tips of my fingers, and at first thought, this is nice. It tingled enough to send a shiver down my spine. If I closed my eyes, it could have been my beautiful wife kissing me with soft, sweet lips. Slowly, she moved down my arm until her lips touched my face. She caressed my eyelids, my nose, and then my mouth. Oh, the feeling of her on my lips. She was such a good kisser. Her sweet taste lingered on my tongue, but the sensation quickly turned sour. The tips of my fingers could have been the wick of a candle for how much they burned. Yet, they weren't even smoking. My hand closed into a fist just so a different part of my body could be exposed and momentarily alleviate the pain. My face rotated like poultry on a spit, but it marginally worked. The torture persisted and a whine came out of my chest until there simply wasn't any more air to produce sound. I didn't bother sucking more in as it would be pointless.

The day slowly wore on as the sun crept across the sky. In all my time in the ocean, this single moment felt longer than the century and a half spent down there. Waves of pain shivered down my body. The willpower from just a few hours ago burned to a husk, and my body hung against the column in defeat. Curls of smoke emanated from my skin now and dispersed in the vast space.

The pain grew so immense that the feeling disappeared from my toes. It came across as odd because they were safely covered in shoes. My neck muscles refused to act normally and as a result, my head fell awkwardly forward after deciding to give it a look. The beautiful separation from day to night caressed the tips of my shoes. Slowly, the western window swallowed the orange globe until the last of its rays climbed up the opposite wall and dissolved into the surroundings. Relief pricked the back of my eyes and overflowed down my cheeks.

The fleeting response dried up as anxiety took its place. Surely, Joseph and John were on their way to retrieve me.

Once again, the night ticked by. Every little noise stabbed at my conviction that they would pop out of the shadows. Twice the wind picked up just enough to tussle the dust into the air, sending it through the building like glitter, resettling in our footsteps. It would be only a matter of time before our presence here was wiped out. Slowly, the burns that formed on my exposed skin healed. Raw, exposed nerves cooled as my regenerative abilities swiftly covered the area in new skin. The process would have gone a lot faster with fresh sustenance. A rat scurried along the top of a glass shelf across the room from me and my mouth watered in response. It would not be much, but it would be something. Instinctually, my hand tugged just to check. Nothing. The vermin disappeared behind a wall, and didn't reappear the rest of the night.

Purple and orange blazed across the glass roof again without a sign of the other two. The thought of going through another day in the sun made me want to weep.

Regardless, I endured. The vicious cycle repeated itself for two more rotations of the earth. By the end of the third day, it felt like any more exposure would shatter me into a million pieces. Every day that passed, my chances of escape became slimmer and slimmer. There simply wasn't enough energy left to pull myself free of the bindings, let alone fight two full strength vampires. My regenerative abilities dwindled to such a snail's pace, a human would heal faster. Even from the previous night, my burns barely closed before the sun blistered them open again. Without blood, I would not last another day. Then again, that wouldn't be so bad. It couldn't be worse than this.

The sun dipped below the glass at last and the bracing breath that had supported my lungs all day released in a frigid grunt. My shoulders slumped and my chin fell against my chest. Just like the three days before, the pain existed into the night, taking longer and longer to ease until today, where the throbbing refused to let go. The prevalence of the sun pulsated across my body even though it itself disappeared. It squeezed my eyes like a vice grip and my skin felt too tight. Solace would only come from shedding out of my skin like a reptile. The idea itched my mind and firmly took hold.

"Hello?" squeaked a sweet voice.

My head jerked up, and I scanned the room. Specks of light danced on my vision, making it next to impossible to see. They wouldn't clear even after a couple of heavy blinks. Everything looked like shapeless blobs when, at this time of night, should be perfectly clear. Slowly, my eyesight adjusted and the shapes came into focus. The deep shadows morphed into the objects I memorized over the last couple of days, like the sheets of wood leaning against the storefront called, "Fizzy Kids" and the cartoonish statue of a cat, half draped in cloth, sitting next to a black piano under the stairs, who stared at me with its one exposed eye. One shop front had mannequins that were easily mistaken for bodies, but after counting them, all five remained accounted for with no extras. My mind was truly gone now that it conjured up voices. The back of my head fell heavily against the column as my eyes closed again.

Then I heard it. *Thump, thump.*

My body lunged instinctively toward the sound, only to be yanked helplessly back by the restraints. The human squeaked, fueling the fire of desperation to reach her. However, fatigue settled deep into my muscles and the fight left me depressingly fast. Instead, I watched. The faintest cloud of dust swirled away from a column at the edges of my field of view, mostly concealed behind one of the center staircases. Further encouraging my hypothesis that she hid behind it were the beats of her heart pumping erratically from the same area. The sound made me see red, while venom filled my mouth, threatening to spew over onto my chin.

Another puff of dust, close to the floor where she stood, appeared just as the girl turned and peeked a single eye out from around the column. Long blonde hair swayed into the space around her head. Her pupils filled her irises, trying to make out the figure in front of her in the near darkness. A hungry moan caught in my throat, but it would do no good for the situation if it came out and instead, swallowed it. With any luck, she would be dumb enough to step closer; close enough to latch on with my legs and then my teeth. With a conceited effort, my eyes softened and begged her to come closer. Hopefully, she was dumb enough to get caught in the snare.

"Hello?" she repeated, a little braver.

"Help. Me," I croaked.

With that, she leaned a little further out. A petite nose poked out, exposing her just a little more. My eyes followed her intently. A glob of venom made its way down my throat so it wouldn't dribble onto my chin. I could not risk scaring her away. My weight shifted and the noise scuffed the shoe on the floor. She jumped and retreated behind the pillar. However, she didn't remain hidden for long. She held onto her personal rectangle and tapped the face of it until a light blazed from the back of it. At first, it formed a cone of light directly under it, facing the floor. Then, she lifted it and it seared into my eyes.

A groan came out of me while recoiling in pain.

"Sorry!" she breathed and lowered the light immediately.

Blinking did little to alleviate the gaps in my vision. It left me wishing she hadn't just done that.

While waiting for the white spots to disappear, her timid footsteps made their way out from around the column. They tapped so quietly on the floor; they could have been mistaken for a mouse. The girl kept a wide berth until she stopped behind the stacked wood directly in front of me, about ten meters away. Her heart beat as fast as a rabbit's, and yet, her body remained still. She should have been shaking with adrenaline at the least. No matter. Her stupidity would lead her directly to me. I swallowed my excitement and waited.

She stepped out from behind the wood as a silhouette, and only her most obvious features were discernable. She had slight shoulders, hair that went to her navel, not terribly kept, but still loose. The way she held the light cast a glow around her feet, and it reminded me of an angel. Her steps landed so softly, it looked as though she floated. Only a meter more and her blood would be mine. My chest and head leaned forward hungrily. Foolish. This caused her to pause just outside of my reach. She needed a little encouragement.

"Please, help me." The words croaked out of my mouth.

Then she said something wholly unexpected.

"Are you a vampire?" she asked with bravado.

Her words slapped me as if she physically made contact. Her heart fluttered as she waited for an answer.

"I-I," I stuttered, trying to find the right words. "What did you say?"

"Are you a vampire?" she repeated. This time she spoke sounding …hopeful.

Who was this girl? My eyelids blink rapidly, desperate for a clearer view of her. Encountering a human educated about my status as a monster wasn't entirely unexpected, but extremely improbable. Normally, this kind of question came from villagers holding torches and pitchforks, yelling over a priest who thrust a cross in our direction. Their actions were laughable. When an angry mob grouped together to rid their village of Satan, we left simply out of boredom. Mostly. Every once in a while we would gorge ourselves. As a result, the legend of our kind continued and the humans learned about keeping a healthy distance. Though, they did get it wrong a lot, and I had been to quite a few pyres with innocent people tied up to them.

There was something about her tone that alarmed me.

The woman did not move while she waited for an answer. No doubt she could see the glint of my eyes staring at her, studying. Her damn light pointed in a way that blocked me from seeing her properly. Even though it pointed at my chest, the beam swallowed her face and made it impossible to read her expression. The longer she stood there, the more her heart calmed.

"Help me, I am trapped." My second attempt at coercion came out softer than before. She needed to come just a little closer.

"I don't think that's a good idea," she admitted and shifted her weight back.

The words came out more aggressive than intended. "Why not?"

This did not help and she took another step. My jaw tightened and my lip twitched. She noticed this too and her heart sped back up. In an attempt to comfort her, my body relaxed back against the column while my eyelids dropped closed and counted to twenty. A gross effort was put into making sure the next words out of my mouth were approachable.

"Please, I will not survive another day here." The sentence came out as soft as a feather and laced with the truth. This seemed to appeal to her and she took a step closer again. Just one step.

"You won't hurt me?" she asked.

"No, I will not hurt you." The words came from deep in my chest.

She chewed on my answer for a moment, then moved her light from the ground, across my face, and settled it on my hands. My eyes flinched from the pain as spots danced behind my eyelids once again. Through the spotty gaps in my vision, the woman turned away and determinedly marched down the building, away from me.

"Wait!"

With her head turned away from me, she answered, "I'll be right back!"

She half jogged down the corridor and the light scanned from right to left. Three times she dipped into one of the stores and emerged. Eventually, she went out of view and her light danced on the wall in a faint glow on the other end of the building. Then, a stack of wood tumbled to the ground, sending a thundering clatter through the length of the structure. A cloud of dust puffed out and the girl coughed as a result. After about a minute, she grew quiet, but the silence only lasted a second or two before she started clambering through a stack of wood, clanging something metal against another piece of metal, then footsteps. She jogged back to me.

The optimistic part of me hoped she had forgotten her earlier hesitation and would step closer, or at least, close enough to get a hold of her. My legs tensed just in case. However, she didn't forget. She stopped well within her safety bubble. To add insult to injury, she shone the damn light right into my face again as it passed up to my hands.

"Okay, so I found a crowbar, but I'm not confident about getting those pins out of your hand. Weak muscles. Plus, there is the matter of squishing your hand…" she trailed off.

"That won't matter." My tongue raked the back of my teeth.

"Well, umm, okay, but I'll need two hands. Shoot…" She stopped. "This thing is heavy. Let me go get something to stand on. Hold on."

"I think you can do it. Why don't you try?"

The crowbar clattered to the ground. Her little light started scanning the room again while my teeth clacked together in irritation. She walked wide enough around the column that it was pointless to try to catch her and to an area behind me. Something she did caused another ruckus that sounded like a couple of boards falling to the floor, followed by a sneezing fit.

Metal clambered at her side with every step as she made her way back over and proudly proclaimed, "I found a ladder!"

Curiosity had me wretched as far as the bindings would allow me to try to get a better look at her. She fiddled with the thing directly behind the pillar and perfectly out of view. It banged and scratched against the floor as she tried to get it to open. The rustling calmed and the sound of her exuberant breathing filled the otherwise quiet place. Burdened footsteps made their way closer and suddenly, the V-shaped ladder appeared next to me. She settled it close enough that the metal frame brushed up against my nose, making me lean back a few centimeters. She positioned it in a way that the ladder perfectly aligned to block any attempt at grabbing her with my legs. I would be able to grasp the metal, but nothing else. So, when she popped up from behind the ladder, my eyes trained intently on her, waiting for her to make the tiniest of mistakes. Which only made it worse when she dragged the light across my face yet again.

"God dammit, can you stop doing that!" I lost my patience.

The light dropped quickly, but the damage had already been done. My eyelids pressed firmly together, waiting for the pain to lessen.

"Sorry."

"It's fine, just don't do it again, yeah?"

"If I turn off my light, can you see well enough to guide me to the right spot?" she asked.

"Absolutely."

She tapped on her rectangle and the space plunged into darkness, leaving nothing but the white splotches in my vision from that wicked light.

"Here goes nothing," she breathed.

Her approach from the back of the ladder put me at a disadvantage, but no matter. After she freed one hand, it would be easy to grab her. *Patience, Phil, just a little longer.*

The metal rattled against the floor as she stepped on the first rung, then the second, then the third. Her breath tickled the back of my neck, sending a shiver down my spine and the hair on my arms to raise in anticipation. My mouth moistened in response to the sound of her clambering her way up the steps. Like a vision, her face popped up level with mine and my plan to suck her dry evaporated into the ether.

The muscles in my chest clenched and all the air in my lungs came out in a single, forced breath, much like receiving a blow from John straight in the sternum. My mouth hung open. I did not dare blink, fearing the image in front of me would disappear, for the face peering back belonged to my dead wife.

Chapter 5

"Almost. There," she huffed.

The railroad tie clambered to the ground somewhere below us as my arm flumped to my side. The sensation of freedom should have filled me with ecstasy, but my mind could only focus on the delicate features of the apparition. It was her. My dear Cecelia had returned to me from the dead. Or maybe not? Was it really her? Impossible. This woman's heart beat strongly under her bosom and my wife, well, she died. Even so, I could not dismiss the hundred and seventy years that passed. This must have been a hallucination. Had my deprivation of sustenance and exposure to the elements left me so weakened that my mind would torture me with the conjuring of my dead wife? What a cruel punishment.

The woman stepped off the ladder in a shower of creaking metal, breaking me of my trance. The spell shuttered from my brain and revealed half of me was no longer helpless. While she maneuvered the ladder to the other side, my free hand set to work on the railroad tie still fastened to the column. My fingers felt like sausages trying to get purchase under the head of the tie, regardless the thing pressed deeply enough into my palm that there wasn't enough room to pull it out. The ladder reappeared on the other side and she climbed up the rungs much more confidently. Carefully, she tried to wedge the fork of the crowbar between the head of the tie and the meaty part of my palm. It kept flicking out from under it whenever she tried to push.

"Give it to me," I instructed.

She hesitated. She looked from the weapon to my face with narrowed eyes.

"I don't need a crowbar to kill you."

"Was that supposed to make me feel better?"

"I suppose it wouldn't. Now, please, hand it over. Gentleman's honor not to use it against you."

She handed over the crowbar into my outstretched hand. The wedged end of the bar buried itself deep under the head of the pin with my hand controlling it, nonplussed that some skin came with it. The pin stood no chance of staying put when leveraged forcefully against the pillar. It shot out and flew across the room, landing in a stack of unused windows. The sound cascaded louder and louder as the piece of metal made its way through the different layers. All in all, the task took me no longer than a second to do, but the consequences of it echoed loudly for several more moments. I had grown complacent in my solitude and remembered that the two goons would be back.

Equally, I became acutely aware that my fate belonged to me once more. My shoulders rolled in their sockets and my head stretched from left to right. It felt nice to have the ground so solid under my shoes at last. The air touching the wounds on my hands produced an odd feeling. It wasn't what could be described as pain, but more of an unusual sensation in parts of my body that are normally covered in skin. The holes should have started to close by now but showed no signs of healing. The reason is as clear as night. Reluctantly, I swallowed the saliva in my mouth and turned to face the consequences of my choices.

She remained on the ladder, shielding her head and ears from the sudden noise. When she peeked up from the crook of her elbow, her face stung like another punch to the gut. It was her. You couldn't convince me otherwise.

"Oops," she timidly smiled down at me.

My expression mirrored hers as my hand reached out to offer her a steady place to grab onto while descending the ladder. She draped her fingers over mine and it felt like warm milk against my skin. A shutter ran up her arm in response to my touch.

"Oh!" she gasped.

"What's wrong?"

"You *are* cold!"

It wasn't something that naturally crossed my mind, but she was right. In a mere couple of minutes, this woman had disarmed me to an alarming degree of complacency. This attitude put us both at risk. When my hand tried to pull away, she squeezed harder.

"No, it's fine! I've just read stories about it and…" She lowered her voice. "…you're the first I've met."

"First what?"

She blushed deeply and my instincts threatened to take over, but that face repelled whatever desire remained to act on those impulses. The hunger remained, pulsating deep in my chest, toxins oozed into my mouth, and clawed down my throat. Yet, the pain meant nothing if it meant having Cecelia back. Once she had both feet on the floor, I did not let go, afraid she would float away as soon as our hands parted. With every second, she became more real. Her heartbeat reassured me that she lived while the blood flowing through her veins sung to me like a lullaby. She too had a look of content on her face. Not quite like the look of love, but one of a satisfied rebel, surprised she got away with something.

I heard the whoosh a millisecond before reacting. Cecelia huffed when my arms wrapped around her and pulled her unexpectedly into my chest, the force pushing a breath of air out. My hand cradled her head under my chin while the wood beam splintered into a million pieces as it cracked against my backside. The shower of wood rained to the ground at our feet. A second whoosh quickly followed the first, but my grip released Cecelia's head and instead, handily, caught the board before it could hit me. Joseph smirked from the other end of the weapon.

At this point, he was infinitely stronger than me, made abundantly clear when he effortlessly thrusted the end of the board into my face. It bounced off my nose and the surprise of it caused me to lose my grip. With Cecelia in my grasp, we both stumbled back, creating much needed room between Joseph and ourselves. He made his way closer with the board raised like a club. Cecelia now separated us like a shield and put her in a vulnerable position. I gently drew her behind me, pressing her against my back. Our retreat progressed slowly while my attention remained on Joseph. Ideally, we would get out before he could do anything else, but if it came to defending myself, I'd make sure Cecelia was safe.

"Boat's here, Philip. Time to go," he mused. "And no, you can't take your snack. Defeats the purpose of your little siesta."

Silence hung in the air as John moseyed up behind him, unreadable, like always.

"Not this again. Come on." He whistled to me like a dog. When he didn't get his way, Joseph's mouth smoothed into a straight line. "All right, you little shit, come here. You aren't going to win this one. You are so weak, you can barely stand up. Why fight it? I'm starting to think you like having the piss beat out of you."

The thought of having to let go of Cecelia threatened to disintegrate me. That would be the end, surely. The relief of a final death appealed to me more than continuing on, again, without her. Her safety meant more to me than my existence, my health, my blood thirst.

"No," I croaked.

"Very well," he replied.

The two hiked toward us. Instinctually, my arm tightened around her as best it could. The other lifted to protect my face. They approached us dead on and my attention flicked from one to the other, carefully considering who would attack first since both Joseph and John had their arms swinging at their sides like upright apes. They must not have considered me a threat or else they would have been more defensive. As much as it pained me to admit it, they were probably right, but that thought couldn't deter me for my sake as well as Cecelia's. John lumbered slightly ahead of Joseph, so he reached out to grab me first. My muscles tensed, ready to swat him away, but never got the chance. A beam of light lasered out from behind me and elicited furious cries. John and Joseph pushed their hands against their eyes at the sudden appearance of light.

"Run," squeaked the voice from behind me.

For just one stride, she pulled me toward an exit. When I caught on where she led us, my pace overtook her easily. Her feet tripped and dragged at the impossibly fast new pace. The stun from the light would not last long and desperation pushed me to get out while we still could. A tug on her arm swung her in front of me and, with my free hand, swept her legs out from under her. Safely cradled against my chest, we sped up and breezed out of the first set of doors that looked like they led outside. The glass shattered away from the invisible door that we crashed through and sparkled as it fell.

The fresh night air welcomed us into a world of many possibilities. At present, a large space blurred under foot that reminded me of a road, but covered many acres of land. White lines fashioned into a grid painted the entire space. Wayward stems of grass infiltrated the otherwise lifeless yard. Across the field of pavement was a carriageway and far behind it, the city that had become my shelter. My pace already pushed my fatigued body past its limit, stumbling on tiny bumps in the path, but the sight of the distant skyline encouraged me to go even harder.

On top of it, half of my attention remained behind us, listening for Joseph and John, while the other half looked ahead for a place to hide. We made it into the deep throes of downtown and only one set of footprints echoed in our wake. Fortunately, they were mine.

"Stop, stop. Please stop," moaned Cecelia.

Concerned that she was somehow injured, I skidded to a halt and moved her gently away from my body to get a better look. Her skin glistened with beads of sweat under an unnatural shade of green. She squirmed in my arms. Understanding her meaning, my arms dropped so she could stand. Cecelia took a couple of steps to the edge of a building and vomited onto the pavement.

While she took care of her business, my ears twitched nervously, waiting for any sign of trouble. Any scratch of a rat, any flap of a wayward newspaper, would twist my focus in the direction from where it came. My eyes flitted from one building to the next, always hyper vigilant to any change around us. We were somewhat protected in the alley. The buildings stretched high above us and a long length of brick stood guard to our front and rear. Plenty of room to prepare for an ambush.

"Do you feel better?" My nose crinkled.

"A little," she replied.

Cecelia straightened herself, and she looked brighter. Less pale, but no less sticky. Beyond the smell of sick, her natural scent permeated the whole area. It led straight out the end of the alley and, no doubt, all the way back to my imprisonment. All Joseph had to do was follow the trail. The situation warranted a change in plan, but what?

"I have an idea," she broke through my thoughts.

"And what would that be?"

"Can you get me a new set of clothes?"

"Now is not the time for vanity."

She looked at me wide-eyed. "Excuse me? No, I don't care about that. You're worried about them following my scent, right?" With a shrug, she continued. "So give me a new smell. It probably won't last long, but we can at least try."

"It could work. Good idea, Cecelia."

Her reply caught on her lips as she considered my words instead. She moved her hands to the hem of her shirt and the vulnerability of turning my back kept me in place a second longer than appropriate. It would do no good to delay, so I glided over to a nearby house and nimbly undid the window lock before slipping inside. It connected to a petite kitchen, where in the next room over, a moving picture cast the room in a rainbow of changing colors. Pictures on the wall showed a happy couple, where the woman seemed to be similar in size to Cecelia. At the top of the stairs, a bedroom had a couple of racks of clothing lined up around the outside of the room. Blouses and pants strewn about the floor and bed. From the smell of things, the hanging items were the cleanest option. I snatched clothes from the hangers without much thought, as long as it ended up with a full outfit. The window attached to the bedroom allowed for a much hastier exit. With full arms, the drop from the second story deposited me next to Cecelia, who was just pulling the shirt over her head.

She jumped at my reappearance before continuing to undress. The articles of clothing draped across my outstretched arm with my back turned to her, while listening very carefully to anything that moved. She shakily grabbed each piece and put it on as quickly as she could, but the task took ages before she spoke. "I'm dressed."

She rejected a skirt and jacket, so with their usefulness expired, they were tossed into a nearby pile of garbage. The amount of time we spent here made me nervous, but there was still one thing that needed to be done before leaving. Cecelia's scent clung to her old clothing just as her new clothes smelled like their old owner. Her old stuff needed to be deposited into a place that would lead the goons away from us and buy a few extra minutes. Just down the street, the Hudson shimmered against the edge of the city.

"Wait here."

Her reply would have been to an empty space for how quickly I left. With the clothing wadded into a tight ball, it catapulted halfway across the river before breaking apart and fluttering down to the surface. The current swiftly caught the articles and carried them downstream. The mature smell of the water gave me an idea. I jumped over the railing and splashed into the water below. My head briefly dipped under the surface before thrusting back onto the railing. A spray of water joined me and struggled to keep up with the pace back to Cecelia. Only my backside remained wet by the time we met back up.

Her heel slipped into a shoe as if suspended in time for how fast she came into view. Without slowing down, my hands plucked her from the ground and threw her over my shoulder. She did not approve.

"Stop!" she cried.

So, I did.

"Put me down."

When her feet touched the ground, she ran an angry hand through her hair to smooth out the wild mess that had accumulated thanks to the mad dash. Her eyes turned on me and my chest clenched with resurfaced feelings.

"Do you even know where you are going?"

"I do not."

Her eyes softened before pointing to her left.

"Go toward Harlem. There is a white apartment with graffiti of a bald eagle on the south side. Fourth story, third door on the left from the elevator."

Harlem made sense, but the rest of what she said meant nothing. She didn't complain about being scooped up the second time. Perhaps she appreciated being held like a baby instead of slung over the shoulder. We took off toward the north and it wasn't long before she pointed to a cross street. With a slight change in direction, a building shorter than its neighbors popped up. As promised, a painting of the aforementioned bird decorated the majority of the south side. I slowed to a walk and marched toward the entrance.

"Put me down," she demanded.

"Not a chance," I grumbled.

"It's going to look weird if you parade me through the building like a prize. Put me down," she repeated.

She got what she wanted, but not until we were almost through the doors. The building was a bit rough around the edges. The walkway leading up to the front had cracks that crumbled around the edges. Rust licked the edges of the stairs on the fire escape. She used a key to get in and the lobby didn't have a greeter. A lingering smell of mold hinted that they did not have a regular housekeeper either. A couple doors lined the bottom floor, but she led me past them. The short hall ended at a shiny wall with a seam down the center. This sparked a sense of deja vu. Of course! It was the room that moved vertically down Miles's building. She pressed a button with an arrow pointing up and it lit up at her touch. Then we waited.

I aligned myself to keep a watch on the entrance door, wondering how long we had before John and Joseph appeared in the entrance. Something dinged behind me and the two halves of the shiny wall split to reveal another one of the small rooms. She walked inside with me following close enough that my jacket brushed against her. Her finger deftly pressed the button labeled four on a panel located near the closing doors. The room shivered and started to lift. A little light illuminated the numbers as we rose through the building.

The number stopped at four and the room bounced to a stop. Anxiety boiled through my body waiting for the doors to open. They started to slide apart and my body stood ready to pounce on our pursuers. Yet, they weren't there. It didn't stop me from rushing out of the small room and inspecting the new space. It mimicked the first floor in that it led to a short hallway lined with doors. Cecelia hurried out behind me and stopped at the third door. She produced a key from her pocket, shakily inserted it into the lock, and turned it. In one swift motion, she swung the door open and removed the key from the lock.

I leaned into the doorway and listened, while pulling in as much air as possible, smelling for any sign of either Joseph or John.

"You can come in," she invited, very quietly.

"Thanks?" My eyebrow rose.

The home took up very little space. The front door opened to the left of the kitchen, which took up about half the room. The cabinets wrapped around one corner with storage above and below the limited counter space. In the kitchen's nook, a small, square table nestled in the middle with two chairs. Her bed sat a shoulder's width away from the eating area, also pushed as far into the corner as space would allow. The headrest pressed against the left wall and aligned so that her feet faced to the right. Her desk took up the remaining width of the room, facing the only window in her home. In the little gap between her desk and the kitchen, she boasted a bookshelf brimming with novels, stacked two deep. A door on the same side as her headrest was cracked open just enough to see the reflection of her shower in the mirror. I peeked inside the room, just in case there was more to it than how it appeared. It too supported a washbasin and a place to relieve yourself, but it also had a doorless cabinet filled with her personal items. Trinkets littered the home here and there, a dirty plate sat in her wash basin, and a few articles of clothing sat unkempt on the few pieces of furniture.

Satisfied that we were alone, my gaze fell back to Cecelia. She stood next to her bed, holding her elbows. Her golden hair fell around her shoulders, windswept and wild. I breathed in the sweet smell of my darling Cecelia. Her natural scent leaked through the disguise of her new outfit, conflicting with what my memories expected from her. The aroma of roses was synonymous with my wife and with a lot of imagination, the scent could be kissed from the air.

She shook ever so slightly, chattering her teeth. Water prickled the bottoms of her emerald eyes and a single tear spilled onto her cheek. I wanted so badly to walk over and wipe it away, but something about her look stopped me. Those eyes looked much too wide. She stared at me like an animal would stare down a predator. Cecelia would never look at me like that. The silence grew heavier as she stared. So much needed to be said, yet my mouth remained closed.

She needed reassurance and an embrace from trusted arms. However, the look in her eyes kept me away, afraid that coming any closer would do more harm than good. Instead, I organized my thoughts into a coherent, encouraging sentence. My jaw slackened and when my lips parted to speak, a pool of venom spilled down my chin.

She yipped and took a step back. Her hand reached to quiet her mouth and remained in place to muffle any more involuntary noises. A few more tears escaped. She stared at me in horror with her beautiful emerald eyes. In the pit of my stomach, an animal tried to claw its way out in response to the cries. The growling reverberated in my spine and settled in the back of my head. My ears pounded in a rhythmic pulse, calling to me. *Blood, blood, blood.* To my horror, the sound came from Cecelia's pounding heart. She danced dangerously close to death by just existing. My body jerked away from the bloodthirsty thoughts. The countertop groaned when my fingers gouged into the edge.

We escaped just to be put into another impossible situation. I needed nutrition, which required leaving this space. Yet, exiting this house put me at a high risk of running straight to my death. Staying here would mean her death. My jaw clenched so hard; something in my head cracked.

Behind me, Cecelia sucked in a big breath.

"This is not at all what I pictured," she whimpered.

Through teeth that acted as a dam to the saliva contained behind them, the reply came out shallow, "What?"

"You, me, the stories," she choked out.

A risky glance revealed she sat hunched shouldered on the bed, staring at me. She did not look at me quite as harshly, but her eyes and cheeks were puffy and red. It didn't take a genius to see that the situation overwhelmed her and that her mind no longer processed the information coming at her with reason.

She looked conflicted, yet scared. There had to be something that could be said to help. The first thing to enter my mind forced its way through a clenched jaw.

"I am not going to hurt you. I can't."

"Well, that's something."

A sarcastic laugh involuntarily made its way out. "As if there is something worse?"

"Well, yes," she responded.

"Like?" The word hung in the air. The conversation helped me stay in control of myself.

"You could leave," she whimpered.

I fully turned toward her, curious. My fingers reattached to the counter, keeping my accountability in check. What remained of my humanity looked at beautiful Cecelia with nothing but love, but the disease in me was just so thirsty.

"You would rather be in the same room as me than risk being alone?"

"You *said* you wouldn't hurt me," she stated.

"I would not put too much weight on that sentiment at present."

"Why not?"

The words came out precise and slowly to emphasize her precarious position. "I'm thirsty."

"Oh," she breathed.

The room went quiet with the weight of the

situation.

"It is a good thing I prepared for this then," she announced.

She stood up from the edge of her bed and walked dutifully toward me.

"No!" Horrified, my reaction flung me to the opposite wall, landing on her desk. She jumped too, unable to keep up with my rapid relocation. "Not now. I won't be able to stop. You will die."

Her smooth face wrinkled in contemplation. She thought about my warning and understanding flooded her face. The blood drained from her cheeks.

"Oh jeez, no," she said. "That isn't what I meant at all. Here, let me get something for you."

She walked over to a large, upright box. The front had a handle and when she pulled on it, the interior flooded the room in light. My eyes shied away from the light just in case, but the intensity inside the box didn't hurt too badly. Still, the contents inside were hard to make out. It looked like the box had a couple of shelves holding an array of unrecognizable labeled goods. Cool air flooded the room and it occurred to me that this thing was a modernized icebox.

"I cannot have any of those things."

"I know," she replied flatly.

My eyebrow raised then, curious as to what exactly she intended to retrieve. She reached for something stored in a bag on the top shelf. They were stacked two high and two across. Her fingers closed around one on the top and closed the door. Cecelia turned and stretched as far as she could, setting the bag down on the table between us. A dark red liquid sloshed in the clear bag, which effectively blocked the smell of the contents inside, but my mouth watered in understanding. Blood. In a bag.

The receptacle of sustenance called to me and the animal in my stomach started digging into my abdomen again. My tongue flicked across my lips, saturated in spit. A tiny voice in the back of my head pulled on me like a leashed dog, however. This wasn't right. It was not safe for her.

"Move." Venom spit out of my mouth.

She shifted, but did not listen.

"More of these bags are in the ice chest, correct? Well, you are standing between me and them. This isn't enough to satisfy my need and once this bag is empty, there will be nothing to stop me from then going after the next easiest resource. I strongly suggest you move."

"Oh," she said again.

This time, she assessed where to go and retreated to the latrine. She closed the door to a sliver as if it would provide her with an iota of protection. Perhaps it would create enough of a mental block to stop me. Hopefully. Her pupil remained trained on me and saw the exact moment the invisible leash holding me back let go. My hands grasped the thing by the middle, causing the top to bulge severely enough that it looked close to bursting. The material containing the blood felt unfamiliar, but similar enough to skin that my fangs had no problems puncturing the surface. Unlike skin, it popped before the blood ran into my mouth. It took two long swallows to empty it. My hand extended for the chest handle and ripped the thing open. The light singed into my eyes, but this task required little sight. Fingers patted the space where the bag should have been and rejoiced at the quick find. The process repeated viciously as the second disappeared in a matter of seconds, the third was more enjoyable, and by the fourth, I merely sipped it to completion.

At some point in my feast, I slipped down and sat on the floor. My back leaned contentedly against the cabinet, with an empty bag clutched in my grasp. Vampires don't experience fatigue in the sense that a human would, so it did not bother me that my body had been treated like a slab of meat and strung up for a couple days to age, but damn did it feel good to just sit. The bag fell to the floor and the last drops of blood stained my lips. A chilly strength oozed into my muscles. Never in my long life did the occasion present itself to drink cold blood. Bodies that sat out for more than a couple of hours turned toxic. It should have been wrong, but the icy tentacles of its nutrition spreading through my body trapped me in ecstasy. It replaced the feeling of emptiness with fullness. Not just in the sense that my stomach bloated, but in the way that my muscles felt stronger, my mind keener, my senses more sensitive. The beast that dictated my every move was satisfied for the moment, freeing up my mind to think reasonably. So much so, that the woman in the latrine would be safe. Her emerald eyes blinked when our eyes met through the gap in the door.

"It is okay to come out now."

The door creaked open, but she did not remove herself from the doorway. She watched with one hand on the doorknob.

"You look better. Not so sunken in," she said, but then added, "or sunburned."

A smile lifted the corners of my mouth.

"I feel better. Look, no more holes." My hands rose

so she could see where the flesh had been split apart. Now, skin smoothed over the wound as if it never happened.

"Do you have any more?"

"Erm, no. That was enough blood for four transfusions. Do you need some right now?" she asked hesitantly.

"No, I do not require any more tonight," I replied, emphasizing the last word.

She looked uncomfortable again, inwardly thoughtful.

"It's not easy getting those," she said. Quickly though, she realized how it sounded and backtracked. "But, maybe, Vince can help me get more."

"How, no, why do you have blood in a bag?"

"We took it from the hospital," she admitted.

"Hospitals have blood bags? Huh. Moreso, I meant, why do *you* have blood in a bag?"

Her cheeks blazed with my question.

"You do not have to answer, just curious."

"This sounds really bad, but I've been expecting you. Well, not you exactly, but I've been looking for," —she paused and the next words came out choppy— "your kind."

"You mean vampire."

"Yes," she affirmed.

"Huh…" Her response mulled in my thoughts for a moment. "Does that mean my kind is common knowledge?"

"Oh, no! Definitely not. Well, yes, everyone knows what a vampire is, but in a fictional sense and not in a sense that they are real and walk among us and have been hiding in plain sight for millennia."

"I understand. People consider vampires a myth."

"Basically, yes."

"That is promising. No more pitchforks and torches," I mused.

Cecelia walked out of her latrine and folded herself down onto the floor next to her bed, keeping an eye on me. Her body remained rigid, but she had her legs crossed, and casually picked at her fingernails as she thought about what to say next. The tips of her blonde hair brushed the tops of her legs.

"Your name is Phillip?" she asked, though her sentence ended fairly flat, since she already heard it from Joseph.

"Yes, Phillip Shevington. I go by Phil."

"Okay, Phil. That's nice. When we were back in the alley, you called me Cecelia. Why?"

"Are you not?" My eyebrow raised, genuinely confused.

"No, I'm not. My name is Olivia."

Instead of answering her, my mind went completely blank. Of course, it made sense that this woman was not my dear Cecelia, but it burned deep into my soul, regardless. She looked exactly like her. The cheekbones, her lips, her eye color, even down to the shape of her body, convinced me that my wife lived in this woman, and it paralyzed me.

"Who is she?" she asked very carefully.

"The woman who saved your life." The sentence came out sternly, leaving no room for further questions on the subject.

She took the hint and remained silent. The minutes started to pass by and she now breathed in and out in a consistent rhythm. Cecelia, no, Olivia fell asleep with her head leaned against the lip of her bed. The window filled with morning light. I pushed off the floor and made my way over to her. One arm slid under her knees and the other cupped her back. She rolled into my chest and a wave of her natural scent danced in my senses. Roses. My nose tickled her hair and inhaled more of her fragrance before setting her in her bed. It was easy to ease her out of the stolen jacket, but left the rest of her attire untouched, except for the one shoe she wore. It popped off easily.

My fingers lingered on the edge of the bedspread after pulling it over her. She looked so peaceful in her slumber, and it felt right to run my fingers along her arm, but the harsh reality came back to me. Cecelia is dead. Instead, I pulled myself away from the bed and took a seat in front of her entrance. The door swung inward and with my body pressed against it, would hopefully slow down anyone who tried to get in.

As she slept, a leery eye kept watch on the progression of the sun. The little house was fully illuminated by mid-morning, but her window faced north and never received any direct exposure. Regardless, Olivia sniffed in a deep breath, leaned up, closed the curtains, and then collapsed back onto her bed. She fell asleep again within a minute and stayed that way until mid-afternoon.

While she slept, the current situation enveloped the entirety of my thoughts. First and foremost, what was I doing here? More specifically, what kept me in this spartan house? With the blood bag supply depleted, Olivia would be next. In my gut, though, it pained me to think about harming her. Yet, this woman meant nothing to me and I owed her nothing.

That wasn't true either. If she had not showed up, John and Joseph would be escorting me to my death. She riskcd her life by climbing up that ladder, and then again to pull out the ties, and yet again to take me to her home. It seemed like she had little regard for her life. Odd humans. There was no getting around the fact she freed me and such a deed couldn't be dismissed. Surely, leaning against her door like a guard dog counted as paying back a debt. Did that not make us even? Not even close. Her home served as a hideout and put her at risk. Without me, they would have no reason to look for her. Then again, she helped me escape and Joseph wouldn't forget that. Would it not be an act of kindness to kill her now and leave this place? She would not feel a thing. A repayment for her generosity. It would be quick.

My shadow hovered over her sleeping form. She lay on her side, softly snoring into her pillow. Locks of golden hair curled around her face. As if she felt my presence, she rolled onto her back and the hair fell away from her neck, exposing her satiny skin. Eager eyes studied the shape of her face, her lips, and no matter where they looked, Cecelia filled my vision. Her beauty transported me to our home in Heathrow. She laid the same way on our bed, only dressed in a shift, and smiling into my hair as my kisses found their way down her bosom.

The memory tore me away from Olivia's bed and back against the front door. Damn this woman! A wave of grief fluttered down my chest.

Where did that leave me? I could not kill her, and bringing her across the ocean seemed disgraceful. In her current state, she couldn't hold her breath long enough to make it out of the harbor, let alone the entire Atlantic. It looked like leaving her to fate was the best choice. If only her existence could be erased from my memory and go back to before we met. My best option now would be to learn not to care about her and leave without looking back.

Then it occurred to me, did I not just fulfill my debt to her by *not* killing her a few minutes ago? She would be free to live a long, healthy life after my little intrusion. As they say, there is no gift more precious than time and she just won the grand prize. Who is kidding who? She lived because, at my core, I am selfish. The mere idea of harming the face that reminded me so deeply of my wife caused pain that cut deeper than my feral hunger.

One enormous problem remained: The Don wanted me dead. Not even one hundred and seventy-three years was enough time to forget about me, apparently. Even if something were to stop John and Joseph, he would just send someone else. It would never end. Could some reason be talked into him? Surely not. At best, he'd put me back in a coffin for another couple of centuries to 'swim with the fishes', as they say. At worst, he'd kill me. Neither option sounded pleasant. My head dropped into my hands. The whole thing had my head swimming, leaving me with no idea what to do.

Olivia sucked in a quick breath, indicating she awoke. Her slim limbs stretched, pressing against the wall above her. Her toes created little points at the end of the fabric and the motion pulled the top of the blanket down, revealing her bosom. The shirt she wore draped over her breasts, just enough to shelter her from indecency. It perturbed me. I wanted indecency. Cecelia would have welcomed me openly. Then again, in the perfect world, she would have woken up to the gentle caress of my touch as we lay together. My lip twitched in frustration from across the room, sitting on the floor like a dog.

"Oh, my god!" Olivia huffed.

I sprung up at her exclamation and scanned the room. We were still alone.

"What is it?"

"You." She sighed.

My brow furrowed while studying her face. Her jaw hung slightly slack and her eyes were soft. The center of her eyebrows rose slightly, giving her a look of wonder. She stared at me as if she saw an angel.

"You stayed," she repeated.

"Where else would I go?" The question rhetorical.

This seemed to please her and she smiled, holding me in her gaze for several long moments. She hesitantly pulled her eyes away, but when she did, came back to herself and shuffled to the other side of the bed. Her hand found the little rectangle and tapped the face of it. It lit up at her touch and showed a small picture with the time stamped at the top. It read 3:25. Curiosity brought me a couple of steps closer to her bed to get a better look at the thing. They had been in almost everyone's hands and yet, their purpose remained a mystery to me.

"What is that?"

Her cheeks turned a brilliant red again and her eyes narrowed, crinkling in the corners. Her mouth smashed into a flat line, making no attempt at answering my question. She looked up to watch me make my way over to the bed.

"May I?"

Olivia stared at my outstretched hand uncertainly. She thought for a moment before shifting uncomfortably, and then set the thing down on my palm. It weighed almost nothing, and the surface slid across my thumb like polished, black glass. It reminded me of looking through a window into the void that held me prisoner at the bottom of the ocean. On the back were three black dots nestled in the upper corner, ringed in sky blue. I flipped it back over and tapped the front as she had, but nothing happened.

Olivia's gaze watched me from her bed, bouncing from the thing to my face.

"You weren't asking about Eric, were you?" she said with relief in her voice. Olivia became contemplative for a moment, then asked, "Do you not know what that is?"

She pointed at the rectangle in my hand.

"No."

"It's a cell phone…" She trailed off incredulously. "You've really never seen one before?"

"Yes, but only in the last couple of days. The people around here seem to be transfixed by it."

"How do you not know what this is?" She seemed bemused.

"I spent some time," I paused to think of the right word. "…away."

Her eyes narrowed again at the wide array of possibilities in the meaning of the word 'away'. Instead of answering her, I handed the cell phone back and reached for the gold watch in my pocket. It slid out easily and offered it to her in my open palm. Her fingers brushed mine as she carefully lifted the object from my hand. The tiny clasp opened and she immediately found what she needed to see.

"Eighteen fifty-one? What is so significant about that?"

She scanned the blank side of the watch where Cecelia's picture had been and my jaw tensed, hoping she wouldn't say anything. Her eyes crawled back up to mine. Bright green orbs stared at me through blonde lashes and my heart clenched in my chest. Sweet Cecelia.

"The two men after me are named Joseph and John. Their boss is very, very angry with me and the last time we met, they condemned me to purgatory. Let's say a lot of things have changed in my absence."

My possessiveness gently pulled the pocket watch from her hands and replaced it where it was safe. She kept looking up at me, more curious than scared. As she thought, a shadow of doubt crept over her beautiful face.

"What did you do to make him so mad?" she asked.

"I killed his daughter."

Her face smoothed before she answered, "That's it? Isn't killing kind of your MO?"

My head titled, wondering who the hell this woman was.

"What?" she said matter-of-factly. "You need to sustain yourself somehow. I hoped you'd be one of those that found 'alternatives'."

"Alternatives? Like the bag of blood you provided."

"Well, yes, but more like vegetarian or synthetic."

My expression must have gone blank, since Olivia

mirrored the lack of understanding on her own face. She gave up first and muttered, "Never mind."

"Olivia, you aren't grasping the gravitas of my situation. The Don is after me. He is not going to stop, not even after one hundred and seventy-three years."

"Eighteen fifty-one?" Realization dawned on her wide-open eyes and she finally understood. Olivia possessed every reason to be frightened. Vampires were after me and, by extension, her. She had a vampire less than a meter from her throat. Her life hung in a precarious position. Yet, when she finally spoke, her head nodded and asked, "Do you know what *anything* is?"

This woman's disregard for her own life was absurd. Did she not understand that her life could be cut horribly short by just being near me? A growl formed in my chest and crawled out of my mouth on the word, "No."

"Aww, that's okay. I'll teach you." She jumped out of bed and started scurrying to different parts of the room.

She prattled off excitedly. My impromptu history lesson temporarily distracted me from the piling mound of shit. With everything else going on, might as well take the time to know the new reality that refused to stop battering me. My head shook inconceivably.

"…and this is a blender. It is used for all sorts of things." She paused to take a breath.

"How do you get the fire in the glass?"

Olivia looked at me questioningly until her eyes followed where my finger pointed: the recessed dents in the roof that were ablaze with light.

"You mean a light bulb?" She looked at a loss for

words.

"Light bulb." The word sounded cumbersome coming out of my mouth. "How does it work?"

"Well, it comes from electricity. Which, you probably don't know about either."

At that moment, her stomach growled loud enough that even she heard it.

"Whoops, I forgot about food," she said thoughtfully. "What to do with you while fixing something to eat?"

Olivia snapped her fingers and pointed at something behind me. She brushed past and grabbed the flat square she called a laptop from the end of her bed and carried it to the desk in the corner. The thing split in two and the glossy black screen lit up when it opened. Her fingers drummed the word "DamonStefan4ev3r" on the letter pad and it jumped to another screen.

"Come, sit," she said.

She took a step back and pulled out the chair that was tucked under her desk. I squeezed between her and the space she created. Her hair rested against my shoulder and her heart beat quickly. Olivia typed something on the screen, but my interest stayed on her beautiful emerald eyes as they flitted from left to right and back again.

"Okay, this is a mouse." She picked up a small, round lump. "Use it to click on different things on the screen," she pointed at a little dot that moved in correlation with the mouse. "Use the keyboard," —she pointed at the rows of letters— "to type in words into the search bar. Got it?"

"Yes, thank you."

"Good. I'm going to get out of these awful clothes and make myself some food, but let me know if you have any questions."

She walked away and left me a document on the screen that read, "Notable inventions of the 19th century". One of her hands lingered above my shoulder, wondering if it was appropriate to set it down. Inevitably, she didn't touch me before walking over to the edge of her bed. The bedspread covered drawers that were hidden under the frame. She pulled one out, grabbed a couple of items, and slid it shut. Once she closed the door to the latrine, I turned my attention back to the laptop. The words were fascinating, but a part of my mind listened to the happenings behind me. The shower turned on and, within a minute, steam crept out from under the door. Twice, she dropped something which then clambered around the basin before she turned off the water. Water dripped from her hair when she reemerged and walked over to the kitchen, leaving a trail behind her. She clinked through various glasses, opened and closed the ice chest, well, the fridge, and finally crunched on something fairly hard. The food did not last long and before five minutes passed, she already hovered over my shoulder.

The chair swiveled to face her, its legs scraping against the floor, but Olivia sidestepped quickly to avoid getting brushed aside by my body.

"I need to go."

Panic furrowed her face. "No, not yet. You just got here."

My eyelids closed to refocus my thoughts before the images of Cecile saying the exact same thing melted me into complacency. It was so much easier to focus when not looking at her.

On a grumble of an exhale, she got her response. "Do not mistake my words for misplaced admiration, but you are a problem."

She shifted her weight. "I realize that the allure of my blood is probably hard for you, but we can get more from the hospital."

Olivia received the full force of my glare then.

"You think your blood is why I need to leave? Olivia: mob boss. Vampire henchmen. ME. You are not safe with me around. Do you have a death wish?"

"It's a little soon, but the thought has crossed my mind. I'm open to it if you are," she stammered.

"To what?" Her statement took me aback. Her eyes cast downward, with red flushing her face even deeper. My hand found its way to her chin and delicately lifted her face so our eyes could meet. They sparkled in anticipation, but a hint of strain suggested she still possessed some common sense. It was fear. She started to tilt her chin to the side, exposing the side of her neck, and closed her eyes. Her little heart fluttered and her veins pulsed wildly under my touch. What a foolish woman to give herself up so easily. To be accepting of my kind and wish for sacrifice. My lips tickled her neck as her true meaning dawned on me. I jerked my head back and met her fevered gaze.

"You want me to turn you?" The weight of the question ripped out of my chest with a bit of spittle.

She shrugged, waking up a different kind of monster that scraped just below the surface, wearing many faces of emotion. My mind couldn't grasp the concept of her wanting this, this curse. She had no idea what she asked me to do and how much danger this put her in. Her blood sang from inside her body and she invited me to take pleasure in it *if* I gave it back. Olivia couldn't have asked me for a more substantial favor and with such callousness in her intention.

My fingers dug into her skin and if they gripped any tighter, it would cause harm. A film of moisture covered her eyes, making me realize she didn't know what she asked, not really. Her head slipped from my grasp and disappeared behind me, forcing me to walk away.

She found her voice, and it emerged a little more than a whisper. "Sorry, I thought we were on the same page. It's okay though, this is something I should be better prepared for, anyway."

The rage that filled my body must not have been as contained as what it felt like internally. While there wasn't a desire to punch a hole through her wall, Olivia took a cautionary step back when our eyes met again.

"Don't ever ask me to turn you, unless you are prepared to die."

Olivia grabbed her elbows and gazed downward for a single breath before nodding. The corners of her lips pulled down in a way that made her look like Cecelia when she didn't fully agree with me. My top and bottom jaw ground against one another, much like the clashing of memories separating the likeness of Olivia from my dear, sweet wife. Dammit, I couldn't stop making the comparison! This woman, right here in front of me, still breathes the ticking clock of mortality while my wife's time stopped a long time ago. Maybe this fact would finally sink in.

It wasn't just her appearance, though. It was the way she expressed her emotions, the little crinkle at the corners of her eyes, the way she squared her shoulders when she got defiant. It was her horrible lack of self-preservation to associate with someone like me. It took everything in me not to pull her into my arms and treat her like the woman she had nothing to do with, as if that would heal all my open wounds. At this point, the cure to this burden was distance. My time with Olivia needed to end, right now, before this relationship became inescapable.

I soaked in every detail of her uncanny face, hoping to imprint it in my mind so the memory of Cecelia could last just a little longer. She didn't make it easy to leave. Her eyes drifted from my own and studied me the same. It pained me to see her fine brows pulled together in a crease, with the frown still securely pulling at her lips. The grief that stabbed at my heart never lessened with time, not really, and looking at her reminded me that the hole Cecelia left still wept. Trying to walk out the front door felt like leaving her all over again. If I walked over to Olivia to comfort her, to touch her satin skin, I would never let her go.

"Thank you for your help." My comforting smile didn't reach my eyes.

"Please, don't." She panicked.

"Goodbye."

Bang, bang, bang broke through the moment like a crack of a whip. The glassware in the cabinets next to the front door rattled in response. They weren't done shaking by the time my arms formed an iron-like cage around Olivia, pressing her against me. Her head vibrated against the rumbling growl seeping out between my teeth. In that moment, it became clear; my reaction doomed us both.

Chapter 6

I listened carefully to the person standing outside of her door. To my relief, it had a heartbeat. My grip on Olivia slackened, but she did not relax. Her arms squeezed my waist as if she clung onto a buoy in a storm.

"It is not one of my kind." My voice remained low so as not to carry out to whoever stood at her door.

"Right." She hesitantly released her hands and took a step away from me. "Better see who it is."

The door banged three more times in response.

"Jeez, I'm coming," she yelled at the door.

Olivia unlatched the chain, turned the deadbolt, then swung the door open just enough to peek a single eye at whoever stood on the other side. My muscles were rigid, ready to react at the first sign of danger. It could have been a trap, after all. Joseph could have sent this person as bait.

"Vince," she exhaled. "What are you doing here?"

"You've got to be kidding. You had me worried sick. The last thing you tell me is that you are going to the graveyard mall and then nothing for two days? I thought you were dead," he accused.

"Sorry, Dad," she remarked sarcastically.

"Don't call me that. Olive, you better have found something for how much worry you put me through."

He pushed his way into the room, leaving Olivia

grasping for the door sill to regain her balance and continued. "Did you find anything?"

She caught the door and slammed it behind them. The new human continued to take his jacket off, setting himself up for a long visit, all the while talking about the many ways she could have been hurt. He threw the jacket across one of the chairs pushed up against the table and only then did he notice she wasn't alone.

"Oh-livia," he sputtered. "Who is that?"

He eyed me suspiciously from across the room. I too judged the man. He was average. He carried more weight than me despite being a nose length shorter, but certainly not fat. While being clean shaven, he also kept the hair on his head short, styled in what seemed popular right now. He wore a soft, yellow colored short-sleeve shirt on the top and matching pants on the bottom, reminding me of prison garb. A badge hung off his neck with a little picture of him on it. Olivia hung back near the entrance, looking sheepish.

"Vince, this is Phil. Phil, Vince," she introduced.

"Pleasure." My reply came out like ice. Olivia received my opinion with slightly more warmth. "He needs to leave."

Vince raised his eyebrows incredulously at me, challenging the declaration. He opened his mouth to voice his opinion, but Olivia interrupted.

"No, Phil. He's fine. He can help," she stuttered.

"Help? Him?" Vince pointed at me. "No thanks."

"Agreed," I added.

Olivia sighed heavily and pushed off from the front door. She walked into the kitchen and bent down, picking up my trash from the floor. Meanwhile, Vince and I were locked in a stare, sizing each other up. It would be easy to remove this man from the mortal coil, but Olivia seemed to know him and she mentioned that he could help. It didn't make me trust him anymore, however.

Vince jumped when Olivia slapped her loot onto the counter.

"Look." She pointed at the pile like the meaning was obvious.

He walked over and picked one up, looking at the bite marks on the top.

"Seriously, Olivia?" he whined. Remembering that they weren't alone in the house anymore, he glanced at me from over his shoulder and continued much quieter. "Do you think it was a stray dog again? Dammit, Olive. These are really hard to get and I told you to only leave *some* out at a time. Not four damn bags all at once."

"And I told you, if you wanted to catch one, it wouldn't be enough. Guess who's right," she replied smugly.

The tone of his voice changed. He lit up in excitement. "Did you see something at the mall?"

"You could say that." She looked at me.

Olivia's words dawned on him then and he fully turned around with a look of horror on his face. His eyes grew wide and full of understanding. So were mine.

The realization warranted an interruption. "Were you trying to catch me?" The next words that came out of my mouth punctuated my irritation. "Were you *hunting* me?"

Images of angry villagers and pitchforks flashed behind my eyes. Scenarios like this started off with one person with an idea and before you knew it, a whole group of people screamed profanities at you, threatening to burn you at the stake. A chill settled in the room and the two humans looked at me with ashen faces.

"God, no! It isn't what it sounds like, sir," he faltered. "We just wanted to know if, if your kind was real."

"Real, huh," I growled.

Vince never saw me move. One second, he stared at me from across the room and the next, my fingers squeezed around his neck, pushing him into the wall between the kitchen and the latrine. Plaster cracked under the pressure and the wall molded around his shoulders.

"Is this real enough for you?" Hissing at him through a clenched jaw, proudly showing him the two fangs that overlapped onto my lower set of teeth.

No words came out of his mouth as his face turned purple. Tears overflowed onto his cheeks as he stared into my eyes. Olivia's hand reached up and started yanking on my wrist. She cried out for me to let go, that I was killing him. Her second hand joined in and pulled. Her words entered my consciousness like molasses, slowly creeping through the pounding anger pulsating across my thoughts.

His body slumped to the floor in a fit of coughing. Staying near him would only make matters worse and the desk chair provided the perfect place to recompose myself as well. It sunk a few centimeters from the new weight. After a few minutes of wheezing, the man uttered, "Sorry." His apology sounded much more believable this time.

"Leave us," I commanded the mass on the floor.

He started to pull himself off the floor before Olivia joined his side and placed a hand under his elbow to help him up.

"Sorry, Vince," she implored. "This all happened so fast. There hasn't been a good time to tell you. We can talk about this later."

"Later," he puffed in a short laugh.

The two of them gathered Vince's belongings and made their way to the door. The day's warmth nuzzled my backside through the closed curtain, igniting an idea.

"Wait," I said.

Vince stiffened, but obeyed. He turned to make sure he wasn't going to get attacked again.

"You are the blood bag supplier, yes?"

"Yes," he answered hesitantly.

"Would you be able to supply more?"

He looked at Olivia expectantly. A flora of emotions processed across his face, but he finally settled on relinquishment.

"Sure," he answered.

"Thank you."

The sincerity of my words surprised even me. This one man took a huge responsibility off my shoulders, freeing up the mental space to conquer other problems just as pressing.

Vince pulled on Olivia's arm so that their faces almost touched. He lowered his voice to a level that should have offered them privacy, and said, "I'm not going to be his fucking Renfield." He slammed the door behind him and the picture frames on the walls rattled.

Olivia looked at the dent in her wall before she mumbled, "Great."

"My actions toward Vince are shameful. You should know my tempter is very short. Please, forgive me."

"I'm not the one you should be apologizing to," she retorted.

"Right."

Anxiety came off her like waves on the shore. She stood by the door, hugging her arms to her chest, staring at me like she was waiting for me to say something. My thoughts remained in my head, and she'd be thrilled to know what they were. Some things should remain private, while others are too boring to share, like mine right now. I thought about how she probably didn't even realize that she blocked the exit. Olivia made it clear that she wanted me to stick around and, truth be told, a part of me didn't want to go either, but this little interaction with Vince reminded me it wasn't right dragging her into this mess.

"Does this mean you are going to stick around?" she finally muttered.

Yet, she remained stubborn to her cause. My head shook at the audacity of it all.

"Well, for a few more minutes, anyway. It would be rude to leave when Vince is due back within the next couple of hours with more sustenance."

Her shoulders relaxed, and she dropped her arms down to her sides. Olivia took a couple of steps to her right to lean against the counter. A million thoughts clouded her eyes as she stared through me. I had to repeat her name twice before she blinked me into focus.

"Could you help me with something while we wait for Vince to come back?"

"Right, yes. Anything." She grinned.

"The sun is still up, so it is doubtful Joseph and John are out and about. This would be a good time to sneak out and get some new clothes, unless you have some lying around?" She just shook her head. "In that case, we should find a shop somewhere nearby and get something new. There are a few hours before dark. Might as well get some fresh air before returning to hide."

"Aren't you worried about the sun too? Will you start to sparkle?" she asked.

"Sparkle?" I grimaced. "Hell no."

"All right, Phil, yeesh. It still doesn't answer my question."

"It isn't pleasant, but I won't start burning." A grimace wrinkled my face remembering my time in the mall. "Immediately, that is."

"What about our smell?"

This answer wasn't as straightforward and required a careful answer. She was right. Inevitably, even if we simply walked across the street, they could run into it before it dispersed. Leaving this place in any capacity came with risks. However, there were also things we could do to minimize those risks. An idea came to me.

"A shower certainly wouldn't hurt, but after that, we could travel to the shop a little more modernly. What do you call the horseless carriages that are crowding the roads?"

She answered through a fit of giggles, "Do you mean cars?"

The sweet note in her voice infected me, bringing a much-needed smile. "Yes, I suppose I do."

"Let's see…if we are lucky, we have about three hours of light left. There is a department store down the road that might work."

"Lovely. Do you mind if I borrow your facilities for a wash?"

"Oh, sure. Um, have you ever used a shower before?"

"We had showers in the 1850s, Olivia."

"Right."

She marched into the small room and dug around for some things for me. First, she grabbed a folded towel, then a much smaller towel, and set it on top. She turned to bring them over to me, but jumped when she discovered that I stood right behind her instead of at the desk where she left me.

"You are *so* quiet!" she chastised.

"Sorry, I can't help it."

"Well, let me know if you need anything. I'll just be at my desk." She timidly smiled up at me.

In order for her to get out of the bathroom, she had to squeeze past me, even though my back was already pressed against the door frame. She mumbled, "Excuse me," as the crown of her golden hair brushed past, leaving a trail of her rosy smell. The door clicked closed and signified the first time she'd gotten out of my sight since she changed her clothes in the alley the previous night. It didn't stop me from listening intently to her every move. She didn't fib; she walked over to her desk, pulled the chair out, and took a seat. The clicking of her nails on the keyboard in little bursts soon followed.

Even before my time in purgatory, it brought me great pleasure to use water so hot that 'it would poach an egg'. The temperature of the water had no effect on my kind, but it made me feel alive for those precious few minutes while submerged. Olivia's shower consisted of one lever for hot and one for cold. My fingers went straight for the red label and turned it up all the way. Steam curled up and around the curtain that lined her tub. Separating it to climb in burst the barrier, and the fog rolled out to fill the room.

A sigh of relief hissed reactively out of me and flowed down my body with the rest of the first droplets. The deeply pleasurable experience left me paralyzed in its warmth for many minutes. My eyes drifted down to see the water that swirled into the drain first stained the sides of the tub a light shade of brown, with flecks of rusty-colored blood. My hair clung to my skin like seaweed and cooperated just as much when washed. The bar of soap traveled from the top of my head, down to my pits, around my abdomen, and focused on the difficult bits between my toes. By the end of the shower, not even the fine lines of deeply embedded dirt remained.

Too soon, the water stopped falling from the spigot. The fog in the bathroom swirled upon my exit from the shower. A rush of air filled my nose, testing to see if my plan worked. The earthy, borderline unsanitary smell that clung to me since arriving disappeared with the shower. Now, the charming smell of cherry clung to my skin and followed me around the room.

I swiped the dew from her mirror to get a clearer view of myself. The person staring back at me looked more alive than dead. Olivia's blood bags did wonders, filling in my usually sunken eyes. My blue eyes even looked a little glossy with life. The man in the mirror looked passable as just another human, except for one thing. Olivia surely had something sharp in her bathroom. She didn't have anything usable in the cabinet with the towels or in the drawers under the washbasin. However, in a little wooden box stored in a pile of other odds and ends, were some scissors.

****

It would have been nice not smelling like dirty water for a change, but until this current outfit could be replaced, there really wasn't another choice. Between the soap and the musty clothes, neither smelled like me and that is all that mattered. My hand combed through my hair one last time before stepping out of the little room.

"Ready to go, Olivia?"

"Yeah, let me just get my shoes on…" She paused and stared at me from the desk. Her eyes grew wide and her jaw hung open. "You, you cut your hair."

"I figured it would make it harder for someone to grab onto. Do you like it?"

"Like it? Phil, it's like, four inches long. How did you manage to style it so well?" She gaped.

Her compliment lifted the corners of my mouth. "Maybe the skill comes with age, or it is just being observant. Seems like everyone cuts their hair this way. No reason not to fit in."

"Wow, it, uh, looks really good."

"Thank you. Now, shall we get this little adventure over with?"

"There is a department store about a mile down the road that would work for you and, if my phone is correct, there are about two hours before the sun is past the horizon."

"Helpful. We best get going then."

"I hope you won't be disappointed."

"At this point, what could possibly be disappointing to me?"

"Clothing has changed a lot from back then. You probably won't be able to find a black cloak."

"Shame." Her heart rate rose when she noticed my wink.

Olivia grabbed her satchel from a hook on the wall and swiped the keys from the counter beside her. With a couple long strides, I loomed right behind her, listening for hidden danger. All the buildings in this city had a natural breath to them. Groans escaped from the walls, water dripped sporadically, chit-chat murmured from different homes. The constant noise of people going through their lives filled the background. In my long life, this never seemed to change. Even now, I could hear the progression of time in the hallway in front of us and none of it seemed out of place. The only thing unnatural in this setting was my kind, perfectly blending into the background without making a peep. That is how we hunted; monsters that escaped the cruel march of time, unable to blend into those who were still on the mortal coil, and *that* is what made me nervous about her opening the door.

I wedged myself between Olivia and the exit, forcing her to take a half step back. The brass doorknob felt cold in my hand. As a backup, my foot served as a stop far enough away from the door so a single eye could peek into the hallway. No one occupied the space up until the elevator, but that didn't answer if anyone hid around the corner to the left. I pulled the door open a little wider and quickly stuck my head out. Empty. Though not entirely surprising, relief eased my nerves.

We made our way down to the first floor and out into the late day sun. She sprung to the curb and started waving her arm wildly. One of the yellow cars pulled over to her and stopped. Olivia didn't waste any time getting the door open, so when she looked up to me, her gaze landed where she thought I'd be standing, but in reality, remained under the protection of the building's shadow.

"Well, come on," she encouraged.

There was maybe two meters between me and the car, so I pulled at the collar of my jacket and hunched my way over to the open backseat, claiming my spot on the side closest to the curb.

"Scooch." She encouraged me to move over with a swift motion of her hands.

"I'd rather be on this side. Less bright."

She looked irritated until she realized what that meant. Olivia nodded, closed the door, and hurried around the back of the car. She found her seat next to me and asked the cab driver to take us to some place called "Casey's".

"This place has lots of options for varying styles, but there are other stores close by that might work too," she eyed my clothes dubiously.

"Your attention to detail is appreciated, but really, this isn't the time to be picky."

As promised, the place was no more than ten minutes from her home, even with the stop and go flow from the traffic. Our conversation stayed to a minimum since my focus remained on everything going on around us. The ever-present crowd of people walked alongside us, but none of them looked suspicious. The cars funneled into a formation that flowed in our same direction. Their occupants looked tired from boredom and more importantly, harmless. The lucky ones sat in a restaurant with food in front of them, happily munching away on their meals. Just because Joseph and John weren't present, didn't mean that couldn't change in the blink of an eye and precisely why my head remained on a swivel.

The cabby dropped us off in front of the store after Olivia swiped her poker card shaped rectangle into a little box in the back of the seat. Once inside and out of the sun, my curiosity prompted another question. "What is the stiff card people are using in lieu of paper bills?"

"It's a credit card. It is linked to your bank account so that you can use it instead of carrying around a bunch of money."

"How does it know how much money you have? Do they just take the money from your safe whenever you use the card?"

"Erm, no. Money is basically a number on a screen now."

"That's ridiculous! You could just fake that number!"

"True, but with investments, bitcoin, and business assets, wealth is kind of fluid now."

"What in the hell is a bitcoin?"

"Oh boy, that's a tough one to explain. You might have unlimited time on this earth, but I don't, so maybe we should stay focused on the task at hand, yes? What kind of clothes are you looking for?" asked Olivia.

"I've always been fond of a well-fitted suit. Not so different from this." My hand tugged on the bottom of the jacket.

"Then follow me."

Olivia led me through a warehouse of clothing. Rows upon rows of articles that looked suited for more feminine taste. Several shirts were printed with words over cartoon characters, while others were cut in ways that looked like they had been attacked by a wild animal. Large displays showed a vast array of pant options in varying lengths, but very few options for skirts.

Our journey led us toward the back of the space and to a second story stairwell. Only, these stairs moved! The steps glided up until they reached the top, disappeared, and reappeared at the bottom. Olivia took a step on the first available ledge and let it carry her up. I hesitated, trying to get the timing right. My foot met the stair but wobbled as half of the step lowered into a different tier. Once at the top, the thing flattened out and dumped me onto the solid ground. Olivia must have seen me eyeing the contraption, since she offered a single word of explanation, "Escalator." My head shook in disbelief.

In front of us, more rows of clothes continued. This time, it appealed to a more masculine crowd. Olivia did not have to lead me anymore before spotting a manikin wearing a suit exactly to my taste.

"Perfect."

My eyes drew away from the example and scanned the store for an employee. Stuffing a shelf with boxes, a lonely woman worked, softly muttering to herself.

"Miss?"

The word carried quickly to where the woman worked. She heard me easily and looked around for the source. Her gray hair bounced against her head as she turned to look at me. She held up a single finger in acknowledgment before getting back to her task of putting away the box that she already held in her hands. The walk over caused her spectacles to slowly work their way lower onto her nose, but she didn't seem to notice.

"What can I help you with?" she offered when she reached us.

"I would very much like this suit. Do you have one premade? Regrettably, there isn't enough time to get it fitted today."

She eyeballed me from feet to head and said, "Shouldn't be a problem."

Just to the left of the manikin were various sizes of the same suit. Nibble hands sifted through the hangers and neatly plucked one out once she was satisfied. She repeated this with the undershirt and pants.

"You'll need a different pocket square," she added when she led us past the display. Oh, I liked this woman. She took a second, quick glance, and chose a silky square that looked like liquid gold. My wicked grin showed approval of her choice.

She finished her tour by leading me down a hallway lined with five oak doors on just one side. She opened one of the rooms to reveal a space the size of a closet. Only, this closet had a bench, a couple of hooks on the wall, and a body length mirror. She hung my clothing choices up and left me alone. It occurred to me that the room would be cramped if my coat went in with me, so I draped it over a chair in the waiting area nearby.

The woman did an exemplary job of finding the right pieces. Each one fit like someone tailored it specifically for me. Making adjustments to the fit would be woefully unnecessary. The dark fabric absorbed the light like the last moments of day. The gray threads had a slight sheen to them that caught the light like emerging stars. My undershirt was comparable to twilight, a blue so deep, you could go swimming in it. As a focal point to the ensemble, the pocket square poked out of my breast pocket in the shape of a rose. Pressed against the rose from the interior pocket, my gold watch butted up against it. Both objects close to my non-beating heart. I took one last look at myself, smiled in approval, and strutted out of the changing room, leaving my rags on the bench.

Olivia gazed at a shoe that reminded me of something you'd wear while at home, smoking a pipe, while seated next to a fireplace. She had my coat draped over her arm. When she spotted me, her heart skipped and then sped up. My grin widened.

"You like it then."

"Who wouldn't?" she mused. "It is very nice, if a little impractical."

"Not at all. I always dress like this."

We walked over to the cash register and by the time we reached it, Mile's wallet was already in my hand.

"If it isn't too much trouble, do you mind disposing of my old clothes left in the changing room?"

"No trouble," she answered.

She read off a price that would have eaten up the rest of my cash, so with Olivia's education, pulled out one of the credit cards to use instead. The woman took it, stuck it into her little cash box, and waited for something to happen. Beside me, Olivia stiffened. Her attention stressed wholly on the wallet in my hand. It troubled her, evident by the wrinkles creasing her forehead.

"It's declined," said the woman behind the counter.

"Declined?" My eyebrow rose.

"Can you pay with another method?" she asked, still unamused.

Miles had more than one credit card, but it didn't seem worth the hassle, so my fingers strummed through the bills in the fold and pulled out enough to cover the balance. She took the stack and stuffed it into a drawer before handing me a paper receipt. Wasting no time, I ushered Olivia to a more private area of the store.

"What's wrong?"

"Where did you get that wallet?" Her voice trembled.

My answer came out defensive. "I found it."

She paced away a few steps, clenching her fists under my coat mumbling, "This is so wrong."

"What part did it finally cross over to being 'wrong'?"

"Miles Cage!" she spat.

I recoiled, surprised she knew the name.

"Who is he to you?"

"No one," she replied. "But his name is *all* over the news."

"So?"

"So! So, that means the police are looking for his murderer, *his wallet,* and *you* just used his credit card," she pointed out vehemently.

Still not understanding, my face stared blankly back at her expectantly. She just threw her hands up in the air and muttered something under her breath.

"How does his credit card and his missing wallet

have anything to do with each other?"

She shot daggers at me for a moment before her look softened.

"Right, you wouldn't know. It said 'declined' because the bank closed his account. When you tried to use it, an alert was sent back to whoever checks that kind of thing and it probably went to the police, since this is an active police investigation. Phil, they know where you are. They are probably on their way right now."

Olivia pointed at some dark bulbs on the ceiling. My shoulders shrugged, still not grasping the urgency.

"There is no way they can connect me to it. I was very careful." My attempt at reassurance went over like dropping a cat in water.

She inhaled sharply. "Ignoring the fact that you just admitted to murder, they have your freakin' picture, Phil."

She plunged her hand into her satchel and rustled around for a moment. Olivia pulled out a newspaper clipping and shakily unfolded it before shoving it in my face. I recognized it. The date aligned with the paper from a couple of days ago. The headline confirmed it; 'Vampire Killer'. There was only one glaring difference: instead of a shapeless black mass under the headline, you could make out the man in the picture, down to my dimples.

For Christ's sake.

My irritation came out in a heavy sigh as the realization flooded over me. It all made so much sense. Joseph and John would have seen this and recognized the figure instantly. This is how they found me so easily, even a world away. Surely, this wouldn't matter so much now. The damage had already been done. Besides, the picture barely looked like me, anyway. It showed my old clothes, hair that went down to the waist, and a face that looked like something that crawled out of a swamp. Compared to now, anyone would have a hard time making the comparison.

"Give me my coat, please." I held out my finger like a hook.

She grasped it by the collar and let it hang down and said, "We need to leave, like ten minutes ago."

"It will be all right, Olivia. The police will not recognize me. We can just walk out of here."

She didn't look convinced. With one arm through my coat sleeve, Olivia stopped me with her hand on my wrist. "Look at mister perfect here. Should have allowed enough time to get a new coat too." Olivia poked a finger into the space on my coat just under the right shoulder.

"Stop fussing. It's just a bullet hole. Barely visible. Besides, we've already met." He pointed at the result of our lasting meeting before finishing putting it on. "It wasn't an issue then. It will not be an issue now."

"Unbelievable," she huffed, eyeing the hole. A shiver crawled across her body.

"Yes, I do recognize that face. He's right over there," said the woman who helped me.

A glance over my shoulder sent a growl rumbling through my chest so low, the words barely ripped out, "You've got to be kidding me."

We made eye contact and in an amount of time that impressed even me, they yelled, "Stop! Police! Hands in the air!"

Once again, I looked down the barrel of not one,

but two guns. The humans weren't recognizable, but they certainly knew who they were dealing with as they started to sidestep closer to us. Several rows of clothing racks created a maze between us, along with a family of mannequins blocking their clear shot. It would take them a while to weave their way over to our location.

While the broad part of my chest squared up to them, my right hand gently pushed Olivia behind me. She cowered into my back and grasped firmly onto my arm.

"Hands in the air!" repeated one of the policemen.

They stayed together for the most part while worming their way closer to us. It made it easier to put myself between them and Olivia. My own welfare came second to hers, knowing full well that she couldn't withstand gunfire like me. We slowly backed away, but without a plan, the police gradually closed the distance. Annoyingly, the partners split up and I had to decide which one posed the more imminent threat. They seemed equal in their composure with unwavering focus. The tips of their pistols remained steadily pointed at us.

There were a couple of routes out of the building. We could retrace our steps down the escalator and through the front. The likelihood of that path ending in gunfire was high. On the opposite side of the store, behind the officers, were windows that we could easily slip through and escape via the alleys. Also, probably resulting in gunfire.

"Hands in the air!" They took turns yelling.

My patience slipped and "Oh, shut up!" huffed out, while taking a step toward them.

Unappreciative at my outburst, gunfire rang out.

The store employees screamed and flung themselves to the floor. The poor manikin family fell first. They didn't stand a chance. Limb and leg shattered into powder. More than one head rolled toward me, staring at me with blank eyes. Olivia screamed, digging her nails into my shirt and belt. Both of my hands pressed her closer into my body.

The police in this city had better training than the men back home. No less than five bullets hit their mark, one of which annoyingly landed on my face. When they paused their barrage, it opened the door to take the offensive. At my feet was the male manikin's head. Clawlike fingers grasped it like a ball and hurled it at the officer to my left. It hit its mark, and the officer dropped. The other one covered the rest of the distance to us, gun pointed. He pushed the barrel into my side before it popped. Olivia jumped and I just stared into the wide, brown eyes of the officer. My hand found the muzzle and wrenched it out of his grip before pistol whipping him with his own gun. Blood burst from his head, freezing me in place. It smelled so good. Would anyone really notice if I skimmed a little off the top? Blood already oozed from his face. No one would notice. Just a little.

"Phil," whimpered Olivia from behind me.

The sound of her voice broke all train of thought. She had a hand pressed against her side and her shirt slowly soaked with blood.

"No," I gasped.

A sweep of the leg knocked the policeman's feet out from under him and he thudded to the ground. His gun bounced out of his hand and landed between Olivia and me, just out of reach. Immediately upon hitting the ground, he started to scramble to get his feet back under him, so I set my shoe on the lower part of his back and pressed down. His limbs flumped out to the sides, but he started squirming, struggling to free himself to no avail. His tactics changed when he saw me grab the pistol, clawing at another weapon on his belt instead.

It took me a moment of fumbling to figure out the modern piece of technology, but the chamber release remained in relatively the same spot. Four rounds remained and more than enough. I cocked it and took aim at the dark bulbs on the ceiling. They popped like confetti and rained glass down on the displays below them. Another round of shrieks followed, clearing a path to escape. The gun skittered across the ground after being tossed in the opposite direction of the officers. It settled somewhere under a shelf. Olivia winced as I scooped her up from the ground, but once she settled across my arms, she offered little resistance.

I skipped down the stairs two at a time and elected to go out the back of the store since the front already lit up with red and blue. A door with 'Exit' illuminated above it came into view. An alarm started blaring when it got kicked open, eliciting a strain of curses out of my mouth at the announcement of our location. A herd of boots tromped their way toward us. A dumpster sat just outside of the door, providing the perfect tool to slow them down. With my back pressed against the side of the smelly box, rusty wheels squeaked as it moved across the pavement and in front of the exit. They didn't reach the door before we were well on our way.

The alley stretched out in a straight shot home and allowed me to run uninterrupted. It took less than a minute to cover the distance and the familiar, majestic bird painted on the outside of her home welcomed us back. An assessment of the space made up my mind; the elevator wouldn't be necessary. I repositioned Olivia so she draped over my shoulder instead, but it meant the blood stain called to me at nose level. It only spurred me to move faster. My jump cleared us neatly to the ledge outside of her window. Our combined weight rested on my fingertips as it clung to the row of bricks that stuck out. By slightly pulling us up, my other hand could reach the lock on the window. It fell to the floor in a couple pieces when the whole pane jammed upward.

We squeezed through the opening while Olivia whimpered quietly. A sharp breath whistled through her teeth when laid down on the bed. A sheen of sweat covered her body and she looked quite pale. It looked fatal. The guilt of injuring her wrenched through me. My worst-case scenario was about to happen again.

"Olivia? Can you hear me?" My knees thudded to the floor in front of her bed.

"Phil," she started, but my worry drowned her out.

"I am so sorry—you cannot die. There has to be some way to fix this!"

My eyes stole a glance at the red splotch on her shirt and realized it hadn't grown anymore. It brought a wave of comfort, but also interest. Perhaps her shirt should be lifted and the wound inspected. Maybe it should be cleaned. There might be contaminants in her blood that could be sucked out. Really, her heart pumped strong and could withstand a little more stress.

Awareness flung me across the small space and settled my shameful self into the corner of the kitchen. One glance, one breath of this woman derailed any logical thought toward the situation. The infuriation of living like this, constantly, grated on me when caring about someone was this hard. The temptation, though. It hid around corners and waited to attack at the most opportune times. I would not be the one to kill this woman. My fingers tangled in my hair while pacing around the kitchen, thinking of a solution.

As if summoned with a bell, a familiar heart beat outside her door. Nimble movements undid the two locks on the front door and opened it just wide enough to get a fist full of Vince's shirt. His hand was raised to knock, but his eyes were wide with surprise.

"Don't hurt me," he yelled while being pulled through the door.

His cargo clattered through the opening, bouncing around while attached to his arm. He held a red box that had a white handle. The smell coming out of it made my mouth swell with saliva, but it wasn't the right time. I shuttered the impulse by swallowing the spit like water and turned my attention to Vince.

"You work at a hospital, correct?" He flinched when my hold on his shirt jostled. "Olivia is hurt and she's dying! Please, help her!"

He stuttered a bit before looking away from me and then to the figure on the bed. Olivia sat up now, taking in what had just happened in her entryway. When he looked back at me, his eyes looked on with genuine fear. "I'm not a doctor, just a janitor. I can't help her!"

My answer growled out, "What?! You are around healers all day; you could do something!"

I shoved him closer to the bed and he barely caught himself before falling down.

"Phil," groaned Olivia. "Calm down. It's all right.

The injury isn't that bad."

She caught my attention but did nothing to calm the morbid scenarios clouding my thoughts.

"There is no reason to be brave. You were shot! Vince can help."

His eyes looked at her wildly, and he subtly shook his head.

"Don't be stupid. Look." She peeled away the shirt and unlike her calm demeanor, panic flushed my thoughts at the sight of her skin, sticky with blood.

She gingerly poked at the edge of the wound, winced, and then pressed down a little harder. Her face relaxed and a stressed grin found its way to her face. "It just grazed me! It looks so much worse than it is…" She trailed off when she smiled up at me. She clicked her jaw shut and her eyes became exceptionally wide.

I fear what she saw when looking at me was a blood crazed vampire ready to suck the life out of her body. She wasn't completely wrong. The saliva pooled deeply in my mouth and my tongue swam in its familiarity. Muscles twitched along my jaw with every pulse of their heartbeats. In the lowlight, they most likely only saw the black of my pupils, staring intently at her wound.

What couldn't be conveyed to her was my relief. Olivia bled from a wound that I had caused. The scenario paralleled too close to what happened to Cecelia. She lay, dying, in my arms, and nothing could be done to save her. The emotions sloshing around inside felt the same too. Today could have turned out so much worse and yet once again, caused by my own fault, just because she chose to be in proximity with me. The look Olivia saw on my face was shame.

My focus dragged from her wound and found her weary face. She tensed under the stare, but did not look away.

Without breaking eye contact with Olivia, I ordered, "Vince, please help her dress the wound. I am going to take one of the bags from your basket now. For both of your sakes, do not look at me, do not acknowledge me. Do you understand?"

He nodded in my peripheral vision.

The top of the red and white box flipped open and inside were only two bags of blood. My brow furrowed with disappointment, but rather than saying something regrettable, took the opinion and shoved it deep down my throat, reminding myself that at least he came back.

The bag followed me to the corner of the kitchen, clutched around the middle and decreasing the temperature of my hand. Having more sustenance so close to my last feeding made it easier to sip on the packet instead of emptying it in a couple gulps. Dually, it distracted me from thinking about the fresh and obtainable supply just across the room. Vince and Olivia started conversing quietly while they addressed her injury. My fangs remained latched onto the bag.

"What happened?" asked Vince.

"The police shot me." She winced.

"Olivia! What have you gotten yourself into?"

"We went to Casey's and the police showed up to arrest him. He killed Miles Cage," she admitted.

Vince shot me a glance but quickly dropped his glance to the ground, remembering my instructions.

"I know this is what you wanted, but—" he paused, "—is this *safe?* Is *he* safe?"

The last bit of blood dripped from the bag and,

without a peep, my hand wadded it up and set it on the counter. Their conversation continued without realizing my attention now focused entirely on them. It would be inopportune to interrupt them now.

"I don't know, but he's saved my life. More than once!"

"Before he came, was it even in danger?" he countered.

"Well, no, but so?"

"This isn't you, Olivia." His intensity fell away. "I want my book nerd back."

"Maybe this is who I've always wanted to be. Silly of me to think that would mean something to you."

"He is right, though," I interjected.

They both looked at me like they forgot a third person was in the room.

"Being in my presence is not safe. All this shit is following me around, not you, and now it is interfering with your lives."

The last vestiges of light tried to fight its way around the curtains, indicating the time to leave. For good. These two humans taught me a lot, but they would become fodder sooner than later with me around.

"Are you fucking kidding me?" Olivia stood up, scowling. "Absolutely not. You do not get out of this *shit* so easily. I have stuck my neck out for you time and time again. What is my reward for helping? A bullet wound and the police after me."

"There is no way—"

She held up a finger and kept going. "It doesn't work like that anymore, Phil. Plus, you have an entire coven after you for killing a, what, vampire princess? They saw me with you. Doesn't that make me target *numero uno*? No. I need you right now and you are not going anywhere without me."

Olivia watched me push off the counter and make my way to the front door. Somehow, she looked even more like Cecelia when she was angry. The light-colored eyebrows almost touched when she glared. Her lips puckered into a straight line, with the bottom jutting out just a little more than the top. It looked more pouty than angry. Our arguments usually led to an even better night. I breathed in her beauty for several long seconds.

"You done?" My impatience seeped out.

"Don't you dare," she threatened.

I never got the chance to answer her, since at that moment, a muscular arm punched through the door and started strangling me.

Chapter 7

His fingers wrapped securely around my neck, trying to pull me through the door. The wood creaked under the pressure. It would not be long before my assailant had me in the hallway. My hands clawed at the sausages at my neck, while my legs spread, bracing against the strongest part of the door frame. In front of me, the humans screamed and huddled on the bed.

My upper body jerked left and right, hoping to dislodge the arm enough to get my fingers between his and my throat. The thrashing didn't seem to deter my assailant since the grip remained secure. It was time for a new plan. The arm snaked around me and out the new hole in the door, exposing the meaty part of his shoulder. My head jerked over and took hold of his flesh. A gush of his blood washed through my mouth, tasting like kerosene. Grimacing, it flowed out of my mouth as fast as it flowed in.

The result of my efforts was immediate and effective. He let go, and the arm slithered back out of the hole. Not a second later, the door exploded inward in several large chunks from the resulting blow. John cannonballed through the wood and even though my hands rose to shield my eyes from the smaller splinters, they ended up bracing up against the chest of the larger man. He plowed into me and sent us both stumbling backwards. My legs hit the edge of the bed and we collapsed on top of it.

Olivia and Vince scrambled out of the way. Olivia went to my right and Vince went left into the latrine. The door slammed, but my concern stayed with Olivia. She settled in the kitchen and, for the moment, out of harm's way. John's grubby fingers tried to get a hold of my neck again, but the vehement kicking from my legs made it impossible for him to get a grip. His free hand desperately tried to settle the bucking, and one misplaced blow allowed him to snatch my shirt. He used the advantage to yank me off the bed. My feet tried to reach the floor, but he promptly swung me around and battered me into a shelf. Its contents exploded and followed me to the ground. Different sized books littered the floor along with a few shattered porcelain figures. The little shards crunched against my face while my hand fumbled around for a weapon. A hardcover book brushed against my fingertips, and I swung around, landing square on his cheek with a *thwump*. He flopped over like a fish.

My feet were barely under me before John recomposed himself. As he turned back around, my head tilted and I admired the mark the book left across his face. It read, "Interview with a Va" raised in red across his cheek. I shifted my grip to the corner of the novel before hurling it forward like an axe. He batted it away and jumped toward me. He latched back onto my shirt, but the action was reciprocated. Trapped in a tangle of arms, the two of us tussled back into the broken bookshelf and our feet slipped on the pile of books. My knee thudded against the floor, catching my balance, but neither of us let go. From this angle, the extra leverage allowed me to launch upward and into his clavicle. We careened toward the latrine.

His back hit the wall next to the door and we went straight through. Vince screamed as he yanked open the door and skipped over to the kitchen. Our momentum stopped abruptly when John's body crunched against the cabinet holding the sink. His head hit the mirror and fragments of glass rained down. Chunks of the mirror and the broken wall settled onto his shoulders as well as the dented cabinet below. Water started spurting from the broken faucet, soaking John almost immediately. The blood from his shoulder wound ran down his arm and dripped onto the white floor. He pulled himself from the cabinet and head butted me.

This didn't have quite the effect he hoped for and instead, we bounced off each other. I stumbled and fell into the toilet, where it shattered under the force of the hit. The flood of water soaked my pants and nipped at John's shoes. He took a step back and caught his shins on the edge of the tub. His hand reached out for something to grasp onto and ended up with a wad of the curtain. It ripped from the hooks supporting it and settled over his face.

I jumped into the tub with him and used my bodyweight to trap him under the fabric. His teeth snapped through the curtain, making it easier to aim when my fist started wailing on him. Pretty quickly, a more permanent solution occurred to me than just taking out my anger on him. My fingers probed around his face, trying to find the correct area. He squealed when my thumb stuck into his eye socket. They drifted down to his nose, then his chin, and then wrapped around his jaw. The curtain put me in a tricky situation, but my reach managed to circumvent the obstacle and get a solid hold on the other side. My arms twisted with every bit of strength stored in me. John immediately recognized that he was about to have his head ripped off and started struggling tenfold.

One of his arms found its way out from under the curtain and felt its way around my body. He got a hold of my coat collar, then the back of my neck. He squeezed and flung me to the right. I collided with the inward opening door, causing it to disintegrate the hinges. Both the door and I clattered to the ground. After scrambling to get upright, Olivia and Vince watched me back up to where they cowered in the kitchen.

It didn't take John long to unwrap himself from the curtain, so by the time I looked at Olivia and said, "You need to get out of here," he already pushed himself out of the tub.

"What about you?" she pleaded.

"Just go."

Vince pulled her toward the shattered remains of the exit when John stepped out of the latrine. His eyes drifted across the three of us before settling on me. He marched across the short distance to start round three. There had to be something on the counter that could help me or at least slow him down. A stovetop to my left offered a possibility, but we were both soaked in water. It would never work. Then my hand brushed against it. John reached out, but before he could get a hold of me, I plunged a knife into his temple. He flopped to the floor and started groaning. His limbs were no longer under his control and twitched erratically. It wasn't going to kill him, but it would buy me enough time to get out of here with Olivia and

Vince.

Behind me, Vince started screaming bloody murder. Joseph's mouth was latched onto his wrist, sucking. Then, the worst possible thing could have happened. Olivia started beating on Joseph's shoulder, screaming, "Let go! Let him go!"

He turned to her and his eyes widened. He let go of Vince and the human collapsed onto his knees. Vince crawled into the hallway crying, "I've been bit! I've been bit! I don't want to die!"

His safety didn't concern me as did Olivia's, so his cries remained uninterrupted as he made his way further down the corridor. Joseph stared at her and loud enough that she could hear, he whispered with a sneer, "Cecelia?"

He took a step toward her, but never made it any further.

"Hey, asshole."

He turned to me only to have the second blood bag shoved in his face. The force pinned him against the back wall and the bag burst. Blood exploded everywhere, running down in a thick stream onto his face, chest, and lap. Globs of it sprayed onto the wall, the counter, the floor, and regrettably, me. I scooped up Olivia and threw her over my shoulder, mindful of her wound. We hurried down the hallway and toward the elevator. The last thing we needed was to be trapped in the elevator with Joseph, so the door to the stairwell got kicked open and we hustled our way to the first floor.

Vince leaned against the wall in the lobby, gasping for air. He jumped when the stairwell door flung open. He was not relieved to see us.

"No! You stay away from me. All of this is your

fault." He paused to huff in more air. "I didn't want any of this and now you've doomed me to hell!"

"You are not going to die, Vince." One hand clenched his shoulder to shove him toward the exit.

"Don't touch me," he spat.

"If you stay here, you *will* die."

I glanced toward the stairwell, expecting to see Joseph.

"I've been infected! He bit me!" he wailed.

"Vince," —I grabbed him by the jaw— "It does not work that way. You have not been infected. Now, get the hell out of here before Joseph comes back."

"You left them alive?!" he exclaimed.

His answer groaned in my chest, and Vince took the hint. He pulled away from me and ran for the door, disappearing into the night. With Olivia over my shoulder, I ran to the curb and started waving my hand to get the attention of a cab driver.

"Phil, stop. It's bad enough that you have me over your shoulder like you're kidnapping me, but no cabby is going to stop. You look like you murdered someone."

A brisk look revealed what she meant. Streaks of red swirled and specked my brand-new shirt. My pants stuck to my legs and my coat dripped water onto the sidewalk. A grumble of frustration rattled my ribs.

"Do you have a better suggestion?"

"See the stairs across the street that lead below the sidewalk?"

Instead of answering, we took off through the slow-moving traffic and toward the sign that read 'Subway'. The steps descended into a brightly lit space that was buried deep below the streets above. Quite a few people lingered in the entrance, and it worried me that my appearance would attract unwanted attention. To my surprise, no one gave us a second glance. Everyone had their heads buried in their own business.

People channeled through a series of gates that turned automatically whenever someone passed through. Everyone stopped to tap their wallets, or phones, onto a pad before the wheel would turn. I hopped over the small barrier instead. The tracks stretched out in front of us. An entire rail station buried beneath our feet! The ground subtly vibrated before the tunnel lit up with an approaching train. My mind pictured billowing black smoke choking the air out as it pulled up, but in actuality, a flat nosed carriage squawked its way to the platform without the coal powered engine. It slowed to a stop and like the elevator, a series of doors along the length of the train split apart and people wasted no time spilling out. My shoulder drove a wedge through the exiting occupants and once onboard, Olivia started squirming. After setting her down, she found a seat tucked in front of my standing body. Windows lined the length of the carriage but were set low enough that someone of my height would have to stoop to keep an eye out for approaching unwanted guests. My gaze fixed on the entrance until the train lurched forward, the sudden movement making me sway gratefully.

As we traveled away from the station, the tense muscles in my jaw and neck relaxed. A map affixed to the wall showed this particular line did not loop around for a good, long while. The carriage *cha-chunked* rhythmically, lulling my thoughts into complacency. Only when a soft sniffle emerged from below me did I realize Olivia clung to my coat like a life jacket.

Crouching down allowed me to see her from eye level.

"Are you all right?"

"Yes…no. I could have died back there and then before that. This whole thing, this situation, is a bit overwhelming."

My hand came up and, as gentle as a feather, laid over her knee. Olivia didn't seem to mind, then again, she might not have noticed. Her eyes stared unfocused on her lap.

The words that came out of my mouth were so low, she may not have heard. "I'm sorry."

Of course, all of this was my fault. Vince knew. She had been completely safe before running into me. The thought ground into my thoughts, and the guilt shook me to the core. Even after trying to get away from her, more than once, we came back together like magnetism. A positive and a negative pull that decided our fate. If you pulled magnets far enough apart, the attraction broke and each half no longer felt the need to come together. Olivia must be a very big magnet for how much pull she held over me.

Looking at her now, the effects of what I put her through were apparent. Her skin lacked the flourish of a healthy woman, and a shimmer of sweat persisted along her brow. Red and swollen eyes hid under sagging eyelashes. She looked exhausted. An idea itched the back of my brain, but considering everything that had happened, she might disapprove. My hand moved away from her knee slow enough to give her ample time to object and joined the other behind Olivia's back, pulling her into an embrace. Her head found my shoulder and relaxed against me. Her hair brushed against my nose, tickling me with her scent. Roses.

Her breathing slowed down and her heart rate dropped. Olivia stayed silent except for the occasional sniff through her tears, but eventually, those stopped too. I wanted to stay like this forever, but when the train slowed and stopped, she pulled away, slipping out of my arms. The doors slid open again and people shuffled to allow the inflow, and outflow, of new passengers to make their way. The information scrolling across the screen above the door announced the next stop and it was somewhere familiar.

"I know just what you need."

She narrowed her eyes, but did not fully dismiss the idea. She looked more curious than anything. The train started to slow down again, so when the next station approached, Olivia positioned herself behind me while my attention focused on scanning the platform. The usual crowd waited behind the yellow line, but neither Joseph nor John waited for us to disembark. Yet, the pit in my stomach remained. They could be hiding behind a pillar or stooped in a trash can. I offered my hand to Olivia when the train doors opened and she took it gratefully. We pushed our way out, and everyone's attire around us changed to more like what they wore my first night in New York. The women dressed in revealing clothing, and the men looked like they were posturing.

We popped out of the subway to bright, neon lights and honking cabs. We were a block off from the road that led us to my destination, but close enough. Olivia tip-tapped alongside me as we made our way down the street, watching the various buildings as they went past. The queue came into view before the sign and once around the corner, 'Trap Door' illuminated the night in blue.

The guy who accepted my bribe from the first visit stood watch at the entrance. He caught sight of us as we approached on the outside of the line. One of the last bills from Miles's wallet pinched between my fingers and by the time we reached him, the fifty-dollar bill floated just below his breast pocket. He looked at me, my clothing, then Olivia, and said, "Welcome back."

The man ceremoniously unclipped the velvet rope and let us through. His drifting eyes reminded me of my recent discretions, necessitating the fastening of a couple coat buttons before diving into the building. Walking back through those doors didn't give me the sense of familiarity that I hoped for. By bringing Olivia here, it was supposed to feel safe, like a pocket of normality so we could let our hair down if only for a few minutes. Instead, existential dread pricked the back of my neck, making it impossible to keep my head still. It swiveled in observation of the different areas of the room. Underneath it all loomed an unexplainable duty to keep the woman alive. Most of it was out of my control, except for one thing; getting her some food.

"You brought me to a nightclub?" she yelled into my ear.

"We will be safe enough here and they know me."

We scooted further into the chaos. The female bartender who had, for lack of a better word, helped me bobbed behind the bar and we made our way over to her. I carved a path through the sea of people, while Olivia followed close enough to keep brushing up against my back. A woman left a gap at the bar, walking away with two very full glasses of beer. Another man tried to bully his way in, but by the time he got to the counter, he'd lost his opportunity to me. "Get in line," bounced off my back, but when his retort went unanswered, he lost interest and moved on.

The bartender caught sight of me and walked over, a devilish grin on her face. Her shirt choice covered slightly more skin than the first time we met. It hung off her shoulder on the opposite side of the bite mark and scarcely covered her breast. Under a thick layer of makeup, a nasty bruise creeped out from under the fabric and up her neck. She leaned over the bar so that her femininity was dangerously close to slipping out from its containment. However, her smile broke when she saw the woman whose hand wrapped grasped my upper arm.

"Scotch?" she asked. I nodded and she continued. "What does the broad want?"

"This *woman* will be having whatever she wants." To Olivia, I said, "You must be starving."

We both looked at Olivia. She gave me a dubious look, but continued anyway. "Do you have a food menu?"

"Appetizers only," she answered.

"I'll have the sliders." Then Olivia added quickly, "And water!"

The woman stared at the bill held out in front of me and answered, "No cash, remember?"

Flashbacks of the clothing store reminded me not to try to use the credit card. Olivia understood and promptly pulled out her own.

"Gee, what a gentleman." The bartender rolled her eyes before going about her business. With my drink in hand, Olivia followed me to a booth in the corner, as far away from the door as possible. It butted up against a wall, eliminating the possibility of an ambush. A different bartender deposited water at our table with the promise of coming back with her food. We waited without a word spoken between us. My focus bounced to the front entrance and then to the door that led to the back exit. Olivia glanced around with disinterest, barely registering the people around her. Ice piled on the bottom of her already empty glass of water. Her food arrived steaming and the waiter set the plate down in the middle of the table, but my index finger found the edge of the plate and pushed it over to Olivia.

She started eating the chips one by one, but after a few chews, the amount increased so that she chomped down several slivers at a time. Once they were gone, she dug into the tiny sandwiches in a mechanical way. Biting, chewing, swallowing, biting, and so on until the last bite disappeared into her mouth. Her hand automatically reached for another.

"Hey, pal," said a voice over my shoulder.

A man stood at the very edge of our booth. He was unremarkable, dressed in blue jeans and a white shirt unbuttoned just on the top. A claw of a tattoo peaked out from under the collar. His slim figure hid if he had any muscles. The golden glow of working outside deepened the color of his face. Three other men flanked him, looking just as upset. Olivia looked at them now, swallowing her food nervously.

"Can I help you?"

"You don't remember us, do you," he asked.

The four men brushed across my sight again, but nothing about them triggered any sort of identification.

"No, sorry. You have me mistaken for someone else."

Instead of heeding my warning, the one in front placed his hand into his pocket and dug out a piece of cloth. He threw it on the table in front of me and waited. Recognition tickled the back of my mind. It smelled of salt water and dead fish. Through the dirt and abuse, a very faint pinstripe ran through the faded blue weave, ending at the frayed edges.

"Huh, this reminds me of my old suit." My eagerness extended toward Olivia, but she looked at me with wary eyes.

The memory flooded back to me much like the last time I saw this group. Yes, they all glared at me much the same way. We were crowded together on a life raft.

"You sunk our ship!" roared the man in front.

"You killed our friends," reverberated someone from behind the first.

He came at me swinging. The others pushed into him, trying to reach me too. The group of us ended up wedged in the booth in a pile. They smooshed me against the back of the bench, while four sets of hands clawed at my body. Olivia slipped under the table and used it as a shield. My sigh turned into a growl while pushing myself up and the bodies fell off me like bowling pins. The two in front fell cleanly to the ground, while the two in back caught themselves on other patrons. Several shot glasses bounced on the floor and one woman took a bath in her cocktail.

"Get off me!" raged a nearby man.

He shoved the sailor who caught himself by grabbing onto the other man's shirt and, instead of returning to assault me, swung at the angry customer. The original sailor made his way back to me, with his fists raised. He swung, but it caught in the palm of my hand. He tried to pull back, but his fist didn't budge from my grip. I had zero interest in fighting with these imbeciles and only wanted to get out of there as quickly as possible. With a flick of my wrist, he tipped over into the crowd, angering another group. In a matter of seconds, the fight spread to include all the people in our immediate area. None of the original four sailors could find their way back to me. They all had someone trying to dance with them.

Squatting down to peek under the table, the glow of Olivia's eyes revealed that she was more-or-less glowering at me with her lips pinched into a straight line. My hand stretched out for her, and she wrapped her fingers around mine. She crawled out from under the table and into the firing squad. Projectiles in the form of drink glasses flew through the air and people were getting impaled with shots of liquor. One such cup headed toward Olivia and I caught it before it could reach her. The impulse to throw it back into the crowd almost made it to fruition, but instead, the glass made its way onto the nearest table.

The buttons fell away from their slits as my fingers released them and invited Olivia into the pocket of protection under my coat. She tucked herself in and shielded her face with the fabric. The entire bar erupted into mayhem. Quite a few of the women took refuge under the tables, like Olivia had, while a few of the braver ones were in the middle of the brawl. I saw hair pulling, kicking, slapping, and one guy dragged his foe down by his nipple. Sounds of breaking glass echoed from different parts of the room, and it was time to get out of there. Sure enough, the faint smell of blood started to tickle my nose.

Olivia handled being led to the entrance almost blindfolded with grace. Her feet fell in step with mine and after a few more meters, we could slip out and dissolve into the night. Along the way, several people got shoved out of my way, which caused a new fissure to form, and a renewed sense of justice from the people who were inconvenienced. We almost made it to the exit when the sight of red and blue lights flashing through the entrance doors stopped me mid step. Olivia stumbled around me when our direction abruptly changed. With our backs to the door, a growl burbled in my chest.

Olivia poked her head out and said, "What is it?"

"The police."

There was no easy route to the back exit. We would have to carve our way through the mob, so I started shoving. The humans bounced off my hand easily enough, but not without the occasional swing of retribution. One unfortunate man flopped out of the way by his face. Subtlety went out the door, right next to the law enforcement. We reached the back hallway that led to the bathrooms and kitchen. Olivia popped out from under my coat when she saw the back exit.

"Don't go that way," said a deep, feminine voice.

The manager didn't have a cigarette this time, but her sequined dress danced with every little movement. She leaned against the frame of the kitchen entrance with her arms crossed and an indifferent look on her face, seemingly unbothered despite the scrimmage on the dance floor. Her words were worthy of consideration, but ultimately, it didn't matter, and I ushered Olivia toward the back door again.

"The cops are in the alley too," she added.

She earned my full attention then.

"Why?"

"Don't want any escapees." She smiled. "Follow me and I'll get you two out of here."

The rest of my question fell away and instead, considered her offer. Olivia nodded at me and started to follow the manager into the kitchen. We walked into a connected pantry that smelled like a mixture of rotten meat and vegetable oil. The only door in and out of the room was the one we just came through. The whole thing reeked of a trap, so I pushed past Olivia to scope out the small room. There really wasn't much room for someone to jump out at us. Shelves lined the room, stuffed with canned food, plates, cutlery, and brown boxes. The manager took a moment to roll her eyes at me before she pulled on a handle attached to the floor. It revealed an exit that perfectly blended into the surrounding tiles.

The door thudded against the wall when she let go. The manager looked up at us smugly. "It leads to the subway. You should be able to find your way out fairly easily."

"You literally have a trap door. Ironic. Thank you."

The manager didn't bat an eyelash when my head dipped into the darkness that swallowed the ladder. It led to a sublevel tunnel made of bricks, a meter wide, and completely void of light. Most importantly, no one else inhabited the space, at least, within hearing distance.

"Olivia, give me your hands."

She walked over and sat down so that her legs sank into the hole. She grasped onto me and trusted my grip when she scooted off the edge. The hole swallowed her and even fully extended, her legs hovered over the ground, luckily, by a few centimeters. Dust puffed out from under her shoes when she landed. Olivia moved just enough out of the way before fumbling with her phone light. I slipped down and landed neatly on the bricks below. The tunnel only moved away from us, but split about twenty meters ahead. The rattle of distant train tracks shivered in the walls. Olivia walked away from me in the cone of light from her phone.

"Oh, and Miles, well, fake Miles," the manager started. She stood over the hole, with the door in her hand. "Don't ever come back to my club."

We exchanged knowing smiles, and the light from the room above shrank to a sliver. The door thudded closed, leaving us in the dark. It took a few jogging steps to catch up with Olivia, but she paused at the mouth of where the path split. She moved her light from the left tunnel to the right before turning it on me. A hiss of pain snapped out.

"Philip, is there anyone in this city that isn't out to kill you?" she barked.

"I suppose I deserved that." White dots marred my vision, despite trying to blink them away.

"Well?"

"Well, what?"

"Should I be worried about the local witch coven or….?"

I actually laughed. "No, no one else."

When my vision returned, she was looking something up on her phone. Watching from over Olivia's shoulder, her fingers tap quickly on the screen. She pulled up a map of the subway system, narrowed in on a couple of roads that overlaid the tunnels, and then found us. She dragged the image and followed it to the east. It zigzagged a few times before she stopped and said, "There you are."

She looked over her shoulder to make sure she had my attention and asked, "Do you think you can get us here?"

"Yes. What is it?"

"A safe haven. At least, a better haven than your choice," she challenged. The chaos of the reception upstairs echoed through the bricks, making it hard to disagree. "In any case, it's a long walk, unless we run?"

"We better get going then."

One of my arms took hold of her upper body, while the other swept her off her feet. Olivia grasped her hands at the back of my neck, and we took off running before she could say, "Ready."

The track split off from the main route and the effects of abandonment instantly became visible. More frequent piles of animal dung littered the ground, cobwebs unapologetically strung between the rails and the walls, and a thick layer of dirt coated the greasy parts of the tracks. No train had passed through here in a very long time, if ever.

After a kilometer or so, the tunnel opened onto a train platform. Only, the tracks retreated through a mortared wall at the far end of the station. Even the stairwells to the exits were plugged up with brick. We arrived at the place she pointed to on the map.

The architecture set it apart from all the others. Ornate walls were painted in soft pastels, with accents of white tiles. My shoes tapped across a floor that had once gleamed to a near mirror polish, but now dulled beneath years of soot and dust. Carvings of stone held up the roof from atop their columns. Spiderwebs hung from their gargoyle-like noses. An abundance of brass finished out the fittings with unnecessary quality.

Despite being run down, one area of the platform had so many footprints in the dust, their individuality blended, yet they all originated from the same entrance as where we came from. Seven chairs were arranged in a circle throughout the space. Along the outside, a single wood table held up a couple of recently emptied cans and used up food containers. Pictures suspended along the wall. They mostly contained well-dressed men gazing at you menacingly, or at least that is what it looked like. Three dozen white candles sat half melted around the table and floor. Defining the entire area was a single, well-worn rug.

"Olivia, are you part of the witch coven you jested to me about?"

She just glared at me, grabbed a twig from a little box, and struck it across the side. Fire licked from the end and she set about lighting some candles.

"Don't be ridiculous. This is where my book club meets."

Chapter 8

Olivia scrounged around the table, looking for a food packet that wasn't empty. She unrolled one bag and sniffed the contents, then dropped it back on the table with a disgusted look on her face. Bottles of mysterious liquid accompanied the food, but she chose one labeled water before making her way over to the back wall of the station. Someone brought decorative items to make the space seem more comfortable. One of these items was an ornate black pillow with swirls of red across the front. Many others accompanied it, but she only took the one. Olivia dropped it so it leaned against the wall and plopped down. She folded her legs under herself and cozied up into the bit of comfort it provided. Her hand covered her mouth, shielding a powerful yawn, before tilting her head back and closing her eyes.

In an odd way, this place reminded me of home. The decor reflected a more familiar setting where the colors weren't so lifeless. Maybe the candles triggered the feeling. Their inconsistent flickering cast dancing shadows on the walls around us and it transported me back to a time before this mess. The only sign of the electronic takeover lay in Olivia's pocket, leaving a rectangle-shaped indent. There was no ambient noise from the televisions or music boxes. There weren't any people mumbling to each other through thin walls.

Every minute or so, the low rumblings of a passing train would interrupt the silence, shaking loose fine particles of dust. Only rats made their home here and it made me uncomfortable with how at peace this place made me feel.

A lip overhung where the platform dropped to the rails and I took a seat on the edge. My legs draped over the side and my hands folded in my lap. If someone came through the entry, they would have to go past me. At the far end of the tunnel, just as the walls closed into themselves around the corner, someone had laid a brick, about two meters off the ground, that stuck out about a centimeter more than the rest. My worries locked onto this one flaw and stared blankly.

I was so sure Olivia had fallen asleep that it surprised me when she sucked in a deep breath and asked, "Who's Cecelia?"

My vision narrowed, but didn't budge from the far wall while contemplating how to answer her question. The atmosphere of the place she brought me to already churned up painful memories that strong-armed their way to the forefront of my thoughts and answering her would only make them more substantial.

"You should try and get some rest." The words delicately cut through the air.

Her feet shuffled and she walked over to join me on the ledge. Olivia took a seat so close to me that our arms brushed. My eyes remained fixated on the brick, not daring to look at her and risk giving in to her inquiry. From the corner of my vision, her dewy eyes probed my face.

"I get that Cecelia is the woman who 'saved my life' and I am grateful for that, truly, in some weird way that doesn't make sense, but that isn't enough anymore. Joseph called me Cecelia too. So, no more avoiding the truth. Who is she?"

From someone looking in from the outside, they would have seen a beautiful, inquisitive woman staring at an emotionless stone statue. Not a single muscle twitched as my addled brain constructed an answer for her. She was right and deserved some sort of explanation, but conveying it in a way that accurately answered her seemed insurmountable.

"Well?" she pushed.

"I am thinking."

"Is it so hard to just blurt something?!" she huffed.

"She was my wife." My eyes blazed into hers with the weight of the words.

Olivia shrunk back and breathed, "Oh," before her gaze dropped to the tracks. She studied the little variations along the ground as if the loose bits of cement hid the answers to the things she didn't know. So much time passed, the air grew heavy with silence. After a couple of minutes, her sweet voice broke through. "I'm sorry. You must miss her very much."

"You have no idea."

"So, how does Joseph know who she is?"

No part of me wanted to have this conversation and the chances of ever being ready were low, but she didn't seem like the type to let it go. Then again, my ass dragged her into this mess, and she deserved an explanation.

"The answer is more complicated than just 'blurting something out'. Simply thinking about her reopens the wound of my grief. Please bear with me while I organize my thoughts."

My gaze softened as I looked at her, hoping she could sense the sincerity in my words. She gave me a slight smile. "Take your time."

"Best to start at the beginning, then. If it is not already clearly apparent, I am from London. It was home for my entire natural, and unnatural, life. My existence went along as well as one could expect under the circumstances. A couple of good investments allowed me to purchase a home just outside of town and my connections let me live relatively comfortably. Additionally, living in a city as big as London sheltered my nighttime activities from the suspicions of the citizens.

"It's funny, the little details you remember in memories. A rather decadent carriage stopped in front of the theater and the groom hopped off to settle the two white horses pulling it. The quality of the setup garnered more than just my attention, so when her white gloved hand reached out for support from her coachman, I wasn't the only one staring. While the others shied their eyes away in social etiquette, mine remained transfixed on the beauty stepping out into the night. The sight of her made me feel like someone held my heart in their fist and squeezed. That feeling never went away, by the way. But that first time, wow. Her face, her hair, her dress…

"She floated inside and immediately started chatting with some of her friends, but the cordiality stopped when one of them spotted me approaching. This garnered her attention and when she turned to see who disrupted their conversation, our eyes met, and it became clear that life would never be the same. We talked through the entire play and to the end of the evening. When the production concluded, neither of us wanted to go our separate ways. So, we didn't, and from that moment on, we were inseparable.

"I wanted to spend the rest of my time on Earth with her, but she was mortal and people from my time raised their children to fear monsters who lurked in the night. Telling her about my true self came with a high probability of ripping my heart out, but she had to know. After all, the first time we touched, or kissed, she would figure it out. It took me a week to gather the courage to tell her and, in the end, she noticed how distant my behavior became and asked why. Like our conversation right now, my words came out in a jumbled mess. Yet, my fretting was all for naught. Like everything Cecelia did, she accepted it with grace and reassured *me* that everything would work out. After that, our lives continued in bliss. I built her a house on the west side of town, and we married within a year. We spent ten heavenly years together.

"I am not sure how it works in this time, but in the 1800s, things were run by the monarchy. He had the ultimate power publicly. However, under him, powerful families operated on their own set of rules. Their punishments were swift and their rewards exorbitant. The reason I bring this up is because Cecelia's father led one of these families. Humans and their musings do not scare me, but to say meeting her father made me nervous only touches on describing the emotion. After all, he needed to approve of me and allow the pleasure of his daughter's hand in marriage.

"From the very first moment he welcomed me into his office, it became abundantly clear why Cecelia didn't worry about my undead status. Her father was a vampire too."

Olivia broke her silence when she gasped. "Wait, Joseph works for a mob boss who is mad because you killed his daughter." She locked her eyes onto mine. "You killed your own wife."

My teeth snapped together. "It was an accident!"

I sprung up and started pacing the length of the platform. My hands clenched into tight balls and my mind clamped onto the last memory of Cecelia: her eyes stared up at me, unfocused and lifeless. The blood stopped oozing through my hand covering the wound, only because none of it remained inside of her. The scene replayed over and over until enough common sense snapped into me to start counting. One, two, three.

"Why does everyone keep calling me Cecelia then?"

The control remaining over my actions held on like a workhorse at the end of a hot, sweaty day. Her question came across like a horsefly landing on my rump and biting savagely into flesh. Anger turned me toward her, not knowing if the resulting action ended with mutilation or just answering her. The woman looking cautiously back at me could have been Olivia or Cecelia. The difference was indistinguishable. My anger came out in a huff and all the unforgivable impulses slumped out of my shoulders. Deflated, the words flowed from my mouth.

"I loved Cecelia with my entire being. My life belonged to that woman and her family knew it too. Now, looking at you so soft and vulnerable, a future worth living seems achievable, like there might be something after losing my wife. Yet, strong feelings endure that make it confusing to differentiate between what was and what is, as if the pattern will repeat itself like a sickness. That also means letting go of Cecelia, and I just cannot do that!"

My last sentiment ripped through the space and echoed down the tunnel. In the distance, a rat scurried into its hole. With closed eyes and a lower voice, my story continued. "Joseph must think I have moved on from my beloved wife when it simply is not true. It devalues my dedication to her and, and, ugh! Her face torments me every time my eyes close. The day when that is no longer true brings me great fear. Olivia, you are being compared to a ghost. It's not just me, Joseph sees it too, and he is going to try to use that against me. For that, I am deeply sorry."

Talking to Olivia made the words flow out of me. She listened without judgement and when silence filled the room again, she looked as though she accepted my answer.

"It's okay, Phil," she said.

In a sign of truce, she patted the space next to her. The last bit of anger dissolved while plopping down next to her. Neither of us spoke, but it didn't bother me. It was nice listening to the rhythmic beat of her heart. It reminded me of a metronome, lulling me into a more relaxed state of mind.

"Can you tell me about her?" asked Olivia.

The image of Cecelia filled my mind and a smile crept onto my lips. Instead of focusing on the bad, my mouth ran away with a novel full of stories about our adventures. Olivia listened patiently while my heart poured all over her. For those few minutes, it felt as though Cecelia sat there with us and we were happy.

"If only you could see her, Olivia. Her picture goes with me everywhere, but the ocean water ruined it." My hand reached in the breast pocket to show her the pasty remains.

Panic clenched my chest. The gold watch was not there. Systematically, twice, my fingers probed each possible location of the timepiece and they were all empty. Looking down, threads poked out where a button used to be. The same one that secured the chain.

"God dammit, my watch is gone." My head fell into my hands and whatever pleasure Olivia pulled out of me now spilled out of my eyes.

"Cecelia gave me that watch."

Olivia carefully reached over and rubbed her hand between my shoulder blades.

"It is so unfair. I haven't even had the time to grieve. She died and the next day, those bastards punished me. All that time alone, and it still feels like it happened yesterday."

"What do you mean?"

"After Cecelia died, her father had me exiled. He ordered his goons to bury me in concrete and apparently, drop me off in the middle of the ocean. I've been there until you met me a couple of days ago."

"Oh wow," she gasped. "No wonder you are so lost."

The weight of everything made me want to squirm out from under the pressure and throw things, punch walls, *kill someone.* Every breath that came out of my chest came out sharply and Olivia sensed it too. Her rubbing stopped, and she leaned away from me.

"You should try to get some sleep."

Ever astute, Olivia picked up on the underlying

meaning and picked herself up off the floor. She wandered back to the pile of pillows. Out of the corner of my eye, she lay on her side with her back to the wall, and two eyes locked onto me.

The platform was devoid of light, except for the candles flickering on the table. It made it impossible to tell how much time passed, but all the while, her rest remained interrupted. The world could wait. Her rhythmic heartbeat brought comfort to my otherwise musty thoughts.

The candles burned themselves out before Olivia's breathing changed. It wouldn't be long before she woke up, and sure enough, a groan escaped her lips as she stretched her limbs. She lifted the phone up and tapped on the screen.

"Sleep well?"

"Apparently. I slept for almost eight hours. It's around two thirty in the afternoon. How are you doing?"

"Better."

She got up off the floor and turned the phone light on to use it to locate the matches. After igniting a few candles, the soft glow illuminated a stash of food. Swift fingers dug through the paltry options, but unlike her first visit, Olivia made her choice quickly and popped open one of the bags. Each bite crunched noisily. Instead of settling back on the floor, she sat in one of the chairs and leaned back, balancing the top against the wall. Olivia appeared much more relaxed this morning. Meanwhile, my back remained rigid while watching the entrance of the platform.

"Can vampires have kids?"

"No, why?"

"Well, I've been thinking. You said 'The Don' is a vampire, yet he has a daughter. How?"

"That doesn't make sense, does it. He started life as a human, like we all did. Unlike most of us, his transformation was a business transaction. He did a job for a vampire and they repaid him with immortality. Cecelia had just turned a year old when it happened, so she grew up knowing about my kind. She never knew any better."

"I've heard a lot of different methods to change someone," she started. "Some stories say your saliva is venom and it will turn someone by just a bite, but that isn't true since Vince is still alive. Others mention sharing blood then being buried for three days. The theories go on and on, but which one is true?"

"Essentially, you must replace their blood with our poisoned blood. This involves draining them until they are almost dead and then getting them to drink the vampire's blood. It is highly dangerous for the human, and most do not survive because of the blood loss."

"Were you serious before, about not turning me?" she asked innocently.

"Absolutely!" The anger that came from her question surprised even me, and my mouth snapped shut.

"Point taken, yikes. Someone is hangry." She tried to smooth over the atmosphere.

"Hangry?"

"Yeah, like when someone is so hungry, they are angry. 'Hangry'." She shrugged.

"You are much too callous about being around a hungry vampire. Yet, you are right. Not like I can do anything about it." A hand ran roughly through my hair.

She laughed then and said, "Too bad they don't have delivery for your kind."

Because my life is a series of ironic moments, my head snapped to the tunnel opening. Footfalls crunching on the gravel echoed down the tube. Olivia jumped up at my sudden movement and stood at attention, trying to see or hear anything. The intruders were too far away to hear if they had heartbeats or not.

At first, their voices were only clear enough to hear excited murmuring, but as they got closer, the subject of their chatter turned to brainstorming about finding someone. They insisted that the news was wrong, and that this person did stuff like this, anyway. They then started talking about where they could be hiding and listed several locations. To my relief, the bleating of their individual heartbeats thumped their way over to me. Olivia took a step forward.

"Joseph?" she whispered.

"Humans."

"How many?"

"Three."

Olivia stood next to me, anxiously waiting for them to appear around the last bend. In hindsight, it would have been nice to sneak down the tunnel and get some sustenance, but my reaction gave away their approach immediately and Olivia would have disapproved.

Their bobbing cell phone lights were the first thing that became visible. They spotlighted the ground in three separate cones shapes from around the bend until the hands holding them appeared, connected to bodies that looked like silhouettes in contrast. My mouth watered and I wondered if Olivia would forgive me if one of them died in front of her. The single blood bag

Vince brought me the previous evening wasn't nearly enough.

The next few moments happened quickly, even for me. Subconsciously, my body moved into a crouch, ready to spring as soon as the moment was right. Like a survival instinct bred into modern humans, all three of them simultaneously raised their lights toward Olivia's yelling. She grasped onto my arm with two hands, pulling me toward her. She had been yelling at me, but I only noticed after the three intruders flashed me with their lights. It broke my concentration just enough to hear what she cried.

"Phil, don't! Those are my friends!"

Chapter 9

None of us dared move. Olivia and I stood on the platform, with her arms still latched onto me like an anchor. The three newcomers remained on the tracks below us and in the mouth of the tunnel. It felt like a standoff before a gunfight. The impulse to feed lurked just under my skin, but Olivia's touch helped me feel grounded, so instead of doing something regrettable, my energy focused on the way her fingers gripped against my arm. I rose from my crouch and stood completely straight.

I could only imagine how we looked through the eyes of the people who joined us. First off, we stood in near darkness with only a few flickering candles behind us. My outfit reeked of alcohol from the bar fight. Splashes of liquor smeared into the crumpled-up shirt already stained with streaks of blood and dirty water. My face creased with an animalistic desire that would have radiated death to a stranger. Then there was Olivia, crying out and clawing at me as if she held onto a monster. Maybe she did.

"Olivia, is that you?" said a shaky, female voice.

"Mary, it's me," she acknowledged.

The one called Mary stood in the middle of the three people. She had straight, shoulder length hair and spectacles pushed close to her face. Her cheeks were slightly red on pale skin.

"Thank goodness!" She followed it up much more soberly with, "Are you okay?"

"I'm fine! What are you doing here?"

Mary's eyes jumped from Olivia's to mine and her eyebrows came together, concerned. Our stare-down only lasted a breath before she could not maintain contact anymore. She looked back at Olivia.

"When we saw the news, we panicked. Everyone took turns calling, but it went straight to voicemail every time. We thought the worst had happened and came down here to brainstorm."

Olivia frowned as she pulled out her cell phone. The screen lit up under her touch, but it only showed the time.

"I'm sorry, Mary. We've been down here for a little while now and you know how bad the reception is."

"You should probably call your parents. They're hysterical," said the woman to Mary's right. Her voice grated by accentuating every vowel, but still consoling. "If you can." She looked at me.

My eyebrow shot up, considering the implication of her words.

"There is a city-wide missing person's alert for you, Olivia. It came out a few hours ago," added Mary. "Authorities said you were with the same guy wanted for murder. When they got to your apartment, the report said it was destroyed and suspected foul play because of the blood! What the hell is going on?"

Olivia's heart jumped, and she finally released my arm. She walked back to the circle of chairs and started pacing while muttering, "Oh no, oh no, oh no."

The girl on the right of the trio stepped forward.

When I turned to look at her, she stopped and looked at me dubiously.

"Who is he, Olivia?" interrogated the woman.

Olivia stopped just long enough to answer her. "Jackie, his name is Phil. Phil, these three people are my friends; Jackie, Mary, and Pam."

They looked at me with distrust. Warranted, but their concern aimed at the wrong guy. However, having their approval sat low on my priorities at the moment. The more pressing matter was having Olivia linked to me in my crime spree. At least they thought I had kidnapped her.

"Are you in any danger?" asked Jackie.

"Not from him," Olivia admitted.

"What does that mean?" piped in Mary.

Olivia paced a few steps toward the lip of the platform, ricocheting her stares at me, then to her friends. As she passed me, she softly laid her hand on my upper arm, smiled at her friends and answered, "We have a lot to talk about."

This little gesture calmed them and they shuffled over to Olivia. She kneeled and the four of them formed a lopsided wad of bodies, wound around each other in a close embrace. The shortest one, Pam, had her arms around Olivia's midsection and when she squeezed, Olivia yelped in pain. They all moved to see her face more clearly. Without permission, Mary lifted Olivia's shirt to see the bandage. Her eyes widened and she challenged Olivia to open up.

"Shall we go take a seat?" Olivia pulled her shirt back down.

The four of them made their way over to the chairs, while I backed off to the stairwell that had meant to lead to the surface. Only now, a solid wall enclosed the gap at the top. Sitting here allowed me to stay far enough away so as not to be accused of hovering, but also keep the entrance of the tunnel in view. Nothing sat between me and the tracks except for a support column.

"The news isn't totally wrong," Olivia started nervously.

"Okay, so, let's start with what the news got right," said Jackie.

"My apartment did get destroyed. Vince saw everything," she started, but an accumulative gasp stopped her.

"You've seen Vince? We tried calling him too when the news broke, but his text back just said, 'Leave me alone'," Mary said.

"There was a," —Olivia paused— "bad man, in my apartment and he got into a fight with Phil. There are some people after Phil because they want to take him back to London for a crime he's already done time for. They are all upset because his wife died, and, oh god, do they have such an adorable love story. Anyway, for sure, Phil saved my life that night. The blood doesn't belong to anybody. It came from one of the bags Vince brought me, but Phil used it as a distraction so we could get out. It is why Vince was there, you see, he brought me more bags, since the ones I had were used up."

"Slow down, honey," interrupted Pam, "you're rambling."

Olivia took a big breath and started again. "I found one. I found a real vampire."

Her revelation earned several rebuttals, all on top of each other. They ranged from, "No way" to "Are you for real?".

"Yes, but it goes so much deeper than that, and we are in some serious trouble. That is why we are hiding down here."

"We?" asked Mary.

"Ladies." My introduction came from an empty seat across from them.

They responded by screaming in unison.

"Enough," I snapped when they all paused to get more air.

They clamped their mouths shut, but the echoes of their sounds lingered down the tunnel for a long time. Someone could have heard them and, for several long moments, my attention didn't waver from the mouth of the station.

"We're hiding," Olivia added.

Jackie spoke first. "You have to give us more than that!"

"Cliff notes version: Phil killed the banker for his blood. Since this made the news, he has two other vampires after him to take him to London and, well, kill him. He also has the police after him for said murder. So, we are hiding down here until we come up with a better idea," she summarized.

"How did you get hurt?" squeaked Pam.

"That's kind of embarrassing. I got shot by the police," she answered.

Three sets of eyebrows all shot up. Jackie was the first in the group to acknowledge my presence.

"How do we know you aren't some sort of freak pretending to be a vampire?" She challenged me.

"Come over here and I'll show you."

My lips curled so she could see my fangs even in

the dim light. Her face twitched in aggravation, but she held her stare.

"Phil, don't," warned Olivia. "He is one-hundred percent a vampire."

"Can you turn into a bat?" Pam asked.

Olivia laid a hand on her leg and when Pam looked over, she shook her head discouragingly.

"So, what's next?" said Mary.

"The other 'bad men' need to get off me and that involves more murder," I answered. "If they go away, that means Olivia will no longer be in danger either. However, don't ask me what to do about the police, but they need to go too."

"And the sailors?" Olivia teased.

My head shook, lips pressed into a flat line.

"Hmm, they'd make an excellent meal and that would solve two of my problems."

"Hold on, two problems?" asked Mary, using her fingers to count the solutions.

"I am thirsty." My body leaned back into the chair as my eyes drifted to the ceiling with detachment.

She stiffened before shrinking into her seat.

"Should we be worried?" asked Pam.

"No, well, probably not," reassured Olivia.

The corner of my lip turned down, thinking about the turn of events. Instead of having a conversation with these women, their blood could have stained my teeth.

I sighed and teased, "Any volunteers?"

The sentiment had the exact desired effect and their hearts sped up, even Olivia's. When my gaze turned back to the group, they leaned away from me, looking nervous.

Each word came out enunciated. "I am joking."

The edge of the platform seemed like a great place to stand after my attempt at humor and to, more or less, break the tension. Prey animals liked it when you turned your back on them. It meant that you weren't currently hunting. After getting up from the chair to give them space, they only saw the back of my head. Sure would have been nice to convince one of them to let me take a little off the top. Rumor has it that the euphoria from having your blood drained felt almost orgasmic.

"Are you sure about this guy?" whispered Mary to Olivia.

"Yes," she answered after a moment of silence. "He hasn't given me any reason to think otherwise. He needs me right now."

"But he's wanted for *murder,*" she added.

"True," she said slowly. "But, he's a vampire, Mary. They do that. Besides, life dealt him a crappy hand and did the best he could. Plus, he didn't have us to show him right from wrong. He doesn't want to kill."

While that was not exactly true, I held my tongue since she continued to talk.

"You would feel the same way if you found him under the same circumstances: they dragged him into the abandoned mall outside of the stadium. He looked dead, like *really* dead. I thought about following the three of them inside, but it got too scary. That night, I didn't sleep. The image of him being drug into the darkness wouldn't leave my mind. The thought of calling the cops crossed my mind, but something told me not to. Instinct, maybe? But for the next two days, my ass returned to that mall and watched from the entrance. Mary, they had him strung up by his hands! It was horrible! He struggled and growled like a rabid animal, but by the third day, he hung completely still. He looked *dead* dead.

"When he looked at me for the first time, it felt like the end of my life. His eyes were void of any sort of humanity, like what you see in a serial killer. Yet, there was something else deeper, something buried so deep that it hadn't seen the light in a very long time. That glint is what kept me going. After getting one hand free, he seemingly came back to life and looked at me like a man seeing an angel.

"From that moment, my mission became clear: he needed my help. I wasn't sure how, but those details could be figured out later. It hasn't exactly been easy and every day brings a new terror that makes me wonder if tomorrow is going to come for me. I *do* know that he has not killed anyone since we've met and that must stand for something. Regardless, he needs our help."

It would have been nice to see her face as she spoke these words. The sincerity in her conviction caused a pang of guilt to squeeze my chest. My treatment of her hadn't exactly been fair. She continually stood by me whenever presented with the opportunity to leave. I had no idea she watched me in the mall and on top of it all, she felt the need to come back to rescue me. My foolishness convinced me that she did it out of human ignorance, but maybe my preconceived perceptions had no place here and the time came to replace them with facts. In reality, no one dragged her into this mess. She chose to put herself in this situation from the first time she saw me, hell, even before that. The burden of guilt at keeping her in danger suddenly didn't feel so heavy with the realization.

"Well, okay," started Jackie. "How do we help?"

At this, I turned to look at her suspiciously.

"What? I trust Olivia and if she believes in you, well, we should too, " she clapped back.

The other two nodded in agreement.

The last of my prejudice came out in a heavy sigh and a defeated smile spread across my face.

"You all are dumb, you know that, right?" My quip came out while joining them back in the circle of chairs.

"We've been called worse," squeaked Pam. "Like 'obsessed'. Do you have any idea how gratifying it is to know that we were right?"

The seat to Olivia's right was open and she smiled when I took the seat. The group chatted, and their body language indicated that the atmosphere grew much more relaxed. Their heart rates were also considerably lower, but it didn't help my current situation. The metronomes of their life force rung between my ears, lulling me out of their conversation.

With a sharp intake of air, my request cut through whatever Jackie currently droned on about. "Now that you all have decided to trust me, there is still the pressing matter of sustenance. Soon would be nice. I'm still open to volunteers."

"We could ask Vince," Olivia said.

"I am positive that is not going to happen. We don't need to get anyone else involved."

"Could one of us get some blood?" asked Mary.

"How? They keep that sort of thing locked up," questioned Pam.

"Locked up, how?"

"Well, they keep the bags in refrigerators in a secured room," answered Pam.

"So, behind a locked door?"

"Yes."

No point hiding my amusement. "In that case, I'll just knock."

"Maybe this isn't a good idea," interrupted Olivia.

We all looked at her and she continued.

"Don't forget said bags are at a hospital and hospitals are full of bleeding people. And cameras," she reminded us.

She was right, of course. At this point, the sharp pains of the animal in my stomach began to claw at my insides. I didn't trust myself enough to walk through a ward of sick people and not act on impulse. Sick people secreted a smell of vulnerability, like weak prey, and being in a building full of that smell would ruin the good image they all held of me.

"Could you fly in through a window?" asked Mary.

"Why do you people think I can fly?" A quick pause let me recompose. "But, it is not a terrible idea. Scaling the building wouldn't be a problem. Losing control in the blood room isn't ideal, but better than the alternative." My face fell and once again, the relentless reality of my situation crashed down on me. "That means putting myself at risk of running into Joseph and John."

"We could keep watch," offered Mary.

"Out of the question!"

"No, think about it," she continued. "You work off of smell mostly, correct?"

"Yes…" My eyebrow arched.

"Well, they won't relate our smell with yours, or

Olivia's, since they have no reason to link us together. We could warn you if we see them coming!"

Her logic was good, but flawed. "That would be helpful, but how would you warn us? Any vampire could easily hear anything you did."

"Not a text message," she said.

"A what? It doesn't matter. What you are not grasping is how fast we are. You would have to be kilometers away from the hospital to be of any use, and you cannot cover that much ground without there being gaps. Besides, our movement is faster than what the human eye can perceive. If you happen to see one of them, it would most likely already be too late."

"We can just get in, get out, then come back here," said Olivia.

A low grumble formed in my chest. Their idea lacked substance. Too many holes and there were other, more obtainable, options. A couple of homeless people would do and the world would never be wiser. Slip out, then in, and by the time the group finished brainstorming, my stomach could be full.

"You cannot hide in this cave forever, Phil," stated Olivia.

"I know that." My snippy reply to her came with the full weight of my stare.

"Sounds like we just need to get rid of those bad guys," said Pam.

"Agreed."

The group became quiet as we all fell into our own thoughts. No doubt the humans were busy thinking about keeping my humanity intact. Admittedly, all I could think about was the feeling of blood running down my throat and into my muscles. Just a little drink and my thoughts would clear up making this whole conversation not even worth talking about.

Once again, Jackie broke the silence first. "How do you kill your kind, then?"

It seemed like she was the pragmatic one and earned my respect for it.

"Fire."

"That's vague," she griped. "Does that mean, like, a bonfire? Dipping them in molten iron? Lava? Flame thrower? Electric car fire? Thermite? Dousing them in gasoline and throwing a match?"

My eyebrows drew together. "Stay away from me."

"You aren't invulnerable either, right, Phil? You bit John and he bled," said Olivia.

"True. It is easier to destroy my kind when you rip off appendages, but all these ideas involve getting close to them. With there being two, I am miserably outmatched....and weak because of the lack of nutrition..."

"For me, when the stress gets to be too much, it is much easier to finish my tasks if they are broken up into smaller, more easily obtainable goals," offered Pam.

"Are you saying that we should separate them and take care of them individually?"

"Precisely!" she answered.

"That is so much easier said than done. How would we separate them? Anyone who volunteers to lead one of them away is signing up for certain death."

Not surprisingly, no one offered to help and the conversation grew quiet again.

"How long does it take to make a new vampire?" Jackie smiled.

"For crying out loud, not you too."

This was all too much and my patience wore away into a single thread. My rush to get out of the chair tipped it over. It clattered against the floor, sending out an echo into the otherwise quiet space. I marched toward the edge of the platform. Only when my feet crunched against the gravel on the tracks did anyone get up to follow me.

"Where are you going?" Olivia said, panic painting her tone.

She trotted ahead as the other three lagged behind at a leisurely pace.

"To find something to drink."

Olivia caught up with me at the mouth of the tunnel. She jogged to keep up with my quick pace, huffing out her next sentence.

"You can't go, not yet. We haven't figured anything out."

She didn't expect me to stop so suddenly and ended up bouncing off my chest. An "oof" came out of her and she glared up at me. Her friends hung back on the lip of the platform.

"No, we haven't. Once again, you underestimate the situation. For your sake, I am going to go and fix my needs before your friends are any more appealing. Stay here."

She looked uncomfortable with the idea and countered, "No! You'll need my help breaking into the hospital, or whatever, just don't go and kill someone. Please," she ended quietly.

Olivia looked at me through the tops of her blonde lashes again and it set my heart aflame. It caused me physical pain to see that face and I had to look away before doing something incredibly dumb, like grab her by the back of the head and place my lips on hers.

"Fine, but we have to hurry."

"That was easy," she breathed.

"Incredibly. Besides, you'll have to show me where the hospital is, anyway."

"Right, well…" Olivia turned toward her friends. "Are you in, ladies?"

"Please, no."

She held up a finger. "Take the help, Phil. We can't do much, but we can do this."

The most frustrating part was their incessant need to help. They injected themselves into the situation unnecessarily and it felt like being infested with fleas. My skin itched with the idea of bringing them along, but Olivia had me by the short and curlies.

I started down the tunnel again and asked, "Where are we going?"

This time, four excitable women trotted behind me, discussing the inner workings of staging a stakeout. At least they could cover the corners of the block. The thought of letting Olivia out of my sight brought out my anxiety, which surprised me. Even if we were apart for a short amount of time, it was still enough time for the goons to get a hold of her. They would most definitely use her against me. It wasn't too late to find some place to lock her up, if only to keep her safe.

The group made painfully slow progress out of the tunnel. We walked at their pace the entire way. The thought crossed my mind to scoop them all up and deposit them outside, but they headed in a new direction. I slipped to the back of the group and followed. They discussed everything from what happened since we met, to what came next. Olivia tried to describe what Joseph and John looked like, so they knew who to look out for. Her description wasn't bad, despite only seeing them once, and while under duress. She shared her concerns about the fallout from being wanted by the police. Olivia didn't know this, but my plan for this particular problem was to take the fall for everything. She'd never find out since she would, no doubt, argue with me about it, so my mouth remained shut on the matter.

"Oh!" gasped Pam. We all stopped to look at her, but a quick scan of the path in front and behind us revealed we were alone. Nothing changed, so I glared at her, hoping to get some sort of explanation. "How are we going to get a hold of Phil if we see the bad guys? You don't have a phone, do you?"

"No, he doesn't, and he can't have mine, you know, in case I need to alert everyone too. Going in there with him is out of the question," answered Olivia.

"Surely, we can get him a burner from a bodega or something like that," offered Jackie.

"We'll stop and get one on the way to the hospital," said Olivia.

"We need a rendezvous," chirped Jackie. "You know, in case things go wrong, we can make sure we are all accounted for."

"Good idea!" said Mary.

"How about the cemetery? We could meet up at the plot where we had our first meeting," suggested Olivia.

"That would work. If it gets too long of a wait, we could always leave a flower on the grave," said Pam. "I could leave a yellow flower, Mary could be purple, Jackie's is pink, Olivia can leave white, and Phil has to be red."

"No one would be the wiser." My eyes fought not to roll in their sockets.

Their schemes were somewhat well planned, and more credit should have been awarded to them. However, the idea of having their scents intertwined with mine made me uneasy. It would make me the happiest if they kept their distance, by about an ocean preferably, but regardless, far, far away. So, after seeing the unlikely bouquet at the gravesite, I would leave and take care of Joseph and John alone. No more human distractions.

The end of the tunnel approached, and a faint light brushed against the uneven bricks that lined the space around us. No doubt the others couldn't see it yet, since the source of the light came from the reflection of the stars. Night snuck up on us. Not long after, the crispness that accompanied a set sun greeted us. The air felt lighter and the hair on the back of my neck stood up. Saliva seeped into my mouth.

"Ladies, this is where we need to split up." My announcement came at the tunnel's mouth. "Do you have your plan in place?"

Three of the women nodded, but Olivia's attention directed down at her phone, dealing with the nearly constant buzzing. She pulled it from her pocket and the screen filled with notifications. One would pop up, just to be pushed down by another.

"What is wrong with it?" I asked.

"It must have gotten the signal back. Holy crow, there are a lot of people trying to get a hold of me. Mom, Dad, unknown, unknown, Mom. Didn't you guys say that there is a missing person's report out on me?"

"Yeah, it was all over the news last night and this morning," answered Jackie.

"Shit! They're going to start tracking my phone. Will turning it off block the signal?"

"Maybe?" Pam said, uncertainty flickering in her eyes.

"They can track you through your phone?" A deep frown crossed my face, trying to understand exactly how that worked. "Yet, it didn't work until now? I don't understand."

"Yep, satellites in the sky provide a signal for people to communicate wirelessly. In this day and age, you would think things like skyscrapers and low-coverage areas wouldn't be an issue," responded Mary.

It truly sounded like she spoke in another language.

"Phil, the tunnel blocked the signal," explained Olivia.

"All right, then let's leave the phone in your witch's circle."

"It's not a witch's circle," Jackie remarked with a sly smirk. "Do we have time?"

My hand extended out for Olivia's phone. She hesitated but set it down on my open palm. The women started talking about exchanging phone numbers while my feet crunched on the gravel heading back into the tunnel. Without the burden of waiting on them, I had enough time to set her phone on the food table next to a bag labeled 'potato chips' and joined back up with them before Olivia scribbled one set of numbers on her forearm with a pen.

"Ready to go?"

Mary and Pam yelped while Jackie jumped to the side, shielding her face.

"You just left!" breathed Pam.

"You'll get used to it," offered Olivia. "Give me a sec, Phil. Mary, what's your number?"

Like a nervous tick, my eyes darted around the landscape and my weight shifted anxiously. We stood in a vulnerable position. Since the mouth of the tunnel sunk underground, they could ambush us from above, the sides, or use the high walls on either side to funnel us into a death trap. When Olivia announced that she was done, I marched forward to where the tracks leveled out with the rest of the landscape.

Out of courtesy, and desire to get them away from me, my parting words were, "It has been a pleasure getting to know you. Olivia is lucky to call you her friends." One last thought popped into my brain, spurring me to address the four ducklings following a couple steps behind. They stopped too, but not without bumping into one another. My next sentiment couldn't be allowed any room to be misconstrued, so my voice dropped and addressed each of them individually.

"If you breathe a word of my kind of anyone; I will kill you."

Each one of them gave me a decisive nod. Instinctively, my hand raised for Olivia.

She jogged to catch up, but took my offer with a secure grip.

"Nice to meet you, Phil," said Pam.

"Until next time," added Jackie.

"Be safe," Mary said, with worry etched across her face. "See you soon!"

We reached the top of the little hill and from behind us, the three others started in their own direction, while Olivia brushed up against my side as we continued down the tracks.

"You have nice friends. Is everyone so accepting of new people in this decade?"

"You have no idea." She smiled.

I looked down in time to see her rolling her eyes.

Chapter 10

The building in front of us was obviously a health institute and identifiable instantly. The implications of agreeing to let Olivia show me the way seemed so much smaller back in the tunnel. Sickness oozed out of the place and could be smelled from blocks away. It only gained strength as we walked closer, permeating everything in the area with sweetness. It pushed into my temples like a headache and begged me to act on the sensation. *Death*.

Alas, we stood across the street from the entrance. My collar pressed against my ears as the rest of me kept a vigilant eye on our surroundings from the crook of someone's front steps. Olivia pressed against the wall behind me and peaked around the edge of my coat. Joseph and John remained undetected. That mattered little to me since every interaction with them had been an ambush, but I was learning.

"Ready?"

"One more minute, please. It takes a while to program a new phone. All that is left is to get a group text started."

"Could you please hurry up? My saliva is going to start dripping on my shirt."

"Jeez, I'm done. Here."

She handed me my new phone. This one had a full set of keys along the bottom in the form of buttons, since my lifeless hands didn't trigger the touch screen. She set it so that the device would vibrate whenever it got a new message, and after a quick tutorial, I felt confident enough to navigate through basic commands.

The small electronic slipped into the pocket where my watch should have been. Olivia shrugged out of her shirt and pants. She was easily concealed by my figure, shadowed in part by my long coat, but partly because we were backed into the corner of a stoop. She grasped for the clothing draped over the edge of the railing next to us and stuffed herself into it. One hand lifted the lid of a bin next to us and the other plucked out the top bag. With a sigh, she placed her old clothes in it and watched as they disappeared under the trash bag and lid.

With one more cautious look around, my hand gestured for Olivia to come out from behind me.

"Do you remember your instructions?"

"If either of the other vampires show up, just run. If any of the others see the vampires, run," she repeated.

My teeth repeatedly clacked together in nervousness. "This plan is so stupid; I don't know why I agreed to it."

"You'll be gone for a few minutes and that is enough for us to be helpful. Then you won't be so grumpy after you have eaten," she said.

"Any idea where the blood room is?"

"Erm, it never came up while talking with Vince, sorry."

"Might as well start at the top." My last instructions came out regrettably. "If you start to hear screaming, just leave. Please."

She didn't get a chance to answer. There was a space past the entrance that said "Emergency" that provided an uninterrupted strip to climb up. The designers of the building recognized the view from the back wasn't ideal since it aimed at another building and, as a result, spaced the windows further apart. With the larger gaps between windows, it allowed ample space to hide while peeking into the varying rooms. Less windows also meant less options to enter the building, not that they probably opened, anyway. That left breaking in and would unquestionably cause a scene. This left one good option. A slight crouch and a powerful thrust of the legs landed me close to the roof. My fingers held onto the lip and made easy work of pulling the rest of me up.

Large pipes and clunking box-shaped machines dotted the rooftop. After a bit of slinking, an access door came into view from the center of the building. The staff kept it unlocked and unlit. Perfect. Except, movement triggered the light, and it flicked on when my foot entered the threshold. I hesitated only a second before continuing on.

Olivia told me to watch out for the black bulbs on the ceiling, like what she pointed out in the clothing store. She warned me that they were scattered throughout the hospital, so I needed to watch out for them just as carefully as I watched for the people around me. Sure enough, one of them loomed right inside the door.

Like a raven's eye, it was completely black, except for an almost invisible iris, tinted the faintest shade of red and kept a vigilant watch down the stairs. Made sense to me. People generally didn't trespass from the roof. I zipped past it and slid comfortably around the corner quick enough that the naked eye couldn't see me. Hopefully, these little recording devices were the same.

More worrisome than being caught by the cameras was the increasing presence of vulnerability. The weight of sickness grew thicker while descending into the building, making me think it only became stronger further inside. At the end of the stairs, a paltry wooden door sat between me and the patients. The inlaid tall and skinny window allowed me to snoop through the glass while remaining out of sight of the cameras. Doors lined the walls, each labeled with their respective purpose, like x-ray, waiting room, consultation, and restroom. People busied themselves around a reception-like area at the end, floating around like ghosts in their white coats, and paying no mind to the head floating in the window. None of the rooms looked like anything vaguely close to indicating blood storage, but parts of the building ebbed out of sight and would require further exploration. The door cracked open under my push and a barrage of smells assaulted my senses. Downright unnatural materials burned my nose, making me wonder what they did to these people. Best to try another, lower level. The thud of the door closing vibrated up my arm.

This level looked more like the main part of the building. More people made their way through the area, some dressed more casually, while others matched in their head-to-toe uniforms. Curtains separated the row of white beds pressed to the outside in an otherwise open room. The people here were sicker too. Their irony, rich life force had a consistent presence in this place. One patient actively bled while a nurse bandaged him up. My eyes closed as the rest of me gave up against a wall. Keeping air out of my lungs and nose helped with the ravenous impulses, but nothing could drone out the sound of weak and unstable heartbeats that pounded just on the other side of the door. Making it worse, a machine next to them echoed what their heart already said, making this place my own personal hell. One last glance through the door window proved this floor didn't contain anything useful.

Each level continued in the same manner, but the patients seemed to get worse closer to the ground floor. If there wasn't an overwhelming smell of human suffering, my nose alone could find the blood room, but be as it may, I could only hope it was well labeled.

Level three finally showed something promising. The sign above the door said, 'Medical Supplies', and unlike every story before now, it seemed worthy of risking a little sniff. Cutting through the smell of human suffering, the artificial wrapping of blood bags rose above it, exuding a sharp, chemical-like discharge, but the whisper coming from the contents underneath couldn't be mistaken. That same smell seeped from the medical supply room. A doctor breezed by the door and as soon as he passed, my body slipped out of the protection of the stairwell and silently walked over to the respective door. Locked. A little harder push and the mechanism gave up in a low crunch. The room hosted exactly what you'd expect. Shelves held things like gauze, needles, wraps, splints, and other necessities. Silver doors lined the entire backside of the little room and hummed stoically. The air around the cabinets nipped at me like winter. Shivers ran down my spine and the temperature of the air had nothing to do with it.

Stacked up like soldiers on the battlefield, the red bags waiting for someone to come for them. Greedy fingers didn't discriminate and latched onto one from the top. Four long gulps and the bag shriveled in my hand. Despite my ravenous thirst, the familiarity took me back to Olivia's apartment when everything appeared so juvenile. Her bright emerald eyes stared at me timidly, yet curiously. As a stranger, she hadn't been given any reason to fear me yet and the look on her face stemmed from the desire to learn about someone new. If it wasn't for this artificial sustenance, someone else would be under my fangs with their own story, like Miles, and thinking nothing of it. Somewhere outside, she once again waited for me to finish. Unlike before, the fourth bag of blood in my hand didn't bring relief, just more anxiety knowing every minute away put her further into danger. Curse this wretched woman.

It was unfortunate timing, since whoever stood behind me saw nothing but a man sucking down the contents of a blood bag. Spillage ran down the corners of my mouth. I didn't dare wipe it away. It would only add to the satanic image this person, no doubt, already held against me. The empty bag slowly made its way down until my hand settled near my abdomen, attempting not to alarm them any further with sudden movements. My jaw muscles clenched in frustration. Callousness cost me my anonymity, and this is exactly how a vampire got caught back then. However, instead of someone's son or daughter being harmed, a bag stamped with "O-Negative" took the brunt of the brutality instead. The sight would be alarming, regardless of the circumstances. In a way, though, I lucked out, since the human in the room with me was Vince.

Blood stained my chin and at least four empty bags littered the floor, but surely Vince could see through what probably looked animalistic to anyone else. The friendly smile smattered across my face didn't secure quite the anticipated result, evident by his stiff posture. Vince's eyes widened with recognition almost immediately and he started spouting off, "No! Anyone but you! Help! HELP!"

The empty bag fluttered to the floor when my hand let go of it to replace it with Vince. One of my arms pressed across his chest while the other held his mouth. We crashed into one of the shelves behind him and the majority of its contents tumbled to the ground.

"Shut the hell up, man."

He only mumbled, horrified. His mouth opened and closed under my palm like a fish out of water. At one point, he tried to bite me.

"You said you didn't want to get involved and I am nothing if not a gentleman to respect your wishes. But if you want to walk out of this room, you need to agree to stop screaming for help. Do you understand?"

His eyes teared up with fear and bounced from left to right, looking at anything except for the two orbs just centimeters from his own. After a couple of seconds, he relented and started nodding vigorously.

My grip loosened on his mouth slightly, to test if he would keep his word. When he remained quiet, I took a step back and let the man gather himself.

He pulled down angrily on his shirt where it bunched up.

"Have you killed her yet?" he spat.

"Who? Olivia? Of course not!"

"Well, that's something," he muttered.

"Can you get me a bag to transport some more of this blood?"

"Fuck no, I'm not your Renfield." He turned to go.

Curse words grumbled deep in my chest. Vince noticed that he was being followed and started to yell again.

"Help! The murderer is in here! HELP!"

On the second help, he started running. We made it out of the supply closet when my hand snarled into his collar and his yelp attracted the attention of several curious onlookers. Two women perched behind a desk stopped what they were doing to see what caused the commotion. A man with a clipboard stopped to watch from the doorway of a patient's room. Even the people in the beds looked on in fright.

"Goddammit." The word came out in a full-on snarl while releasing him.

Vince scurried away, and I stormed toward the stairs. Murmuring, then eventually yelling, followed my heels out of the main area and back into the shallow haven of the stairwell. With my back to the door, my foot wedged against the bottom, so when the security guards started to push on it, there was no chance of them getting in. Two stories below, a couple sets of boots clomped their way up the stairs, along with two other sets descending from above.

Never having experienced anything like it in my life, the sensation of the phone vibrating in my pocket caused me to spook. My fingers fumbled for the thing and yanked it out. Mary's name lit up the top of the message with the words —*Is this them?*— under a picture. The phone thunked against my chest as my eyes closed out the rest of the world. A flurry of colorful words pushed past a locked jaw. Joseph and John were as clear as night, looking as ugly as they usually did.

One hand stuffed the device back in its pocket while the other practically ripped the door off its hinges when it swung back open. Two surprised guards fell through the newly opened space, losing their balance in the process. One of them tried to catch me mid-fall, but a gentle push redirected his attempts to the floor without hindering my progression. Several security guards followed me into the main ward and yelled at my backside. The quickest way out would garner even more attention, but it seemed like the best option for the situation. I marched toward the exterior wall and jumped through the third-story window.

Glass showered onto the street below around the same time my feet landed. Pedestrians cowered out of the way, but no one saw what caused the window to break. This side of the building butted up against an alley and on the opposite side as the emergency entrance. Instead of immediately heading for the front just around the corner, I reversed so that my back bumped up against the exterior wall and whoever looked through the broken window would only see the glimmer of broken glass. The tips of the security guard's hats poked into the open air briefly before disappearing back into the building.

My worst-case scenario acted out like a play. Joseph and John were on the same block as me. My plan to sneak in and out of the hospital ended with a herd of police being called to this location, and worst of all; Olivia was alone. No amount of speed would get me to her fast enough, but it didn't stop me from trying. I fumbled with my phone while making my way around the building and managed to type out, —*Run*—, in the group message.

"Curse you, Vince," came out while rounding the corner to the front sidewalk. Familiar red and blue lights lit up the road about a kilometer away. The braying of their sirens cut through the confused conversations of the people around me. As planned, Olivia stood on the corner a block away. She was talking to Joseph. My step faltered and then froze in the middle of the crosswalk. A deep grumble formed and seeped out of my chest. Joseph heard and turned to smirk at me before going back to his conversation. Cars streamed across the road, but it didn't matter. They could just hit me. Something large rammed into my side with enough force to fling me across four lanes of traffic and back through another window into the hospital.

I skidded across the polished floor of the lobby and slowed to a stop by the reception desk. The two people sitting there hustled out of the way, trying to avoid the glass that followed me in. The other humans stared at me while I got up off the ground and subsequently brushed the debris off my coat. My hand combed through my hair as John barreled toward me.

When he reached the entrance, the sliding door did not open quite as fast as he would have liked and shoved it the rest of the way. My fists raised in anticipation of his impact. Predictably, he came at me already swinging. The first whistled over my head, the second aimed for my ribs, but the third caught the underside of my jaw, sending me over the desk in a flurry of papers and pens onto the floor behind it. He walked around the edge and puckered when he saw the rolling chair waiting for him. My hands grasped it by the neck, above the rollers, and swung it like a bat. It smashed into his shoulder and it molded perfectly around his solid shape. While he shrugged it off, I scooted myself backwards enough to get my feet under myself and jumped up.

With John standing behind the desk, there was a clear shot to the front of the building, and Olivia. Sprinting toward the exit didn't work. He pounced like a cat and wrapped his arms around my legs. We both went down like a tree. No matter how hard my legs kicked, they couldn't lessen his grasp. It became all the harder when he sunk his teeth into my calf. A cry of pain filled the reception. Closed fists started pounding the back of his head and when that didn't do anything, my hands unfurled and started clawing at his eyes. Bloody lines trailed across his face with every swipe. John loosened his toothy grip on my leg, but clamped back down, harder and deeper. A couple more of these and he'd gnaw entirely through.

Instead of wasting energy to get away from him, my efforts went into looking for something to weaponize. The hospital lobby held very little, except for the chairs and magazines. Neither of those things would get him off. Outside offered more possibilities, like manhole covers, or a car, so my fingers clawed at the floor to try and get enough purchase to drag us both outside.

We only made it about a meter before the police

poured in, forming a semicircle around us, with more waiting outside. This group armed themselves with clear shields displaying 'Police' across the front. Gun barrels trained on us from in between the gaps.

"Get your hands in the air!" commanded one from the back.

For the first time since coming topside, I obeyed the officers. They rose above my head, parallel to the ground. John stopped gnawing on my leg, but he did not let go. His teeth dug painfully into my muscle. His position couldn't have been any better.

"It's him! It's the murderer, please, help me!" They reacted to my cries by redirecting their pistols at John. The air buzzed with their nervous energy. "You've got to get him off me. He's going to kill me!"

Their circle slowly came in and they were almost close enough to touch, but they needed to come a little bit closer before making a move. Someone stepped down an arm's length from my head and the timing seemed right to start thrashing against John's hold while crying, "Get him off!"

In the chaos, my fingers found their way into his eye sockets and pressed until his orbits squished. In the same breath, the police mob jumped us and started beating him with their batons. Grunting, he let go enough for me to kick free of his teeth. My shoes slipped on the polished floor, making it difficult to get out of the pile, but a couple of hands latched onto my jacket and pulled me to safety.

John did not stay still for long and around five policemen were tossed aside when he stood up. My left leg slumped to the ground and the muscles below John's bite mark refused to work, making the simple task of standing up a balancing act of rolling over onto my hands and knees before pushing up with just one leg. Once vertical, I limped a few steps toward the door before John got me. He wrapped his hand around my throat and dragged me along at his side while he made his way deeper into the hospital. A smear of blood followed behind us, stark against the white floor. My one free hand tried to cling onto anything within reach. A privacy curtain came off its rails with a series of pops and a medical cart overturned in a clattering of utensils, but John didn't slow down. My other hand wrapped around his wrist, supporting my weight. The army of police followed us with their guns raised, but none of them dared to shoot: there was too much collateral with all the patients around. On the bright side, in one sentence, I managed to change my own narrative in their eyes. At least, for the moment.

We continued through another door, pausing long enough for him to snap off the handle that led inside, stirring up a bit of internal panic. Without the human façade to keep me safe, it freed up John to do his worst to me. The broken latch clicked frivolously as they tried to open it and when that didn't work, the thudding of their bodies hitting the barricade followed us down to the basement level.

We reached the bottom of the stairs and John shoved the door open. It bounced off the wall, then thudded against my shoulder. My fingers wrapped around the handle, but only managed to break the thing in half. The inner mechanism came off with the grip and extended out into a pointed tip. It didn't look very sturdy, but it also didn't crumple when it got jammed into John's forearm. Two things happened simultaneously; blood spurted from where the metal broke through his skin and John's hand went limp.

My mass thumped to the floor and scurried further into the space on my hands and knees. The area was defined by a wide, white hallway spotted with blue doors every couple of meters. Just like the rest of the hospital, a label hovered over each entrance. The wall dipped slightly where the silver doors of an elevator broke up the space. They opened to reveal a lump of black clothing stuffed into the space. Around fifteen humans pushed through the doors, so I rolled onto my back and threw my hands up defensively.

"He's down there!"

They looked to the left in time to see John charging down the hallway. In response, they formed a barrier between us right before opening fire. The noise left me cringing in a ball with my hands trying to block out the barrage of noise. All fifteen of them emptied their clips. Peeping through their legs, John stepped slowly, but he still made forward progress, only slightly inconvenienced by their assault.

I used the opportunity to get back up and make my escape. Some of the feeling in my left leg returned, but not without complete disobedience, so it dragged uselessly while the other hobbled along. A double door at the end of the hallway led to more of the same thing, but at the end of the second hallway was a sign that said "Morgue". The lights clicked on as soon as it detected someone slipping inside.

The smell almost took me to my knees. It wasn't the natural aroma coming from the dead, like bacteria and dirt. No, this room pierced through my sinuses like someone submerged my head in kerosene and lit me on fire. Every part of my being screamed to leave, but a peek through the window in the door made me change my mind. John lumbered at the end of the hallway, checking one of the rooms. After a moment, he stepped back and moved on to the next. Maybe the smell in this room would affect him this badly too and he would miss my scent.

Venturing further into the room expounded the smell. The fumes burned into my eyes, blurring the details so that they had to be viewed through tiny slits. My sleeve mopped up more than one spilled tear. On each side of me were the blobs of four shiny metal beds mounted to the ground. One empty bed had a drain at the end, while the others hosted the deceased, covered in white sheets. Tools sat readily on carts that crowded each of the workstations. There was everything from scissors to saws to white bandages. Another door interrupted a wall of shelves and cabinets, storing the overflow of instruments. The terrible smell grew stronger the closer I got in that direction. The source sat grouped together on a shelf in liter sized bottles, printed with a litany of useless words and warnings. One word stuck out: Formaldehyde. I gingerly touched the package to see if it burned, and when it didn't, fully grasped one of the bottles before continuing through to the next room.

The walls were lined with silver doors, about a meter square, stacked from floor to ceiling. Each door had a latch and a number. The smell didn't penetrate here nearly as dreadfully, but it remained. The weight of death lingered heavily under the horrid smell. Decomposition didn't exist here, stripped away by something more permanent. Under the serene stillness, a smell lingered in the otherwise sterile space. Ash.

Situated against the back wall, a coffin-like structure took up almost the entire width of the room. Maybe coffin wasn't the right word. The thing stood on a pedestal with tubes coming out of the top and looked to be made of concrete, or perhaps, ceramic? There was an opening at the end, about the same size as the others dotted along the walls.

The door that led to the morgue creaked open. I flung myself backwards and out of sight, so the intruder wouldn't immediately see me when he entered.

"Ugh!" he moaned.

He clomped his way through the first room, getting closer to my hiding spot next to the door. He took a few steps, then stopped. He took a few more, then stopped again. My hand squeezed the bottle of formaldehyde tight while it rested against my side and slowly untwisted the cap. A thin line of foil spread across the top. It made a *pop* sound when my thumb broke through. Though it was quiet, I might as well have shouted, "Look over here!"

Footsteps walked purposely toward me now. The door opened and left me covered in its shadow. Entrails of the bottle reached up and tried to get me to react to the awful smell. My body remained as still as possible, but tears freely ran down my cheeks. The window in the door let me watch his head sweep the space. A single drip betrayed my location when it landed on my jacket. Two beady eyes met mine through the window, and he growled. The door slammed shut hard enough to shatter the glass.

He had me backed into a corner, with a bum leg, and an escape route that would require going past him, so I did the only thing that any sane person would do and pointed the end of the bottle of poison at him right before squeezing the shit out of it. The liquid came out in a stream and landed, first, in his right eye, then the left as the bottle bobbed back and forth. John started screaming, clutching his face. When the bottle ran out of fluid, it fell to the ground. Then, my shoulder dropped and rammed into his abdomen as hard as possible. The force pushed him into the far side and the doors caved in protest.

He mauled his own eyes instead of getting up, groaning all the while. In his compromised state, he allowed me to get a hold of his collar and fling him around. He thudded against the ceramic coffin head first, and lost his balance, tumbling to the floor. Surprisingly, there wasn't a scratch on the object, giving me an idea. My hands grabbed onto the back of John's neck and manhandled him around to the front. A lever opened the front of the coffin, providing the perfect perch to bend John over and smash his head in. Over and over the door slammed against him until he went limp.

It crossed my mind to leave him there on the floor, but he would come back to life sooner than later and I needed more time. The unknown thing seemed sturdy, even after bashing him into it with my full strength. Battering him with the door didn't seem to damage the closure too badly either. John's deadweight lolled with my various attempts to stuff him into the long, narrow space inside the box. The soles of his shoes were the last thing visible before securing the door. It would have been nice to lock him in with some sort of mechanical pin or something similar to give me slightly more time, but the machine didn't have many external buttons. A few knobs jutted out of the side, one of which was red, so I pushed it. After several seconds, nothing happened.

With John out of the way, my attention turned vehemently on Joseph and Olivia. The morgue door closed behind me when the coffin started clicking. It reminded me of someone striking flint and steel. *Click, click, click, click, click.*

It was nice being right about some things, but not in this case. The flame erupted inside the chamber and only a half second later, the whole thing started to hiss. My hand was still on the handle when the coffin exploded. The shockwave launched the door into me and across the room.

The ringing in my ears alerted me that something terrible had just happened. It drowned out all the other sounds, but details started filling in like molasses. Rain pounded down on the door covering me and streamed onto the floor. It crept under the temporary shelter and soaked into my clothing. An alarm incessantly blared, filling every square inch of the space with noise. Screaming humans scrambled on the floors above me, while others barked muffled orders. The water turned black with the soot. Somewhere close, a little curl of smoke crawled its way up the underside of the door, tickling my nose.

The door clambered to the side, and I lumbered to my feet to take a better account of my surroundings. A lick of flame burned on the end of my coat, so my hand brushed it out quickly and shook away the pain from the short-lived burn. Water streamed down my face, washing away the last remnants of the formaldehyde.

Interestingly, the rain actually came from little nozzles in the ceiling. The heavy stream made such quick work of putting out the morgue fire. All that remained of the explosion was a blackened, twisted mass. Char marks melted down the walls where the water started rinsing it away. The coffin remained relatively intact, but the end with the latch blew out in jagged edges. The metal twisted on the top where the pipes previously attached. They now dangled from the ceiling.

John completely disintegrated. Surely, there would be a crispy husk to identify him with, but no. The only evidence that he had been here was his shoe, which landed next to me. Well, a little bit of John survived. His blackened foot filled the leather. A nudge of my toe caused the remainder of him to turn to ash. Disgusted, I awkwardly kicked it down the hall and the last bit of him poofed out like an erupting volcano.

Mayhem engulfed the main floor. The alarm continued to blare, and some hoarse voiced man tried to bark instructions over the sound. Patients were being wheeled out, carried out, shuffled out, and I limped unnoticed out the front door. Once outside, a crowd gathered of emergency responders, pedestrians, and scattered patients while police vehicles clogged the road. A uniformed human tried to check on me, but he didn't pursue the matter after being brushed off. One thing sat at the forefront of my thoughts, and it consumed me: Joseph had Olivia and he was going to kill her.

Chapter 11

Olivia wasn't on the same corner as when I last saw her. My chest could be plucked and produce noise like a violin for how taut the muscles were. The air filled with a symphony of smells that blended to create a crappy song. Smoke, ash, exhaust, sewer, rainwater, trash, sick people, clean people, on and on my senses inspected the objects around me, but none of them matched what Olivia put on before our departure. Several desperate minutes passed of breathing in the smells and feverishly looking in every direction for a hint of which way to go. She had vanished. Joseph's stink lingered, but anytime it led anywhere, the influences of the street quickly erased it. A headless chicken would have better luck. Panicking in this situation wouldn't help, but it skulked dangerously close to the surface.

The phone bounced against my chest reminding me of twenty-first century options. A large crack crossed the screen, but it lit up when the buttons were pressed. My shaky thumbs hit several letters at once, creating words that no English speaker would recognize, prompting me to start over three times before they typed out a coherent message. —*Olivia, where are you?*—

There was no use waiting for a response, since it would come standing still or actively looking for her.

The pavement pounded hard under my feet after choosing the direction in which Joseph's scent dissolved. My injured leg awkwardly tripped with every step, slowing my progress, but I marched on regardless. After a few blocks, I turned and had the idea to loop the area in a grid. The first pass went by the hospital, then one block further out, and so on. It felt like people waited at every road crossing for another set of emergency vehicles to pass by. The reflection of their red and blue lights danced in the darkness like a beacon.

The phone buzzed in my hand, but my eagerness waned when Pam's name accompanied the message. — *Olivia? Pls rspnd ASAP.—*

In the subsequent minutes that followed, each of her friends reached out as well with no answer. Every time the phone vibrated, a wave of anticipation rushed me, hoping the next one would be her, but each new text resulted in disappointment.

The faintest hint of her rosy smell tickled my attention finally. She passed through here a while ago, pointing me, hopefully, in the right direction. She never deviated from her straight path for over two kilometers and as far as company is concerned, she walked alone. Joseph's scent vanished at the hospital and in all my searching, it didn't come up again. However, my head remained on a swivel and looked down every alley, every crevice, every drain for the face that caused me the most amount of dread. Where there could have been Joseph's steely stare, there was only darkness.

Sniffles that accompany a woman crying resonated through the night. It echoed slightly on the buildings, and it took me a moment to pinpoint where it came from. At last, I saw her. She sat curled up on a bench under a streetlight. Her head buried in her knees, which had been pulled up tight against her chest. Her arms held it all together.

She yelped when my hand caressed her shoulder. Her eyes flitted up to me in fright. Once she recognized me, she calmed, but only slightly. A fresh wave of grief spilled over her. My leg protested when forced to support the weight of my squatting body, but Olivia mattered more to me than a little pain.

"Are you okay? Did he hurt you?" My wandering eyes tried to locate the source of her tears, but she seemed physically fine. All her blood remained inside of her, and she didn't appear to have any broken bones, leading me to believe Joseph hurt her emotionally. Olivia buried her head back onto her knees and shook her head.

For just a moment, I thought about wrapping my arms around her, to squash out the fear, and to let her know everything was going to be okay. Yet, my limbs remained frozen, stuck in the reality of the situation. We were nowhere close to being okay.

"Where is Joseph?"

When she did not answer right away, I grabbed her by the shoulders and gave her a tiny shake.

"Olivia!"

"I don't know!" she wailed. "He, he ran away after the ex-explosion."

She reminded me we weren't in a great spot, warranting a glance around for safety. Other than a few homeless people, we were alone.

"We need to get out of here." The second half of the sentence came out in a bit of a gasp as the pain in my calf radiated up my body.

This caught her attention, and she raised her head to really look at me for the first time.

"What happened to you?"

"Nothing that time won't heal. Let's go." My attempts at getting her off the bench went ignored.

"Phil…" she started.

"It's going to be okay, Olivia." Her fingers intertwined mine as she followed me ungracefully down the road.

"That's not…" She broke off before finishing.

We made our way toward the busiest part of the city, thinking the sheer amount of people would make it harder for Joseph to do something stupid if he showed up again. Our progress was painfully slow, and I mean painfully. The dull ache in my leg punished me with every step. My foot didn't feel like my own and dangled uselessly, but luckily, it supported weight just fine. Most of the blood stolen at the hospital had bled out through the wound, leaving me with a limb that wouldn't heal and a growing craving. Olivia stopped to wait for me every half a block or so. She saw my eyes lingering on flesh as pedestrians walked by and only when she called out, "Phil!" did it realign my focus.

The noise alone assured me we were headed in the right direction. The hum of the crowd seeped around the buildings in a low constant murmur. The glow of the giant screens illuminated the night sky, blocking out most of the stars. We rounded the last corner, and people stood shoulder to shoulder in the square, forming a warm, fleshy fence. Polite prodding fell on deaf ears and the outside edge seemed the most reluctant to let us through. Their aloofness encouraged me to reconsider the route, but equally, our trail would be next to impossible to follow in this exhibition.

Not once did this jungle of steel, concrete, and asphalt make me feel at home, not even a whisper. Every single thing was foreign to me. Standing at the edge of a courtyard, illuminated with screens larger than a *house,* while people recorded videos from devices that could fit in their pockets, I never expected to feel a sense of normalcy. A smile settled on my face. The man waited on the outskirts of the crowd. He stood in the glow of his phone, scrolling through the screen with his thumb. His other hand kept warm in his pocket. Olivia followed me to where he waited and took my hand to balance while climbing into the vehicle.

The carriage attached to a thick, white horse. He had one hind leg cocked and his lip hung drowsily. The horse was obviously no stranger to city life. The driver positioned himself next to the animal's head, not paying attention. He didn't even have a hold of the horse's reins: they were draped over the dash rail. The vehicle boasted gold piping on a white background, something quite ornate for a mode of taxiing around the masses. Olivia sat down in the back on a red velvet cushion. I climbed in the front and took a hold of the reins.

Only when the horse bobbed its head at the presence of a driver, did the man look up from his phone.

"Hey, pal, you gotta ride in the back," he ordered.

"No." I whipped the reins on the rump of the animal.

It leaped forward in surprise, knocking the man backwards. His heel caught on the lip of the sidewalk and he fell on his ass. Instead of pointing the horse around the crowd, a stern pull on the rein guided his head around so that he pointed straight into the thick of it. A lot of things may have changed, but other things will always remain the same. One person bounced off the chest of the horse before the yelling of the crowd accomplished the perfect result. They started to part like the Red Sea, and we were able to canter through the square with ease. The path instantly filled with people behind us.

In a matter of minutes, we cleared Times Square and the horse huffed down the road in an easy trot. The clip-clop of his hooves were peaceful in the cool night air and my tight muscles relaxed into the seat. Olivia climbed over the divider to join me up front. She looked uneasy and gripped the carriage with white knuckles. She found her seat, but did not let go. Olivia remained quiet as we trotted down the road.

She drew in a breath and snarled, "What the fuck, Phil?"

My scrutiny bounced to her in surprise.

"What do you mean?"

"Joseph told me everything." Her glare caught me square on.

"Olivia, be sensible. That could be a lot of different things. What did he tell you specifically?"

"You expected me to believe the bullshit you fed me when I asked you why he recognized me? It all makes so much more sense now. You are disgusting! You are a creepy, SICK man!" she shrieked.

"Oh, you weren't crying before because you were worried about me."

"Why the fuck would I cry over you? Get a clue, Phil, you are a horrible creature. You lied to me and what's worse, you are probably having some perverse thoughts about me since, apparently, my face shares the likeness of your dead wife. Is that all I am to you? An image of someone who is dead?"

My response almost made it out, but she blazed on after sucking in a long breath.

"Unbelievable. The only reason you haven't killed me yet is because of your sick fantasy, right? Newsflash, Phil. She's dead. I'm here. No matter how hard you try and make me into your puppet, it is never going to happen. Cecelia is gone. FOREVER." She had more, but that crossed the line.

"You are talking to me like you are any better!" The words came out in a roar. "What about all your cryptic remarks and hushed conversations? It doesn't take a genius to read between the lines, Olivia. Your little books have painted such a nice picture of my kind, but I am a killer, a murderer and *I like it*. You can try and mold me into one of your fairytale princes, but it's not my responsibility to rescue you from your boring life. You stuck your nose where it doesn't belong and now you're mad because it isn't like your books!"

Our voices bounced around the neighborhood for a moment before it fell silent. The only sound was the horse's feet hitting the pavement. At some point, it had dropped to a walk while we were arguing. A torrent of thoughts churned in my mind, rolling over all the things that sounded better than continuing this exchange. Shove her over the side of the carriage? Drink her blood and be done with this nonsense? Any other nastiness remained locked behind the cage of my jaw, while the rest of me looked around for inspiration.

Sometimes you luck out.

The cop car was parked about two blocks down the street. An officer and her partner leaned against the hood, chatting calmly amongst themselves. With a plan forming, my eyes wandered off the road and looked around the carriage for something that could be used as a lasso. The owner of the carriage left a lead rope under the seat. It wasn't quite right, but it would do.

Provoked fingers grabbed Olivia and tossed her onto the back seat of the carriage. She bounced once before my hands took hold of her and maneuvered her onto her stomach. The lead rope wrapped around her wrists only twice, but it knotted tightly enough she couldn't wiggle out. The whole time she spewed profanities at me, but her efforts went ignored. We were about a half block away from the patrol car when the horse felt the connection of someone in the driver's seat again. He broke into a trot when the reins slapped against his sweaty rump. I placed two fingers in my mouth and whistled loudly before bailing out of the carriage. A lack of judgement rendered me in a heap when my left leg buckled on the landing.

Both of the cops turned at the same time to the sound of my whistle. The man pushed himself from the car first and ran into the road. The female followed and they stood about an arm's length apart. Their arms waved frantically as they both soothed the word, "Whoa!" The horse got the idea and slowed to a stop. The woman grabbed a hold of the reins and stroked its face, while the man clicked on his flashlight and shone it onto the carriage. Olivia cried out for help. The man found her almost immediately and climbed in to retrieve her. His light swept over the street behind the carriage and over my flattened body. He returned his focus to the bindings after barking an order to his partner.

I took this as my cue to leave.

Dried remnants of leaves floated to the ground after falling from my coat. A mature oak tree rose up to my left that held on to the few remaining vestiges of summer. Its thick trunk provided the perfect cover to slip into the gap between the two houses.

A street cat hissed at me from the alley and I hissed back, not in the mood for its nonsense. It jumped off the trashcan and skittered down a window well. Without a destination in mind, the alleys chose my direction. My only goal was to get as far away from that wretched human as possible. Good riddance. The weight of her lifted from my shoulders and my common sense started coming back to me.

The buildings attached to the alley were residential. All of them built in two to three stories, made of dirty, red brick, and occupied. More personal items decorated the surrounding space, like bicycles, planters, broken appliances. A couple strung wire to dry their clothes. The glow of their nightly routine escaped the curtained windows. Some houses had gone to sleep for the night, while others exuded life with light and sound. Someone's dog barked at me from a window.

The night welcomed me into its cold embrace. With nothing, or no one, to tell me where to go, my lopsided gate carried me on. The only constant was the residential neighborhoods that dictated my movements. The sounds of people living their lives distracted me from the more ominous thoughts in my mind.

The wretched phone buzzed in my pocket again. Jackie sent a message that simply asked for an update.

The phone creaked under the pressure of my grip until the screen blew out in a pop. Chunks of the device folded up like a fissure. Bits of the device started to fall to the ground when my hold loosened, becoming clear to me it was now useless in more than one way. I chucked it aside and continued my wandering.

A house emerged up ahead that had the sounds of a couple laughing together. Food sizzled in a pan, releasing a meaty smell infused with garlic and rosemary. Their backdoor wisely didn't open when the knob turned. However, they left a second-story window open. My fingers found the most minute deviations in the siding to pull myself up and slip into their bathroom. Darkness shadowed the upper floor and made moving from the bathroom to the bedroom easy. A narrow door led to some ancient-looking steps. Each layer looked like it could squeak under pressure, so each footfall treaded carefully. Pictures of various family members hung on the wall leading down. Some were old, some young, but all of them smiled.

At the bottom of the stairs was a living room big enough for a loveseat, a recliner, and a television. Various plants crowded the space, spilling out over shelves, encroaching on the couch, and creeping along the floor. Just behind an archway, the kitchen cozied around a man and woman busying themselves around the stove. The light from their room cast short shadows at my feet. Another round of laughter filled the space. I sat down on the couch and soaked in the normalcy of these people's lives. They chatted about their day, what they saw at work, and a funny video they saw.

Their plates clattered with the sound of their meal being dished up. The two sat, the chairs groaning under their weight as they scraped across the wood floor. The silverware clanged while they chatted. The aroma of their food drifted over to the couch and my mouth watered. Not because their food smelled so good, but that they were going to eventually come to me and the constraint on my hunger could be freed. Their conversation slowed and the silverware stopped making noise. My tongue dragged across my lips.

One of them walked into the living room without turning on the light, while the other stayed back and turned on the sink. He walked through the dark room and started up the stairs, completely unaware of the shadow that followed him. He walked over to the toilet and started to unzip his trousers.

He never saw me. I pushed him into the wall over the toilet and sunk my teeth into his neck. Euphoria gushed down my throat and warmth filled my stomach. The man slumped down as his heart slowed, yet there was so much blood left in him. A growl ripped out of me in frustration. He slid down the wall, over the toilet, and caught himself before he hit the floor. The back of his head remained pointed down and he never saw the figure jump back out the window.

My feet caught me easily when they touched back down on the pavement, landing as light as a feather. Mumbling profanities through gritted teeth didn't make me feel better, so I kicked their trashcan, and a cannonball of paper erupted from the force, floating down around me. Olivia invaded my thoughts and constricted my freedom. The stomping of my feet down the street would make it easy to track me, even for a human.

Our argument played on repeat in my head. The

woman got under my skin and said some horrible things, but did it anger me more that she found out the truth or what she said *was* the truth? Why did it matter to her, anyway? Her likeness to my wife saved her life, more than once. How could she possibly complain about being alive?

I continued wandering through the night with no direction in mind. That man's blood saturated my need for the moment, and my thoughts came more clearly. As the night progressed, my temper simmered down to the point that foolishness flushed my cheeks. Blood lust drove me to do something monstrous and if it wasn't for Olivia, that woman wouldn't have a husband.

Olivia. Had she not gone with the police, she could have just as easily been my next victim. Perhaps this was for the best. If anything could be said about the situation, her current company could, hopefully, keep her safe. One less thing to worry about.

Above everything else, Joseph needed to die. This game of cat and mouse grew tiresome and now it would be an even fight, one on one. John performed the grunt work while Joseph was more of the brains. Well, *all* of the brains. The two of us were more evenly matched, and I had a chance of making it out of this fight alive. Really, it boiled down to finding him and fighting him with a full stomach.

Without realizing it, my wandering took me to the cemetery. The black iron arch over the road gave the overgrown ivy a place to climb. Dewy grass bumped up against headstones as old as this country, yet not even as old as me. Then I spotted it; the site Olivia's friends had described. Instead of a headstone, the corpses were housed in a mausoleum. The stone building stood proudly among a spread of impressive gravestones. Carvings of gargoyles protected the corners of the slate roof. Morc ivy clung to the sides of veiled statues, molded into the walls. Wrought iron crossed a thick wooden door painted black.

The door swung open and the breeze stirred up swirls of dust and dead leaves. The familiar scent of the dead greeted me, but so did the faint remnants of the three women. On the altar at the far side of the room, stone hands held up melted candles, pooled with hardened wax that dribbled onto the rosary hanging below. Below the chiseled woman were three flowers. One was pink, another yellow, and one purple. A part of me wanted to see a white one among the bunch, but I knew better. The police held her God knows where, answering questions about how she ended up hobbled in the back of a runaway carriage.

The weight of everything left me slumped on the ground and the silence of the dead seeped into my soul. For hours, not a single muscle moved, an eye blinked, nor breath came in or out of my lungs. Lay me down next to one of the coffins and there wouldn't be a difference. My mind was an entirely different story. No matter how far it wandered from my current situation, it always went back to Olivia. She never should have been abandoned like that. Joseph knew what she meant to me when I didn't realize it myself. Otherwise, he would have never let her walk away like that. Bait.

My original plan always concluded with her ending up with the police to keep her safe, but now it felt like the wrong choice. Would the confines of a jailhouse be enough to deter Joseph from attacking her? He could be at the jail, hurting her, while my dumbass sat here feeling sorry for itself. Anxiety spurred me out of my place among the dead. Time escaped me and the bright pinks and purples of morning lit up the eastern horizon. The streetlights took their turns switching off.

My concern for finding Olivia ran so deep, even the air fooled me into thinking her scent lingered. Her rosiness drifted through the cemetery almost as if someone had laid down a fresh bouquet. If only it were undeniably her. Then again, maybe it was. Sucking in another, deeper breath brought in a stronger wave of her flowery aroma. A familiar silhouette walked toward me, holding a single white rose close to her chest.

"Olivia!"

She looked up to see me jogging over to her. Without thinking, my arms wrapped around her and pulled her into an embrace. She settled just under my chin and her sweet, rosy smell filled my soul. Relief flooded over me and left my limbs feeling like they floated. She was here and unhurt. Within the confines of my arms, Olivia made me whole. She remained rigid however, making me think the feelings weren't reciprocated, so my hold slackened, and she stepped back. Afraid that she'd disappear again, my hand slid down her arms and intertwined with her fingers. As gently, but firmly, as possible, my eyes burned into her. She looked down at our hands before reluctantly lifting her eyes to meet mine.

"Olivia, I am so sorry. All of this is my fault, and my actions were selfish. Any one of these bad things that have happened to you was because of me and I could have walked away to keep you safe, but that meant letting you go. I promise, once all of this is over, if you never want to see me again, you won't."

She did not respond right away as she chewed on my words, but her eyes softened the longer she stood there under my gaze. Finally, she sighed and dropped her stare.

"I can't stand here and act like you are totally at fault. This whole situation is so fucked up. Neither of us are innocent by a long shot, but you hurt me, Phil. What you said back at the carriage was a direct attack on my personality, and I'm still pissed at you. Yet, I apologize for making you out to be something, *someone*, you are not and holding you to unrealistic standards. Also, you didn't deserve to be called all those nasty things back there. You're not a monster."

She finished by leaning forward and letting go of my hand so she could wrap herself around my midsection. My hands settled on her lower back and head, gently drawing her closer to me. After a moment, Olivia murmured, "I hoped you'd be here."

Olivia pulled back and looked up at me. "Oh, we aren't supposed to be seen together. You know, legally speaking."

"We have some catching up to do. Let's go chat in the mausoleum."

"You found it!" she said as we walked.

"Yes, and you will be pleased to know there are three fresh flowers there too."

"Good. Too bad they got involved, though. It could have ended very badly for them."

"Did you ever let them know you are all right?"

"I texted them back and also told them to go home, but you should have seen that. Where is your phone, Phil?"

"It broke."

"Right. Well, guess they didn't design these phones to withstand supernatural fights."

"Hmm, suppose not, or being gripped too tight."

Begging for just a few more minutes of peace, the door of the mausoleum closed behind Olivia. No reason to give ourselves away. She walked over to the flowers and placed hers on top. With the bouquet complete, she took a seat.

"John is dead." My voice reverberated coldly in the small space.

"What! What happened?"

"There was a box in the basement surrounded by dead people. It looked like a kiln of sorts, but the size of a coffin. A pyre, maybe?"

"You cremated him?" She laughed.

"Well, no. He didn't burn as much as blow up. That explosion could have just as easily killed me too."

"Joseph and I saw it from outside. It blew out some windows on the bottom story. Black smoke poured out almost immediately. By that point, Joseph had me by the wrist, leading me away."

"What did he say to you? John found me in the hospital and wouldn't let me leave."

"He told me about Cecelia. I already knew a lot of it, but he told me that we looked practically identical in appearance and that you were too much of a coward to let me, and her, go. He said you'd end up imprisoning me just to have a living memorial to your wife."

My gaze shied away from hers. The truth hurt too much to make eye contact. Just when the awkwardness forced me to apologize again, Olivia filled the void.

"On the bright side, the police know everything." She smirked.

"What do you mean by 'everything'?" A single eyebrow raised.

"Not everything, of course. Your secret is safe with me. All they know is that some guy pretending to be Miles saw me getting into a cab and, kidnapped me, forced me to get some supplies from the clothing store, took me back home to unspeakable things to me, where a fight broke out, I cut him with a knife, which would explain all the blood, and ran out. Unfortunately, he caught up to me, tried to get away in the carriage, but when he saw the cops, panicked, and left me there."

"That story has more holes than a fishing net."

"Well, they believed me. Enough to let me go, anyway. The bad news is, they showed me a picture that is clearly you. Not sure how to explain that one away," she continued.

It took a moment for a possible solution to come to me before remembering what happened just a few hours ago. "In the hospital, I convinced the officers that John committed the murder, at least, enough to point their guns at him. Doing it once turned out to be easy enough. We just need to find someone else to frame."

Olivia did not answer, she just pointed at her face.

"No, not you."

She clicked her tongue at me in frustration and said, "Phil, they have your face on file!"

"Hmm." The tomb went quiet when both of us slipped back into thought.

"Ever heard the saying about killing two birds with one stone?" she asked.

"So, what? Frame Joseph? Could work. Seriously though, Olivia, one thing at a time. The police thing is more of an annoyance than anything. My priority right now is to get rid of Joseph. He must die. With John gone, there is a good chance I can do it.

"Are you going to bake him too?" she mused.

"He isn't dumb enough to make the same mistake as John. Nonetheless, it will have to be fire." I shrugged. "Which puts me in danger, too."

"You need fire, but it has to be controlled in a way that keeps you safe while Joseph burns." She stared up at the ceiling with eyes twinkling in thought, then a smile spread across her face. "I have an idea, but we'll have to lure him there."

Her thoughts crossed her soft features without a single word. Olivia's heart quickened, and yet, she kept the idea to herself.

"Care to share your plan, or?"

Instead of answering, she pulled out her phone and her fingers drummed quickly on the screen. I peeked over the edge of the phone, but she raised it.

"The less you know, the safer we will all be," she muttered, distracted by her typing.

"We? Didn't you just say it was too dangerous for your friends?"

"Cell phone," she answered, as if that meant anything.

My eyebrows furrowed. After a moment more of typing, she hopped up and said, "Let's go!"

She was jogging by the time she got outside of the stone building. Long strides ate up the ground just to keep up.

"Olivia, wait! Where are you going?"

"My idea is going to need some supplies," she huffed.

A nervous survey revealed we were the only ones

around. Mature trees blanketed the cemetery, blotting out large chunks of the morning sun, but my path still zigzagged behind her, hopping from one shadow to the next. Olivia was on a mission, stopping only to hail a cab. As one of the yellow cars pulled up, she turned to me and asked, "Do you trust me?"

"Olivia. What a silly question. Yes, of course. Now, what is this about?" My answer came from the edge of the last shadow.

"I am going to go and get some supplies, alone," she said.

"Absolutely not. You are not leaving my sight again."

"That doesn't sound like you trust me," she observed.

"It isn't a matter of trust. It is a matter of being dumb." I raked a hand through my hair, frustrated.

"Fine, I'm dumb, but in order for this plan to work, you need to do something without me, too," she added.

The word came out snippy. "What?"

"Now listen here, smarty pants. Joseph believes he turned me against you, since the last thing I said to him was, 'He's dead to me.' Hopefully, he still thinks that is true. So logically, he is looking for you and only you."

My jaw relaxed, acknowledging that her point had some merit.

"So, we need Joseph to find you. The best way to accomplish that is by laying down a scent trail. Do you know where the performing arts center is downtown?"

"Yes…"

"Good. Meet me there tonight around seven o'clock," she said as she sprung into the cab.

"I don't like this."

259

"Trust me." She smiled.

The car drove off and my dumfounded stare watched her for several blocks. This woman was going to kill me if Joseph didn't get to me first.

Chapter 12

I stood in the cemetery's entrance for a few moments, not knowing what to do. Olivia's cab melted into the mass of other cars. In less than a minute, she disappeared completely. It crossed my mind to follow her, but inevitably, she was right. Trust came from somewhere and letting her go on this task probably didn't come with much danger. Probably. It would have been nice if she gave me a little more insight into her plan, however. Knowing her, this grand idea could very well be something idiotic, and it would have been nice to have a say in it if she'd lost her mind.

Olivia wanted me to create a scent trail that led downtown. That would be easy enough. All I had to do was circle the city in a web that led to the performing arts center. It would be time consuming, but it would ensure that he'd pick up on my scent. The thought of Joseph possibly showing up at any moment during this exercise made me uncomfortable. Then again, it didn't matter to me where we fought. The next time that man crosses my path will be his last and Olivia would be far away from the conflict. It would make it easier to concentrate without her around, anyway.

I pulled up on my collar and set off down the street at a reinvigorated pace. The bottom of my jacket flapped in the breeze. My hands curled into tight fists, hidden deep in my pockets. A thin wall of clouds affected the sun's intensity, casting a morose veil on the city. I kept to the shadows cast by the buildings, wary of the sunlight that still stung any exposed skin.

My first lap traveled around the city limits, tackling one island at a time. Staten Island, then Brooklyn, then Manhattan. Each lap, the threads tightened, but never touched the performance center. All the paths needed to lead to one place, and it would be vain for him to follow a trail all night. Throughout the day, a part of me kept an eye out for Joseph, glancing at each face for his ugly mug. Less annoying, but worth consideration, were the police. My closest interaction happened when rounding a corner. They headed in the opposite direction, and we almost bumped into one another. Our eyes met and held for a breath until one of the men said, "'Scuse me, Should've been looking forward!"

"No problem. Cheers." My eyes dropped as we brushed by each other.

Several other police crossed my path, and they didn't seem to recognize me, or care. Yet, it only made me feel slightly better. All it would take is one of them to put two and two together. Walking down the street, under the sun, brought out feelings of paranoia and it made me twitchy. Another layer of protection seemed necessary to reduce the chances of being recognized. The purveyor of my solution owned a cart on the side of the road with stacks of hats. He had everything from informal looking caps to straw western wear, fedoras and bowlers, to some sort of open topped thing printed with cartoony graphics. Over all these choices, my heart went for old trusty. The shopkeeper chatted with another customer and my theft went unnoticed. Sticky fingers grabbed a black flat cap and put it on my head before he could question if it came from his store. In the throngs of people walking by, no one said a thing. I slipped into the increased discretion of my hat and continued on with my journey.

The sun slowly made its way across the sky, shifting the shadows from one side of the road to the other. My morning started by following the streets on the eastern side, but now the western side remained cloaked. By the time the sun dipped under the horizon, all of my threads should have tied neatly together and led Joseph directly to us. Olivia wouldn't have to wait long at this rate, but there was a lot of city left to cover and my stride lengthened.

The pressure to get sustenance became more prevalent. After all, it directly correlated with my strength and Joseph could kick my ass on a normal day. Every bit helped, but too much would be better than not enough. Thanks to Olivia and modern societal restraints, my choices narrowed down to something victimless, and this led to an alley where people couldn't see me. They weren't hard to catch, but it would take quite a few to feel anything at all.

When complaining about not feeling at home, the feeling didn't include succumbing to the method some of London's vampires used to sustain themselves, but here I stood, listening for the scurrying of rats. They lingered at the edges of trash bins and sewer drains. The first victim smelled like mold, but my fangs bit into it regardless, letting the nugget of fulfillment outweigh the disgust at having to pick out a bug from my tooth. The second one tasted slightly better, having plucked it from a puddle, but the grit of dirt on its fur rubbed against my lips. The hunt continued, a flurry of snapping jaws and squeaks, until at least a dozen rats had been consumed. My new, lowered standards horrified me, but the energy gained from them outweighed my pride.

The clouds never broke and when the sun popped out from behind them, on the horizon, it took me off guard. Rays of warmth blanketed the buildings in a golden glow. Harlem extended out in front of me and the timing caused a shiver of panic. I took off at a hasty jog since not all the threads were connected and Joseph needed a seamless path to the correct location. At this rate, our rendezvous would happen around seven fifteen or even half past. More people filled the streets with the setting of the sun and it slowed my progress. More than one person spun because we bumped shoulders. Angry shouts accompanied the hits, but they didn't get an acknowledgement.

Streetlights started popping on when I turned the corner to the performing arts center. Surprise hitched my step at the sheer amount of people heading toward the venue as well. It looked like a flood of black water flowing to the lowest point. Splashes of red and white broke up the otherwise solid sea of dark clothing. My head barely stayed above the crowd after throwing myself into the stream, sweeping me toward the front of the building. At this rate, it would be impossible for Olivia to spot me.

Luckily, she waited on the outskirts of the main entrance. Her head swiveled over the tentacles of descending people. Like swimming upstream, it took twice as long to undo my progress, even after cutting across instead of facing the torrent straight on. The building created a pocket free of the crowd and led me directly to her. Olivia faced away, on tiptoes, engrossed in her search and didn't hear me approach. A brown paper bag hung from one hand and two slips of paper in the other.

"Olivia."

Despite the forewarning, she still jumped and turned skittishly toward me. The anxiety etched on her face melted as soon as she recognized who had called her name.

"You made it!" She lunged at me.

Her arms wrapped around my midsection and the paper bag crinkled against my backside.

"Are you okay?"

"It's just good to see you. After we parted, I wondered if leaving you like that was the best idea," she replied.

"Glad we agree." A small smile tugged at the corner of my mouth.

She pulled herself away from me and offered a smile. "How'd your day go?"

My eyes drifted to the heads bobbing next to us. "As well as it could. Surely, he'll catch my scent."

"Good!"

"Are you going to tell me what this is all about now?"

"Not quite yet, but I have a present for you." She held up the bag.

A part of me hoped it was more blood, but their usual smell didn't waft from the container. However, another recognizable scent gave away the surprise. My fingers wrapped around a pullover shirt and trousers, dyed as black as the pit of night.

"I figured you'd want to blend in. Plus, you *still*

have blood on your shirt. It's seriously doubtful they will let you in looking like that." She wrinkled her nose.

Her cheeks blushed after collecting my grateful smirk. Just around the corner, the roof's overhang created a dark alcove—perfect for changing in private. Olivia didn't have time to finish her breath before swapping out my clothes. Once again, the shirt hugged my chest a little too tight and the pants stretched across my thighs, but it worked. The fit didn't interfere with my movement when my evening, inevitably, would come down to a physical confrontation. I shimmied back into my coat and felt for the gold watch that wasn't there. None of this would have happened if Cecelia was still here, and my thoughts turned inward to ask for her forgiveness before stepping out of the shadow.

Olivia's breath caught and it came out in a cough. My hand ran nervously through my hair while taking my place next to her again.

"We aren't going to go in with all these people, right?"

"That is precisely what we mean to do," she said.

"I knew this was going to be idiotic."

To make myself clearer, she needed the full brunt of this reality. "Olivia." She looked up at me. To emphasize the point in case she forgot, my lips uncovered two fangs while my index finger made sure she didn't miss the abnormality. "Vampires! There is a massive amount of people in there who could, one, get hurt, and two, expose us!"

"Don't you think Joseph knows that too?"

"Olivia, just no."

"Phil." She grabbed my hand.

Our eyes locked while she pouted. "Will you at least try? If anything, you set the trap to lead him here. We can lead him out the back and finish him off somewhere else."

"You keep using the word 'we' like I am going to let you get involved in this."

"You keep assuming that it is your responsibility to keep me alive. I chose this, remember?" she snapped back.

This woman was exhausting.

"Fine." She smirked with success and started dragging me by the hand toward the entrance.

The crowd thinned out considerably. The only stragglers were the smokers and the scalpers. Olivia walked up to the woman standing at the entrance and held out the two slips of paper. She scanned the bottom of each ticket and waved us through. We passed under a low, stone arch and into the thick of the chaos.

People stood in lines around food and beer stands, while others crowded around a merchandise booth. The outside of the building had been so boring. Flat, beige bricks stacked in rows to form the walls, but the inside presented ornately decorated fabrics with velvet accents and gold-plated scrolls. No doubt this place hosted theater and orchestral performances, but the class of people that filled the space could only be described as the delinquents of society. Their black clothing alone absorbed most of the already dim light in the area.

To think, we were only standing in the greeting hall. The main attraction waited behind a series of arches blocked off by velvet curtains. The fabric vibrated in beat with the sound pounding out from behind them, barely containing the immense noise coming from inside the room. It must have been music, but unlike anything from my time. The only way to describe it was 'heavy'.

We went further into the venue, looking from the printing on the ticket to the identifying signs propped up on the floor. She changed directions when she saw 'Standing section'. The man perched by this entrance beckoned Olivia with his hand and she gave him the tickets. He looked at them only long enough to see that they correlated to the correct section before handing them back. He pulled back the velvet curtain. The burden carried by that little fabric door was impressive. Without it, everything hit me at once, snuffing out the processing part of my brain.

Fog lurked heavy in the air so thick, for a moment it felt like walking outside, back home in London, on a crisp, fall morning. The mist funneled into the short, narrow hallway that led to the main seating area. Olivia walked through the vaporous screen, and when we broke through, my feet froze in awe. We were in a stadium where the upper bowl had seats focused toward a main stage. Every single chair held a black clad patron standing up while pounding their fist in rhythm.

We stood at the top of a staircase that split through the sea of seats and led to a space that someone cleared for people to enjoy the show while standing up. At the far end of it all sat the stage, and the band was in the middle of their performance. The main lights had been turned off, but the space danced with varying sized beams of color in sync with the music. They flared up in red, before spiraling in white, only to repeat the pattern soon after. The mist prismed perfectly to capture the beams, every once in a while the color passed over my chest.

The room was a cauldron of smells. Hints of beer, fog, body odor, soap, cigarettes, and just about every kind of perfume man invented lingered in the room under the distinct smell of smoke. When the song hit its chorus, it became abundantly clear why.

From multiple sources, placed strategically across the stage, flames shot out of nozzles so high, they licked the rafters far above our heads. The room lit up with the blaze momentarily, before the flames died back, and the process repeated. The warmth from the pyrotechnics could be felt from our spot on top of the stairs. Between the display from the stage and the heat of the moment, it felt like we found a piece of hell on earth.

I leaned over to Olivia's ear and asked, "When you thought of something that produced fire, *this* is what you thought of? How is this supposed to help?"

Her eyes searched for an answer and finally, she responded, "Well, I figured you could come up with the rest."

A sharp breath sucked in through my brazen smile. Idiotic.

"Did you leave a ticket up front for Joseph so he could at least get in and enjoy the show too?"

It was assuredly time for Plan B. I grabbed Olivia's hand and pulled her down the steps with me. Hopefully, the pandemonium would cover our scent. At the bottom, we met a wall of people unwilling to give up their hard-earned position on the floor. A sliver of space existed between a couple big enough to squeeze through, but after an attempt at passing, the man turned to glare at me. No matter, I shoved harder and yanked

Olivia into the new space. In the same manner, we weaved our way through the crowd.

Another exit allowed people to leave closer to the stage, providing a different route than the one we used to get in. With luck, it would loop back to where we originally entered so we could get out of the crowded space. Between the gyrating bodies and their unwillingness to make space for us, my grip on Olivia remained tighter than was probably necessary. Losing her in this crowd would spell disaster. Every so often, my attention shifted backwards to make sure Joseph didn't stand at the top of the stairs.

We were near the middle of the standing section when it unexpectedly opened up. The group formed a wide berth of around twenty or so individuals. One of them ran full speed into me and bounced off. He thudded to the floor and, without a second glance, several people hauled him to his feet and threw him back into the fray. The group shoved and rammed each other like rutting animals. Even though there was more room to go through the middle of this mess, it would be best to go around it for Olivia's sake.

We made it to the edge of the circle when her hand slipped from mine. Turning to see where she went, a pair of hands shoved me so hard, I staggered backwards and tripped over someone's foot. Black pants bombarded me, kicking and running from the confines of their man-made circle. Multiple sets of hands found their way to my jacket and pulled me upright. The strike left me turned around and having no idea where Olivia initially let go.

People closed in, bumping into my shoulders, while trying to knock me off balance. They mostly bounced off, but my patience grew thinner the longer Olivia remained out of sight. Their futile attempts at trying to move me made me realize whoever shoved me down was not human. Panic swelled in my heart.

Attempting to follow her trail would be futile. Her scent blended smoothly with all the other people in the room, forcing me to watch instead. Every once in a while, people's faces would illuminate with the fire from the stage. With one especially bright display, the blonde tips of Olivia's hair retreated just out of view from one of the exits.

One guy jumped up and down next to me, using my coat as a point of leverage to help boost his height. With a gentle push to remove him, he pinballed into several others. No one noticed. However, people *did* notice when I stopped being nice. Like the horse in Times Square, people bounced off my chest and shoulders while barreling in a straight line to the exit until the crowd dwindled. A trail of cursing followed my tracks. The stairs passed two at a time and once at the top, the flinging of the velvet curtain caught the usher off guard, and he skittered sideways.

The air hung so much different outside of the main bowl. The room hoarded most of the show's smoke, but fewer people meant less of their stink to crowd my senses. Individual smells were easier to pick out and Olivia's came to me almost immediately. And Joseph's. A brooding growl rumbled deep in my chest while setting off after their trail.

Their scent followed the corridor that led to the back of the stage. They went through a double door where chunks of the handle littered the floor. Surprisingly, no one guarded the vulnerable gateway between the fans and the performers, prompting me to think something happened to them and being glad for it since it meant less people to deal with. The door swung outward and invited me in. On the other side, the corridor continued with much more spartan decorations that catered toward utility instead of ambiance. Black equipment boxes lined the walls, and snakes of cables ran along the floor in unison. A few stagehands occupied the space, lost in their own tasks, and oblivious to the stranger marching through. Only one man kept an inquisitive eye on me. Olivia's scent permeated the room, but even with my expeditious progress, a strong trail didn't reveal itself, leaving me walking in a circle.

His stare continued until he inevitably raised his head to get a better look at me. My words cut off whatever comment he breathed in to make. "You didn't see a man with a young woman go through here, did you?"

"Yeah, I did."

"Which way did they go?"

"What's it to you?"

I pulled myself up taller and set my jaw. It took one step forward before the man folded.

"Dude, chill. He said the girl was trespassing and asked for the exit."

"And which way is that?"

He pointed over my shoulder, toward a little green sign. The tail of my coat whipped around with the new information. His story checked out, and the trail followed the exit signs. The promise of fresh air lingered as I pressed down the metal bar and pushed the doors open, swirling in the smoke-laden atmosphere with the crispness of night. I stopped though, since Olivia's trail stopped too. They did not go outside. The door clicked shut and my steps retreated angrily. Hastiness had blinded me.

A dark stairwell swallowed Joseph's trail. At the bottom, the space was even more industrial, with hydraulics, pipes, and cables woven throughout. Steps to the stage protruded into the small space and an array of props sat waiting on tables situated near the opening, waiting for their time to be used in the show. The ceiling rattled and thudded in time with the pounding of the performance. Sound penetrated so hard into my chest, it felt like my heart restarted and beat in rhythm to the music.

The clattering of a metal pipe falling to the floor narrowed my focus and Olivia's eyes flashed in the dimly lit space.

"JOSEPH!"

He weaved his way through the jungle of pipes on the far side of the stage while Olivia struggled to keep her feet under her. I beelined it for the prop table and grabbed a handful of tools from a box. The biggest thing in my hand was a wrench and I flung it with all my strength. It whistled in the air and nailed Joseph in the back of the knee. He stumbled, taking Olivia down with him. It bought me a few seconds to charge him, but he recovered too quickly and pulled his captive in front of him.

"It would be a bad idea to come any closer, Phil."

His hand clamped around Olivia's neck, squeezing so tightly that her skin wrinkled under his fingers. Tears streamed down her cheeks and her lips pulled down into a frown.

"Let her go, Joseph. She has nothing to do with this."

"Doesn't she, though? Clearly you care for her. How could you not?" He stroked her hair. "Sweet Cecelia reborn. Quite frankly, it's kinda sick. There are no second chances in life. She's dead, Phil, and your reckoning is coming."

He backed up. Part of me tried to anticipate his next move, while the other searched for a way to get Olivia away from him.

"What if I give myself up?"

"After all this? No, that can't be true. You're lying, Phil." He laughed.

"Gentleman's promise. Please, just don't hurt the woman."

"There's an idea. A terrible one, but an idea. I do wonder. Will you look as broken when this girl dies as you did when Cecelia passed?" he readjusted his grip on her throat.

"Wait!"

He raised his eyebrows and said, "Yes?"

"I'll do anything—just let her go." My voice pitched higher in a desperate, pleading attempt.

An evil grin spread across his grotesque face. "Anything?"

Understanding flashed between us and the words came out fast.

"Not that."

"That is my offer. Either way, she dies. It is up to you, Phillip!"

Anxiety stroked my feet as my weight shifted uncomfortably. A rumble deep in my chest formed around a torrent of thoughts. There must be another solution, but nothing came to me. The lumpy wad of tools shifted in my hand, weighing out if any of them could incapacitate him. After throwing the wrench, a couple pencils and a screwdriver remained. If any of them made it past Olivia, the damage done to Joseph would be comparable to a mosquito bite in terms of all the damage it would cause. The coward stood almost entirely behind her, and the chances of harming her weren't worth the risk.

"Tick, tock."

"Fine!"

"Fine, what?" A wicked grin spread across his face, revealing the predator beneath.

"I'll do it."

Joseph perked up at my revolution and moved his hand around so that he held Olivia by the back of the neck. She stiffened and her body went as straight as a board, sniffling.

"Do what?" She shivered.

"Don't worry, darling. It won't hurt for long," teased Joseph.

My answer came out quiet, hardly loud enough for a human to hear, let alone over the music. "He wants me to turn you, Olivia."

"Oh," she breathed. "All right. It'll be okay, Phil."

I doubted her sincerity, since she didn't sound convinced herself. Her shaky reply crippled me, knowing she didn't fully understand what she agreed to. The fissure of my grief cracked open again and everything that led up to this moment oozed out.

The only sentiment I could offer her was, "You don't deserve this." Sharp eyes challenged Joseph, and he reacted by winking. "Give her over so we can get this over with."

He shook his head and answered, "Not a chance. You'll just run away again. You can do it with an audience."

My face folded into a pensive scowl as I reluctantly made my way over to them, but Olivia squeaked when Joseph tightened his grip on the back of her neck, stopping me.

"How do you expect me to turn her with you hovering so close? That would put me in a vulnerable position where you could just rip my head off."

"Gentleman's promise." He grinned.

"Promise what?"

"That I won't attack you until you've given Olivia all of your blood."

"Don't be daft, Joseph. You know how weak that will make me."

He shrugged. "Fair is fair, now that you took away my muscle."

"Scared of being beaten by someone weaker than you?"

"Well, I'm not stupid."

"Arguable."

"You're stalling, Phillip."

"Not really, just thinking…"

"That isn't a good look for you."

"Why? Haven't you ever tried it?"

"Last chance to get over here or I will break her neck."

Olivia whimpered with her eyes closed, sending a fresh streak of tears down her cheeks.

"Fine! Fine."

Joseph held Olivia only a few meters away and it

took a couple of steps to close the gap before a chest's width separated us. Her uneasy breath tickled my flesh while the sadistic glint in Joseph's steely stare caught the dim light behind her. Olivia's eyes remained closed. I leaned in with painstaking slowness, careful not to alarm her further, letting my cool breath graze her skin—a ghostly touch that raised a trail of goosebumps from her collarbone to her wrists. My lips brushed her ear and I whispered, "I'm so sorry."

My left hand struck out like a snake with the screwdriver. It met its mark, piercing Joseph's hand and sticking out like a porcupine quill. A dribble of blood leaked from the tip where it went all the way through and trickled down onto the back of Olivia's shirt. He did not, however, let go. He readjusted his grip and pulled her closer to his chest, wrapping his free arm around her and grabbing the opposite shoulder.

"You idiot, you thought that was going to make me let go?" He laughed.

"No, I didn't."

It took him longer to notice little drops of blood that ran down his forearm. They sprung from a scratch along Olivia's cheekbone. The stream followed her jawline and fell from her chin. His demeanor changed instantly. His eyes turned black and he sunk his teeth into her shoulder. Her scream echoed through the space.

I leaped onto them, sending all of us tumbling to the ground. Joseph landed in front of me, firmly attached to Olivia. Scrambling to get to him, my fingers probed the edges of his mouth and when they got enough purchase on his teeth, started pulling in opposite directions, forcing his teeth open. A cracking sound came from his jaw and he shifted his demeanor.

Joseph released Olivia and started clawing behind him with both hands.

Joseph tried to bite down and instead of risking getting my fingers bitten off, I let go. He flipped over like a cat and jumped on top of me. He straddled my midsection while trying to get a hold of my neck, but my hands slapped him away. All the while, Olivia lay in a heap on the floor. She hadn't moved since Joseph dropped her and the music made it impossible to hear if she had a heartbeat or not. Playing defensive grew irksome, so Joseph got a right hook squarely in the jaw. He flopped over like a fish, freeing me to crawl over to Olivia.

Her name bellowed from my mouth and she twitched, but Joseph hooked my leg and flung me like a doll. A support beam caught the full brunt of my weight. Though it didn't collapse, it stopped me from flying any further and deposited my bulk onto one of the tables. Props bounced in protest and settled in the nook where their resting spot folded in half. Furious hands fumbled around the pile for anything to throw at Joseph. Unconventional, but useful, a stack of goggles hurled toward Joseph one at a time while he walked over, swatting them away like bugs. The last one left my hand, so my legs curled under me in anticipation of searching for something more promising. However, Joseph was already on me, swinging like a boxer.

His punches whizzed through the air before a miscalculation ended up with me taking a direct hit across the face. Stars danced in my eyes, while staggering backwards. He then sucker punched me in the stomach and my body folded in on itself. I reached up and got a fistful of his shirt. Before he could punch me again, my weight shifted so that he spun around and thudded into one of the supports, face first. He collapsed to the ground with an "oof." This gained me enough time to stagger toward Olivia, who remained prone on the floor. Her hand dozily inspected her bloodied cheek.

Joseph grabbed the back of my coat and yanked hard. My foot stumbled over something on the ground and landed me on my back. Watching from the tops of my eye sockets, Joseph grinned as he stepped toward me with something long and straight in his hand. The thing was about his same height, but he snapped it in half, exposing a jagged edge. He held it like a javelin over his shoulder. His slog continued until he loomed over me, pulling back his arm, when my shiny black shoe kicked up and landed square in his balls. The weapon dropped and he clutched himself, bent over in half.

Olivia lay on her back when my hand gently touched her chest. Her heart beat beneath my palm, steady, but frail. I shrugged out of my jacket, then my shirt, and wadded up the softer fabric against the wound at the crook of her neck. The bleeding slowed, but stubbornly refused to stop.

"It's okay," she said.

"I'm going to get you out of here."

"Look out!"

Her warning gave me enough time to flinch and instead of going straight through my chest, the jagged metal pierced through my shoulder and sparked against the floor next to Olivia's head. Blood coiled down the shaft and dripped onto the floor. He pulled it out just as fast and flexed to try again.

The back of my hand landed straight on Joseph's cheek. He recoiled but remained on his feet. Instead of going for another cheap shot, all of my body weight went into lunging onto him, teeth first. They latched onto his throat and sweet blood poured into my mouth. Instantaneously, I realized why it seemed so familiar. Olivia's blood coursed through his veins and the very thought sent me into a fury.

He stumbled back, but only made it two steps or so before he caught his balance on one of the support beams. With his body pressed up against the structure, he stabbed me with the end of the stick until it grew dull. When it no longer worked, he dropped it and started using his fingers to claw at my midsection. As hard as he tried to get me to let go, my effort equaled his, by trying to chew his head off. Without letting go, my hand caught hold of one of his and stretched it away from us. His other hand continued to try and disembowel me.

We twirled, we dipped, we swung, yet neither of us could get the upper hand, until my leg caught on the stairs to the stage. We toppled over, landing against the steps. One of the edges landed directly on a stab wound and the pain twitched through my body. My grip loosened on Joseph and he pulled away. He scampered up the steps and out of view.

I cursed and flipped over to my feet.

A row of lights shined directly into my face that robbed me of my sight and even if one hand managed to block some of the rays, a dozen others filled its void. Stumbling further on stage didn't ease the assault and neither did turning away from the crowd; it only opened up the overhead projections to invade. Though disorienting, I needed to press on. Joseph had to be up here somewhere and surely, he wasn't immune to the abuse either. My body tucked into a crouch, lowering to a place the lights didn't reach, and saw Joseph cowering behind the man on the drums. A growl rumbled in my chest, alerting him to my intentions. He scooted out from behind his hiding spot and ran in front of the performers. He didn't make it to the stairs before he got tackled. We crashed onto the metal grate flooring to the resounding approval of the crowd. They screamed in excitement.

He used the gaps in the floor to help pull himself along while my fingers grappled with his midsection. Joseph wormed his way out from under me and maneuvered his shoe so that it sat firmly on my cheek. He pushed and despite the strong hold around his waist, he pushed me off enough to get out of my grasp and dashed for the safety of the basement.

The lead singer stood next to me as I stood up. He held what looked like a wide-barreled gun, except a large tube connected to the end that wound around his waist and ended at the bottom of a square, metal backpack. The man glimmered with sweat from head to torso. His heavy-duty pants and gloves surely didn't help either. He lost his weapon so fast; he didn't give up a fight when it was ripped from his hands. My eyes scanned the gun to see how it functioned. It had a grip and a trigger, which is all I needed to know. Securely settled, my index finger squeezed. A waterfall of flame came out of the end and doused the stage in fire, consuming Joseph in a ball of red and black smoke. The audience roared behind me.

After several seconds, my finger let go of the

trigger and the torch quieted down. Joseph no longer stood in the throngs of the flame or anywhere on the stage for that matter. The confused singer wrenched his weapon back, liberating me to run back down the stairs. The effects of the flamethrower seasoned the air, but pinpointing which direction Joseph had gone proved troublesome. A scraping noise betrayed his location. He slowly crawled along the floor in the direction of the original exit and nowhere near Olivia. Without the urgency, my stride slowed too. My shadow loomed over him for a moment before my foot pressed into his calf. Flesh and bone crunched under the weight, pushing a groan out through his blistered mouth. With his clothing charred and black against his skin, bits of it had broken apart and curled under the heat, making it impossible to see where the fabric ended, and his skin began. Joseph was already turning to ash.

"It didn't have to be like this, Joseph. You used to be my friend, and we could have worked this out."

He kept dragging himself forward, refusing to give in, his movements slow as he clawed at the ground.

"Your dad is going to hate me even more after this."

My foot stepped off him so that we could meet eyes one last time. Crouched next to him, he looked up at me with a face wrinkled in disbelief and laced with hatred. "I really am sorry about what happened to your sister, my wife. If it is any last consolation, I know it is my fault."

He opened his mouth to argue, but the action caused his cheeks to flake and nothing but a swirl of ash interrupted the otherwise still air. Joseph's eyes lost their focus as they dulled over. He stopped moving altogether and started to crumble under his own weight. The substance of his body dissolved into his clothes and remained in the general shape of what it used to be. Joseph was no longer recognizable, figuratively, or physically.

Looking at his charred corpse sprawled out on the floor gave me a brilliant idea. The wallet that accompanied me from the beginning slipped out of my back pocket. I tossed it close enough that the police would see it and said, "Goodbye, Miles."

Oliva laid motionless with her limbs pulled up into a loose ball. Crouching next to her allowed me to get my ear against her chest and under it, her heart beat slow, but strong. Whines accompanied every breath. Her eyes fluttered, but it didn't convince me that she was entirely lucid. Even shuffling her around so that her body leaned against mine didn't startle her into a more alert state of mind. Olivia's head lolled against me.

"It's okay, I'm here. You're safe now." The gentle sweep of my fingers moved her blood-soaked hair out of her face.

She blinked into a more alert consciousness and her eyes searched for something to focus on, yet she didn't try to speak. I pulled back the makeshift bandage at her neck and saw little blood had come out. Perhaps her body naturally clotted the wound to stop it from bleeding anymore, but deep down, it terrified me that Joseph nearly drained her. An idea suddenly came to me like getting slapped in the face. Acting on it would mean facing the one demon that haunted my every move, my every choice and once again, resulted in life or death. Thanks to my bite on Joseph, Olivia's blood churned inside of me poisoned with eternal life. If it were returned to her, the transformation process would begin. Then again, the amount was so little, it might not be enough. She could also die from her heart giving out from doing nothing. Left with an impossible choice, my mind went back and forth, running through all the worst-case scenarios, until one remained.

"Not today."

My arms scooped her off the ground and her body settled into mine. The exit seemed so much closer now that the anticipation of violence no longer lurked around the corner. We breezed up the stairs and once at the top, the same stagehands lingered, buzzing about the pause in the show. The sassy man who provided directions from earlier looked up at us wide-eyed. His alarm shifted down to the unconscious woman draped in my arms, held by a shirtless man covered in stab wounds and blood.

"Help her, please. That man tried to hurt her."

He punched a three-digit number into his cellphone and a minute later, a medical professional appeared. This new man instructed me to lay Olivia on the ground while he got to work. She remained conscious, but barely. The paramedic lifted the soggy shirt from her neck, wafting a fresh plume of her life force up into my nose, reassuring me that this life she lived wasn't done with her yet. These people would take care of her and keep her safe. After all, Joseph was dead, John too. The thought hit me like a train. The pent-up anxiety of the last couple of weeks washed out of me like a tsunami, swaying me in the realization. We were safe.

The corridor filled with more people. Some were curious bystanders, while other, more authoritative, people started showing up. The familiar wail of police sirens started to pile up outside. A voice in the back of my mind told me to disappear before they could question me.

Listening as if fog shrouded my attention, someone nearby started interviewing people in the area. She repeated her question twice before realizing they weren't listening. It took too long to register that she spoke to me. A kind eyed woman looked up and asked softly, "I said, do you need medical attention?"

"No, ma'am."

"Humph," she responded, judging the smattering of slowly healing wounds across my chest. After a moment, she continued. "Do you know this woman?"

Looking at Olivia, pale on the floor, the question sounded so shallow. We just met and yet, we've gone through more adventures together than a lifetime could hold. Not *great* adventures, but moments that anyone would hold onto for the rest of their lives. What a whirlwind of a relationship. Time and time again, she showed me what a strong, brave, and smart young woman looked like, even in the darkest moments. A woman that anyone would be lucky to know. It occurred to me then that she no longer reminded me of Cecelia. There were too many differences between them and though similar in appearance, their personalities shone in completely different ways. To answer the paramedic's question, I knew without a doubt, my words were true.

"No, I really don't."

The woman started to ask another question, but a more important matter justified interrupting her, "Another man dragged her away from the show and it made me concerned for her safety. He did not look like he had good intentions. He's, uh, in the basement."

The woman looked down the hall where my finger pointed and by the time her next question came out, it addressed air. My interests already moved on. Olivia rested on a gurney, and they wheeled her toward a boxy truck parked just outside. As they lifted her in, my concern came out in a gravelly voice, "Is she going to be all right?"

"She seems to be a little faint, but with a trip to the hospital, she should be okay," answered one of the men.

A faint grumble of conversation came from the front entrance as the police walked in, indicating it was time for me to leave. Olivia got one last longing look, wishing things had ended differently. The doors closed on the vehicle and they whisked her away. It would have been nice to say goodbye, but she'd understand. Silent steps carried me away from the scene and into the darkness.

The night sat at its deepest when my gaze landed upon the stars. They were hard to see with the city lights, but I breathed them in deeply, enjoying the temporary freedom allotted to me. Instead of slipping down the nearest alleyway, humanity invited me to join the living if just for a few hours. So, I went for a walk. A nice, slow walk.

Chapter 13

"Can you tell me the headline one more time?"

Olivia fought through the laughter, but she plowed through it. "Banker's Murderer Fired!"

She readjusted the paper so that she could read the notes under the bold print and continued. "In a turn of events, the man wanted for murdering banker, Miles Cage, was found severely burned at a popular metal concert. Police pronounced him dead at the scene. Witnesses claim he briefly appeared on stage with another unknown individual who turned the flamethrower on him and pulled the trigger. When we asked the lead singer for his take on the bizarre death, he commented that he thought it was a planned part of the show. Police say the murder is still under investigation and the identity of the man is still unknown."

"Did they have to use *that* headline, though?" A rumble of a laugh interrupted Olivia.

"At least they didn't go with 'Vampire mobster goes up in flames.'" She grinned.

Olivia became quiet again and continued to read through the story. Deep shades of twilight grew stronger behind the Statue of Liberty. She was a silhouette against the colorful horizon and what she represented finally made sense to me. I found my freedom here, even if that freedom lasted just a little while. The Don would eventually find out that Joseph died and he would not be so scant with the people he sent after me next time. For the moment, though, life could stay like this for as long as it liked. Olivia shared a bench with me, leaning against my side. Her warmth soaked into my body as she scanned the contents of the newspaper. Water lapped up against the rocks below us.

It took me a few minutes to realize Olivia no longer read the paper. She watched the horizon change from vibrant shades of orange, red, and violet to blue, just as I did. My arm moved from where it laid in my lap and wrapped around her shoulder. She snuggled into the newly formed crook and let out a big sigh.

"So, what's next for you?" she asked.

"Watch the sunset, then hope the night never ends."

"All good things must come to an end," she replied with sadness in her voice.

"That is true."

"Are you going to go back home to Transylvania?" She elbowed me in the ribs.

"You have very bizarre references. However, yes. Not Romania, but it is time to return home to London and face my demons. I am curious, though, to see if my house is still there. Hopefully, they laid Cecelia down in an easy to find place. It would bring me no greater love than to say a proper goodbye. Then, there is her dad." The implications hung in the air, in no need of further explanation.

"What about you?"

Olivia let out a huge breath before answering. "I've messed up a lot of things too. For starters, my friends think psychiatric help is warranted, my parents want me to move back in with them since almost dying, twice, and Vince won't pick up the phone."

"He'll forgive you. He likes you."

She rolled her eyes. "What, no. He's just a friend."

"Uh-huh. No friend would do the outlandish things you asked of him like Vince did." The next words came out of my mouth selfishly. "You could always come with me."

Her heart skipped a beat and went wild in her chest. She let it settle before giving me an answer. Olivia's emerald eyes lifted to mine and gave me the warmest smile.

"Thank you for the offer, but it isn't the right time. I grew up reading about your kind and it made me want that life so desperately. For crying out loud, my biggest fantasy involved a charming vampire showing up to sweep me off my feet. Well, turns out you need to be more specific about those kinds of requests. You swept me, Phil, but not in a good way. Never have I feared for my life more than after meeting you. It's clear to me now: you're not human and what you consider as just another 'day in the life' is potentially going to lead to me floating face down in the river. Your life is just too scary for me. We shared something incredible over the last couple of days, but it's time for me to go back to my boring, human life and that is fine by me."

Olivia gave me a warm, reassuring smile.

"You know, I almost turned you. Back at the concert, my greatest fear was losing you, even if it meant damning you to this life."

"A part of me wants to be mad that you didn't, but in hindsight, you made the right decision."

"No, you don't get it. The very idea of trying froze

me, paralyzing the thought from turning into action. That alone could have killed you."

"But it didn't!" she replied. "Sure, a little banged up, with a scar on my face that will remain there for the rest of my life, but I'm here to lie about how it happened, aren't I?"

My teeth ground together, wondering how to make her understand. She leaned forward and looked at me expectantly.

"I killed my wife." The words came out all at once.

"You've said that." She shrugged.

"Yes, but never how."

She gave me a sympathetic smile and placed a hand over mine. "You don't have to tell me."

My confession stumbled over her words. "She died when I tried to turn her."

Olivia sympathized as she scanned my face, but her gentleness shied my gaze downward. My palm turned up and her fingers intertwined with mine, providing a temporary distraction to organize some sort of explanation.

"It is always dangerous for the human when you turn them. They must almost be completely empty of their blood and when you let them drink yours, it is like giving it back to them, tainted with our disease. I took too much, and her heart wasn't strong enough to accept the new blood. She died with my mouth still bloody from sucking her dry."

"That is why Joseph asked you to do the one thing that would break you." She comprehended. "Oh, Phil…"

Studying deep into Olivia's eyes, my memories tried to conjure up what originally reminded me so much of Cecelia. Echoes of her danced across my mind and they were so vivid, it felt like she sat beside us. Yet, Olivia and her no longer held any resemblance to one another. Inspiration sparked one last crazy idea.

"Do you mind if I try something?"

"Anything."

Very slowly, my free hand ran along her arm, up her neck, and caressed the bandage that protected the wound on her cheek. Delicate fingers moved under her chin to tilt her head back as my upper body leaned in. Her warm breath tickled my lips just before they connected. Our touch ignited a feeling of fire within me, sizzling from my mouth, through my fingers and smoldered deep inside. Her rosy smell lingered as we pulled apart.

The moment brought out sentiment and a hushed feeling of gratitude, reflected in a whisper, "Thank you."

"Did it work?"

"You misunderstand. That was for you."

She blushed and dipped her eyes down to our hands. As if a bug reached out and bit her, she jumped and said, "Oh! I forgot your gift!"

She reached into her pocket and started digging around. Out popped a small, square box. A blue bow secured silver wrapping, tied neatly at the top. Excited, she handed it to me.

Suspicion couldn't stay out of my question. "What's this?"

"Just open it," she commanded.

The ribbon melted in my hand when my index finger and thumb pulled. Under it, her gift busily ticked away on the little cushion that it rested on and if we weren't so busy becoming intimate, I would have recognized the noise long before she pulled it out. Gleaming in the young night, my gold pocket watch was hardly recognizable. Someone took the effort to polish every ornate etch on the face to perfection.

"Olivia, where did you find this?" Tears blurred my vision, necessitating a hasty wipe from my sleeve.

"In my apartment! After returning home to see the disaster that waited for me, it was laying in the bathroom. Luckily, my parents know a guy who fixes these kinds of watches, so I asked him if he could get it running again." She beamed. "Open it!"

A part of me didn't want to see it ticking with the correct time as if acknowledging it erased what happened, but ignoring it only elongated my punishment and there wasn't a valid reason to be reminded of that terrible time every time I wanted to think of my wife. Sure enough, the correct date and time now reflected on the face of the watch, but the most unexpected of all was the picture of my wife replaced in its cubby.

The word nearly choked me. "How?"

"Do you seriously think a famous mob boss's daughter didn't have a single photo taken of her?" Olivia grinned from ear to ear.

Grateful arms grabbed her in a bear hug and squeezed until she squeaked. When we leaned apart, her tears dribbled down ruby cheeks.

"You're welcome. Now, enough of the mushy stuff. I seriously thought of dressing up in period clothing and putting a picture of myself in there instead." She laughed while wiping away her tears.

We took our spots, nestled together on the wooden

bench. She wiggled in close against me while my arm wrapped around her shoulders. For once, it felt like everything was right in the world. The pocket watch clicked open again. The beautiful face of my wife looked up at me and breathed life into her memory for a few more minutes before the lid closed over her. She settled back in the inner pocket of my jacket.

My question seemed so final, but curiosity spurred me to ask. "Will we see each other again?"

"I'm not sure," answered Olivia.

"In that case, let's just enjoy the rest of our evening since we aren't promised another, shall we?"

She laid her head back down as the sound of water nipping at the shore below us filled the otherwise quiet evening. A few stars poked out into the night sky and I listened as Olivia pointed out which shapes had names. We stayed curled up on our bench and chatted carelessly deep into the night.

Epilogue

"Cheers, mate."

The guy nodded his thanks as he handed me the receipt from behind the counter.

The idea of leaving my pocket watch with him didn't thrill me, but Olivia was confident that this method would be safer than trying to waterproof it. Without a passport, the easiest way to get across the pond would be to swim and after expressing my concerns about damaging my watch, she recommended shipping it. Olivia also said it would probably arrive at the post office before me! A leery eye remained on the postman as he wrapped it in protective film and then double boxed it. He set it down with a group of other outgoing parcels and moved on to his next task.

He noticed my hesitation to leave and asked, "Anything else?"

"No, no…." My eyes ripped from the little box to search for solace somewhere outside.

I was in a decidedly bad mood. We already said our goodbyes and now this. In her kindness, she gifted me a coat worth more than my house back home. The black, Marino wool felt like butter against my skin. She chose a double-breasted cut that ended just below my calves. The last remnants of roses clung to the threads of the fabric, and it would be a sad day when it no longer smelled like her. She didn't want me to part with it across the ocean, so she supplied me with a backpack and a waterproof bag to stuff it in for my voyage.

With that, my time in New York creeped to a close. Little flakes of snow fell around me and furnished the perfect deterrent for people to mingle outside. Meaning, less people to accidentally see me swan dive into the frigid Hudson. Regardless, my plan was to sit on the pier and wait for the sun to set. The sight of a familiar group of people changed my mind.

I spotted them through the wavy, stained panes of a window in a run-down pub. The wood outside was peeled with old paint and the inside didn't look much better. Cold air followed me in, and everyone braced against the chill. The floor stuck to my shoes from years of built-up beer spills and the place emanated a moldy overtone that the humans probably couldn't detect. In the corner, a jukebox crackled while it attempted to play something from the last century. To the left of the entrance, a couple of bikers played a game of pool. The cold air from my entrance caused them both to glare at me.

The men hunched over their beers in the back of the pub. Clearly, they hadn't seen me yet, so I wandered over to the bartender and asked for four beers and a shot of scotch. When he set the alcohol in front of me, my greedy fingers grabbed the shot glass and downed the liquid before handing the bartender a fifty.

He tried to give me change, but my instructions were clear. "Keep it."

With two mugs in each hand, my boots squeaked across the floor. The group never bothered looking up from their spot in the corner. Six empty steins already decorated their table, but the appearance of four more turned their heads. A brief moment of elation lit their faces, but then I had to speak, ruining their perfect moment.

"This round is on me." A wicked grin spread across my face.

The four sailors looked up and the smirks dropped from their leathered faces.

A word about the author…

Laurel Hanlon was born and raised in Colorado, rarely seen without a book in her hands. Drawn to supernatural tales from an early age, she soon began crafting her own ideas on paper resulting in four completed manuscripts before publishing her debut novel Unbury The Dead. Between writing books, she found herself in the car industry for over ten years in various positions, acting in a handful of productions, and training horses professionally. Underlying it all is the passion for creativity and sharing this enthusiasm with others.

http://www.laurelhanlon.com/

Thank you for purchasing
this publication of The Wild Rose Press, Inc.

For questions or more information
contact us at
info@thewildrosepress.com.

The Wild Rose Press, Inc.
www.thewildrosepress.com